BREAKING THE RULES

A DIFFERENT KIND OF LOVE NOVEL

LIZ DURANO

Velvet Madrid

CONTENT NOTE

This book contains depictions of domestic violence, including physical assault and strangulation. The story addresses military PTSD, including violent episodes, flashbacks, and the impact of trauma on relationships and families. There are references to suicide by a secondary character, though not depicted in detail.

The narrative explores themes of survivor guilt, both from military service and domestic abuse. Characters experience panic attacks and trauma responses. There are discussions of military combat, casualties, and war-related injuries.

The story includes a custody battle involving allegations of mental instability, and depicts family conflict and emotional manipulation. There are brief references to substance use as a coping mechanism.

The book ultimately focuses on healing, recovery, and building healthy relationships after trauma, but readers sensitive to these topics should be aware of their presence in the story.

PROLOGUE

Alma

I DON'T FEEL his hands around my neck until it's too late.

His fingers tighten like a vise, robbing me of breath, of voice, of everything except the terror that floods my system like ice water. I can't scream. I can't move. Fear overwhelms every cell in my body as he shouts at me in a voice I don't recognize, calling me by a name that isn't mine in words I don't understand.

Tears blur my vision as I claw at his hands, trying to pry them loose, but he's too strong. My nails dig into his arms, his face, anywhere I can reach, desperate for air that won't come.

Drew, wake up! You're dreaming again!

But the words are trapped in my throat, emerging only as desperate gasps as my lungs burn for oxygen.

Suddenly he releases me, a heart-wrenching sound tearing from his lips as I fling myself off the bed. My knees hit the floor first, shooting pain through my legs, but I scramble to the wall and press my back against it, arms raised defensively. He's still deep in whatever nightmare has claimed him, thinking I'm the enemy.

Wake up, wake up, wake up! Please wake up, Drew!

The silence that follows these episodes is always the worst part.

"Alma? Baby, you okay?" His voice emerges confused, human again. Then a groan. "Fuck, what happened? What did I do? Are you hurt?"

When I don't answer—can't answer around the fire in my throat—he crawls toward me, his eyes frantically searching my face. He looks hollow, haunted, like he's aged years in the minutes since the nightmare took hold. Dark circles ring his eyes, and his cheeks are sunken from the weight he's lost these past weeks.

"Baby? Talk to me." His voice cracks with fear as he reaches me.

I want to tell him I'm not okay, that this time felt different, more violent, but I can't speak. My throat feels raw and swollen. I shake my head instead, and his eyes fill with tears at the simple gesture.

"Oh God, Al, I'm so sorry." When he gathers me in his arms, I don't fight him. I'm too exhausted, too scared, too tired of being afraid in my own home. He pulls away to examine my neck, recoiling in horror when he sees the evidence of what he's done. "Jesus, I'm so sorry."

The sobs come then, hard and desperate. What if he hadn't woken up this time?

"I'm sorry, baby. I'm so fucking sorry," he whispers over and over, rocking me like a child. "Say something, Alma. Please."

"You need help, Drew," I manage hoarsely. "Real help. What you've been doing isn't working anymore."

What he's been doing is drinking himself unconscious

each night—the only way, he tells me, to silence the voices in his head, to keep the faces of the dead from visiting his dreams. The pills from the VA make him feel like a zombie, he says, but the alcohol lets him be himself. I'm not sure this version of himself is someone I recognize anymore.

"I know," he says, his body trembling against mine. "I know I need help."

Since returning from his final deployment—cut short due to what the Marine Corps termed "combat stress"—Drew has been a stranger wearing my husband's face. The structure and purpose he found in leading his unit are gone, replaced by civilian chaos he can't navigate. Each day without mission or meaning seems to chip away another piece of the man I married.

"You could have killed me tonight," I whisper, one hand moving to my throat, the other to my belly where our son grows. "Both of us."

He releases me so suddenly I almost fall backward. The guilt on his face transforms into something darker—disgust, fear, self-loathing all twisted together. "It won't happen again. I swear to you, it won't happen again."

"But—"

"Promise me you won't tell anyone," he says, gripping my shoulders with desperate intensity. "I'm not the monster you think I am. I haven't become like them." By *them* he means the enemy he fought in Afghanistan, the faceless figures who planted the IEDs that killed his men, who turned him from protector into hunter over six brutal years of deployment.

"I never said you were a monster—"

"Promise me, Alma. Don't tell anyone about this. I can't have people knowing what I've become."

"What you've become is sick, Drew. You're sick, and sick people need help."

His grip tightens, his eyes boring into mine with an intensity that makes my skin crawl. "I'll fix this. I'll do everything I can to make this right."

"Then get into inpatient therapy. Call your case manager tomorrow and tell them you need intensive treatment. The weekly sessions, the pills—they're not enough anymore."

Drew stands and begins pacing, raking his fingers through hair that's grown too long, too unkempt. I can't reconcile this man with the confident Marine who swept me off my feet in an Oceanside bar ten years ago, who rescued me from a date that never showed and made me believe in happily ever after.

That man is gone, left behind in some Afghan valley along with too many of his brothers-in-arms.

"I can help you with the paperwork," I offer. "If you tell your case manager what happened tonight, I'm sure they can expedite—"

"I told you, I'll handle it," he snaps, grabbing jeans and a shirt from the dresser he punched last week, its panels still hanging loose. "I don't need you making calls for me."

"Where are you going?" I ask as he pulls on his boots.

"Out."

"Drew, you can't just walk away from this—"

He kicks the dresser, splintering the wood further. "I'm doing my best, alright? I'm not a fucking child that you need to manage."

I don't respond. We've had this conversation before, this dance of his anger and my careful words. He tried to get help two months ago but walked away when he realized other

Marines might see him there. His pride, the same pride that made him a decorated soldier, now stands between him and salvation.

"If you don't call someone about inpatient therapy today, I won't be here when you get back."

Drew drops to his knees in front of me, his hands hovering over my rounded belly where our son sleeps, unaware of the chaos surrounding him. At thirty-six weeks, I can feel Tyler responding to the tension in my body, shifting restlessly inside me.

"I thought you promised to be with me through everything, Alma. Sickness and health, richer or poorer..." His eyes search my face desperately. "What happened to those vows?"

"It's not just about me anymore," I whisper, covering his hands with mine. "Our baby is due in a month. I need you to think about him too. What if this happens again after Tyler's born? What if you don't wake up next time?"

Drew's expression hardens. "I told you. It won't happen again."

"I want you to get better. I need you to call your case manager today and ask about inpatient programs. Will you do that for me? For Tyler?"

I reach out to touch his face, but he turns away and stands abruptly.

"What are you doing?" I ask as he grabs his wallet and keys.

"What do you think?"

Before I can say anything else, Drew stalks out, slamming first the bedroom door, then the front door hard enough to shake the walls. The sound echoes through our small house like a gunshot, and I flinch involuntarily.

I sit on our bedroom floor in my nightgown, one hand pressed to my bruised throat, the other protective over my belly, and let the tears fall. None of my wedding vows prepared me for this—for loving someone who's become a stranger, for being afraid in my own home, for choosing between my husband and my unborn child.

The silence stretches on, broken only by the settling of the house and my own ragged breathing. I need help, but who can I call? Drew's parents think he's perfect, incapable of anything but heroism. The other Marine wives live too far away now that we've left base housing. And the one person who might understand, who's been through his own version of hell...

I retrieve my phone and scroll through my contacts until I find his name. Sawyer Villier was Drew's closest friend until that day a month ago when everything fell apart between them. Drew accused him of making a move on me, which wasn't true—not exactly. Sawyer had been checking on us, concerned about Drew's behavior, and when he asked if I was okay, there had been a moment...

But nothing happened. Nothing except Drew's paranoia turning friendship into betrayal.

Still, Sawyer is the only person who might understand what Drew is going through, who's fought his own demons and won. My hands shake as I dial his number.

Four rings, then his voice, distant and professional: "Villier here."

"Sawyer, it's me, Alma."

A pause. The background noise suggests he's working. "I know."

"I was hoping you could talk to Drew again..." The words

tumble out in a rush, desperation making me bold. "I'm scared, Sawyer. Something happened tonight, and I can't keep pretending everything's fine. He needs help."

"You know I can't do that." His voice is careful, controlled. "You know what happened the last time I tried."

"I know, but—"

"I'm the last person he'd listen to right now, Alma. He needs professional help, not interference from someone he sees as a threat." Someone calls his name in the background. "Look, I have to go."

"Sawyer, please—"

The line goes dead, leaving me alone with the dial tone and the crushing weight of my isolation.

I stare at the phone for a long moment, then at the holes Drew has punched in our bedroom walls, at the broken dresser, at the mirror that's been missing from behind the door for weeks. This isn't love anymore—it's survival. And tonight proved that sometimes, survival means making impossible choices.

I place my hands over my belly, feeling Tyler's strong kicks against my palms. "I'm going to keep you safe," I whisper to him. "Whatever it takes."

By morning, I'll be gone. By morning, I'll have chosen my son's life over my husband's pride. By morning, I'll be living with a decision that will haunt me until the day Drew decides he can't live with his demons anymore.

But tonight, in the aftermath of violence and broken promises, I pack our bags and prepare to save the only life I still can.

Sawyer

It's too early in the morning to start drinking.

But I brought the beers anyway—one for me and one for the man lying six feet underground in a place that looks more like a city park than a cemetery. With its perfectly manicured lawns, meditation gardens, and man-made lake reflecting the California sky, it's not a bad resting place at all.

The morning fog is just beginning to lift, revealing glimpses of the Pacific Ocean beyond the rolling hills. Drew's grave even overlooks that endless blue expanse he used to talk about missing when we were deployed in the Afghan desert.

I look down at Drew's name etched into the black granite headstone, one man's life condensed into a rectangular piece of stone and a few carefully chosen words. *Loving son. Faithful husband. Devoted Father.* And beneath it all, in bigger letters that somehow feel like they should matter more: *United States Marine Corps.*

They must have added the part about being a devoted father later, because his little boy didn't come into the world until after his military funeral. I should know—I was here the day they buried him, watching as Alma's face turned pale with each contraction that gripped her swollen belly.

She held it together through the entire service, standing ramrod straight as the honor guard fired their rifles into the gray sky, as they folded the flag that had draped his casket with military precision. I heard from the others that her brother-in-law drove her straight to the hospital afterward, where she delivered a healthy baby boy with Drew's blond hair and those same piercing blue eyes that used to light up when he talked about becoming a father.

How I wish I hadn't been here that day. If I hadn't been, it would have meant Drew never pulled that trigger. It would have meant he'd finally gotten the help he needed, that we'd found a way to pull him back from whatever dark place had swallowed him whole.

Only he never did, because his demons found him first.

I take a deep breath, the ocean air filling my lungs with salt and the faint scent of jasmine from the nearby gardens. At least I learned how to handle those fuckers—the night-mares, the flashbacks, the way your mind can turn against you when you least expect it. It took time and hard work, therapy sessions that felt like battlefield surgery on my psyche, even bodywork that left me feeling like I'd been put through a meat grinder. But I was willing to try anything, to fight for every scrap of normalcy I could claw back.

I only wish Drew had been willing to fight that hard too.

Fuck. I wish this were all just a nightmare I could wake up from.

But this is no dream. My best friend, Staff Sergeant Drew Thomas, is dead. After all the bullets we dodged in Afghanistan, after all the IEDs that missed us by inches, after seven months of keeping each other alive in a desert that wanted to kill us—this was the one bullet he couldn't dodge. It had his name on it all along, its wound festering inside him the whole time, long after he'd come home to parades and yellow ribbon magnets and people who called him a hero.

But who am I kidding? They all had our names on them —every single bullet, every roadside bomb, every moment that could have been our last. Smith, Jonas, Thomas... even me, Sawyer-fucking-Villier. I may have dodged mine so far, but one day it'll catch me when my guard is down. Maybe it already has, in ways I don't want to think about.

I close my eyes and will myself to relax, letting the ocean breeze cool the sweat that's beaded on my forehead despite the morning chill. The sound of waves crashing against the distant cliffs mingles with the whisper of wind through the eucalyptus trees that line the cemetery's edges.

Calm down, Villier. You didn't come here to rage at a dead man.

I didn't come here to raise hell or pass judgment. I'm here to pay my respects, to visit him one last time before I head back to my new life in New Mexico, and maybe get a few things off my chest that have been eating at me for the past year.

Getting down on one knee beside the headstone, I wipe away a few fallen leaves with my hand, my fingers lingering on the carved letters of his name. The granite is cold beneath my palm, solid and final in a way that makes everything else feel unreal.

"You had everything, man," I say quietly, my voice barely audible over the wind. "A wife who loved you, a kid on the way, a future most guys would kill for." I sigh, rubbing my temples with my free hand as the familiar ache builds behind my eyes. "Why couldn't you have called me? Someone, anyone? Hell, I don't care who. Why'd you listen to those demons? Why'd you let them win?"

I let the words hang in the air, half-expecting some kind of answer, some sign that he can hear me. But there's only the sound of sprinklers starting up somewhere in the distance and the occasional car passing on the road beyond the cemetery gates.

I can feel my frustration building, that familiar knot of helplessness tightening in my chest. It's the same feeling that hits me every time I think about Drew and what could have been different if only I'd been there for him the way he'd been there for me. If only I hadn't let my own complicated feelings get in the way of helping my best friend when he needed me most.

What's done is done, Villier. Just pay your respects and go home.

But I don't leave. I'm not about to let guilt chase me away from the first real conversation I've had with Drew in over a year. Instead, I force myself to remember the good times—all the crazy shit Drew and I went through as Marine snipers in what feels like another lifetime. Seven months of watching each other's backs, of dark humor and shared terror and the kind of bond that only forms when every day could be your last.

We were good at what we did. Damn good. For seven months, we kept ourselves and our squad alive in a place where one wrong step, one moment of inattention, one lucky shot from an enemy sniper could end everything. We had each other's six, always. We trusted each other with our lives because we had to.

Until that day two weeks before we were supposed to come home, when Smith stepped on that IED and our world exploded in a shower of dirt and shrapnel and screaming metal. We'd been so close to making it home in one piece. So fucking close.

I still remember every detail of that moment—the deafening boom that seemed to go on forever, the way time slowed to a crawl as bodies flew through the air like broken dolls. I remember Drew's face when he realized I was down, the way he'd looked at my mangled leg and somehow found the strength to drag me to cover while bullets whined past our heads like angry wasps.

As he worked to secure the tourniquet around my thigh, his hands steady despite the chaos around us, I thought for sure I was going to lose the leg. Hell, I thought I might lose a lot more than that, with pieces of shrapnel buried so deep the surgeons weren't sure they could dig them all out. But after months of surgeries and physical therapy that redefined my understanding of pain, I still have both legs. Sure, pieces of that damn shrapnel still set off airport metal detectors, and there's always the chance that one infection could cost me everything, but I'm walking. I'm alive.

"You should have seen us at Walter Reed, man," I continue, and despite everything, I find myself grinning at the memory. "All of us grunts giving each other hell just to prove we could still take it, that we weren't broken beyond repair. Some assembly required for a few of us, but we were alive. We were going to make it."

The slam of a car door echoes across the cemetery, snapping me back to the present like a slap. I turn my head to see a petite, dark-haired woman lifting a baby from the back seat of a silver SUV parked about fifty yards away. My breath catches in my throat as I get back to my feet, my leg protesting the sudden movement.

She's still as beautiful as I remember, though she's lost weight since Drew's funeral—too much weight, the kind that comes from stress and sleepless nights and forgetting to eat because you're too busy just trying to survive each day. As she approaches, walking carefully across the uneven ground in low heels that probably weren't designed for cemetery visits, she frowns when she sees me. There's something almost fragile about her now, despite the familiar intensity in those dark brown eyes that used to dance when she laughed.

Alma Thomas. My best friend's wife.

No, his widow. I have to remember that now.

A swirl of emotions hits me like a rogue wave—anger that she never told me how bad things had gotten with Drew, sorrow for everything she's been through since he killed himself, and beneath it all, something I refuse to name. As she leans in to give me a careful hug, one arm protectively holding the baby against her chest in some kind of carrier, I catch a whiff of her perfume—the same light, floral scent she's always worn—and for a moment I'm transported back to happier times when the three of us were inseparable.

No. Not here. Not now.

"Hi, Alma. It's been a while." My voice sounds steadier than I feel.

"Hi, Sawyer. Have you met Tyler? Ty for short?" She shifts slightly, angling the baby toward me with the careful pride of a new mother.

"No," I reply as she leans in to give me a light kiss on the cheek, the kind of greeting old friends share. As she steps back, I can see the dark circles under her eyes that weren't there before, the fine lines of worry and exhaustion that have etched themselves around her mouth. This isn't the carefree woman who used to make Drew laugh until his sides hurt.

"It's been a year," she adds softly, kissing the top of Tyler's blond head as he squirms in his carrier, tiny fists waving at nothing in particular.

"Yeah... a year since the funeral." A year I spent deliberately staying away, not making a single phone call to see how she was holding up, how she was managing as a single mother with a newborn and all the weight of Drew's death on her shoulders. But heaven help me, I've lost count of all the times I wanted to pick up the phone, wanted to check on her, wanted to do something—anything—to ease the guilt that's been eating me alive since that last conversation with Drew changed everything between us.

I clear my throat, trying to dislodge the words that seem stuck there. "How are you holding up?"

"Could be better, but I'm managing," she says with the kind of automatic response that people give when they don't want to burden others with the truth. She pauses, her eyes studying my face with an intensity that makes me want to look away. I'm still in my suit from this morning's business meeting, my dress shirt unbuttoned at the neck, the tie I'd worn folded neatly in my jacket pocket. "Are you in LA on business?"

"I was, but I'm off the clock now." I move the unopened beer can I'd set aside for Drew and help Alma spread a small blanket on the grass beside his headstone. The fabric is soft, well-worn, covered in a pattern of baby animals that speaks to her new reality. "My client flew in this morning for a meeting, but my flight to Santa Fe isn't until this afternoon. Thought I'd pay the big guy here a visit while I had the chance."

She smiles, but it's a careful, polite expression that doesn't reach her eyes. We used to be comfortable around each other—the three of us could spend hours talking and laughing about everything and nothing. Until that one day when everything changed, when comfort became tension and ease became awkwardness, and it's all my fault. I fucked up in ways I'm still trying to understand.

Alma unsnaps Tyler from his carrier with practiced efficiency and settles him on the blanket. At ten months old, he's all chubby cheeks and bright eyes, wearing tiny jeans and a striped shirt that makes him look like a miniature version of his father. "How long have you been here visiting Drew?" she asks as she sits cross-legged behind Tyler, pulling him into her lap where he can see the world around him.

I glance at my watch, surprised to realize how much time has passed. "About half an hour." Thirty minutes of standing here wishing I could turn back time, wishing I could have one more conversation with my best friend, wishing I could convince him to put down that gun and ask for help instead.

"I'm glad you came," she says, and there's genuine warmth in her voice for the first time since she arrived. "He would have liked knowing you were here. Some of the other guys from your unit stopped by yesterday—Marcus and Kevin and that group. Tyler and I were here for a few minutes while they were visiting."

The mention of the other Marines makes something twist

in my chest. They're the ones who called me when it happened, because Alma was in no condition to make phone calls to anyone, certainly not to me. Not after our last conversation, when I'd failed her so completely.

"Yeah, I would have been here yesterday, but I was still in Tokyo finishing up another job." The words sound hollow even to me, like an excuse for something that doesn't really have one. The truth is, I've been avoiding this moment for a year, avoiding her, avoiding the guilt and the complicated knot of emotions that thinking about either of them brings up.

"Well, I'm glad you're here now." She adjusts Tyler in her lap, and he reaches for the plastic giraffe toy she pulls from the diaper bag, his tiny fingers grasping it with the determined focus that babies bring to everything. "He looks like Drew, doesn't he? His mini-me."

The resemblance is unmistakable—the same wheat-blond hair, the same bright blue eyes, even the same stubborn set to his jaw that Drew used to get when he was concentrating on something. It's like looking at a ghost, a glimpse of what Drew might have been like as a child, innocent and full of possibility.

"He sure does," I agree, and Alma beams with the kind of maternal pride that transforms her face, making her look more like the woman I remember. For a moment, the weight of grief lifts from her features, replaced by pure love for her son.

Suddenly I wish there was more I could say, something profound or comforting that would bridge the awkward distance between us. For someone who had been best friends with her husband, who'd spent countless evenings in their living room watching movies and sharing stories, I feel like a fraud. Like I'm pretending to be someone I'm not, someone who deserves to be here.

"Look, Al, I should have called to let you know I was coming. Given you some privacy to visit without having to deal with... well, with me being here."

Alma shakes her head quickly, almost urgently. "No, no need to call, Sawyer. But for future reference, so we don't run into each other again unexpectedly—"

"That's not what I meant." The words come out sharper than I intended, and I see her flinch slightly.

"—Tyler and I come here on Fridays after Reading Hour at the library. I let him crawl around the garden over there, although he's more hobbling than crawling these days. He just started walking last month." She gestures toward a fenced-in area with benches and a white gazebo where I can see other families scattered about, children playing while parents watch with the vigilant attention that comes with the territory. "It beats sitting at the apartment all day, you know?"

I exhale slowly, feeling the weight of how badly this conversation is going. The awkwardness between us keeps growing with every exchange, but I also don't want to leave. Not yet. Not when this might be the last chance I have to talk to her, to try to make some kind of peace with what happened.

"I drove by your old house on the way here," I say, and her eyes widen in surprise. "I don't know why—it was almost like muscle memory. Before I realized what I was doing, I'd turned into your old neighborhood, onto your street. But the house looked different. Same structure, but the front lawn had native plants instead of those roses you used to grow." I rake my fingers through my hair, a nervous habit I thought I'd outgrown. "That's when it hit me what I'd done, and I realized you'd moved."

"The house was too big for Tyler and me," Alma says quietly, her gaze dropping to the grass beside the blanket. "And it was... difficult to find a roommate, considering what happened in the garage. The new owners tore that down and built something else. A workshop, I think."

The silence that hangs between us fills in all the details we can't bring ourselves to say out loud—how she must have come home to find the police cruisers and ambulance outside their house, neighbors gathered on the sidewalk in that way people do when tragedy strikes close to home. How she would have known, even before anyone told her, that her world had just ended. I push the thought away because I can't bear to imagine how she must have felt in that moment, eight months pregnant and facing the unthinkable.

"Your neighbor told me you'd moved out a month before it happened. You never told me that." My voice carries an accusation now, as if all the anger and guilt and frustration I've been carrying for the past year is finally bubbling to the surface. "Why didn't you call me, Al? Why didn't you tell me how bad things had gotten?"

She stares at me in disbelief, Tyler still playing contentedly in her lap, oblivious to the tension crackling between the adults around him. "But I did call you, Sawyer. I did try to tell you. But you couldn't give me the time of day, remember?"

I frown, genuinely confused. "That's impossible. I would have picked up if you'd called. I would have listened."

"Oh, you picked up all right," she says, and there's a bitterness in her voice that I've never heard before. "But you told me it wasn't your problem anymore. Don't you remember?"

The words hit me like a physical blow, and I feel the blood drain from my face as the memory comes rushing back with perfect, horrible clarity.

Could you talk to him again, Sawyer? Please. I'm scared. Tell him to ask for help. I can't take it anymore.

I'd been in the middle of escorting a high-profile client across the tarmac to his private jet during a security detail in Saudi Arabia. The one time I couldn't afford to let my guard down, when lives literally depended on my complete focus, she'd called me. I'd answered without thinking, heard the fear in her voice, and done the unthinkable—I'd told her that Drew wasn't my problem anymore.

God knows I'd tried to help Drew before that call. I'd driven down to LA specifically to talk to him about getting more help at the VA, about trying some of the alternative therapies that had worked for me when my own PTSD was at its worst. I'd found him alone in the house, too drunk to hear the doorbell, sitting in the backyard with heavy metal blasting from speakers at eleven in the morning.

I remember kicking off my shoes and settling in with him like we always used to do, trying to keep things casual while I gently suggested he needed more help than he was getting. The nightmares, the flashbacks, the insomnia, the way he'd started forgetting things—it was all textbook PTSD, and I knew from experience that it would only get worse without proper treatment.

But Drew kept insisting he had everything under control, that he just needed time to adjust, that the VA doctors didn't understand what real soldiers went through. When Alma came home from work that afternoon, I knew I had to speak to her privately. Something was off with Drew—more off than usual—and I needed to know she was safe.

For the first time since I'd known him, I wasn't sure I could trust my best friend. He was drinking too much, talking about seeing our dead squad mates around town, becoming someone I didn't recognize. I'd seen how PTSD could destroy a person from the inside out, and I was terrified for Alma and the baby she was carrying. After three previous miscarriages, she was so excited to have made it through the first trimester. She and Drew had wanted a child for so long, but this time Drew seemed almost indifferent to the pregnancy.

When I pulled Alma aside in the hallway to ask if she was okay, she didn't have to say the words. I could see the fear in her eyes, the way they filled with tears when I gently touched her face, asking if she felt safe. It broke something inside me to feel so helpless, to want so desperately to protect her but not know how.

That's when Drew appeared at the end of the hallway, and everything changed between the three of us in an instant. I had to step away from her, appalled and ashamed and guilty all at once. Drew misunderstood my intentions—or maybe, if I'm being honest, he understood them better than I wanted to admit. Either way, that moment destroyed our friendship and sent me running back to New Mexico like the coward I am.

Two months later, when Alma called me desperate and afraid, I was so consumed by my own shame and guilt that I couldn't see past it to help her. I told her Drew wasn't my problem anymore and hung up on her.

Six weeks after that, Drew was dead.

"I remember now," I say quietly, the words feeling like ground glass in my throat. "I was working, and I—"

"I understand why you didn't want to help," Alma interrupts, her voice carefully controlled. "After what happened that day when you came to visit, after what Drew accused you of, it was probably for the best that you stayed away."

"That's not true," I mutter, forcing myself to look at her even though I want to crawl into a hole somewhere and disappear. "All I wanted was to make sure you were safe. That you and the baby were okay."

Her dark eyes search my face with an intensity that makes me feel exposed, vulnerable. "Was that all you wanted, Sawyer?"

The silence that follows feels deafening, broken only by Tyler's happy babbling as he holds up his plastic giraffe like he's showing it off to the world. Alma pulls him closer and plants a soft kiss on his forehead, and I see her lower lip tremble slightly.

"Forget it," she says finally. "It doesn't matter now. None of this will bring Drew back. He's gone, and we're both going to have to find a way to live with that."

I clear my throat, trying to dislodge the words that feel stuck there. "Look, Al, I owe you more than just an apology. I fucked up in ways I'm still trying to understand. Why don't we talk about this over coffee? We don't have to rehash all the painful stuff—we can just catch up, talk about what we've both been doing this past year. Try to find some kind of normal conversation."

Alma considers this for a long moment, her expression thoughtful. Tyler has started to fuss a little, and she bounces him gently in her lap, making soft shushing sounds that seem to calm him. "There's a diner about three miles from here on the main road. Mel's Place. You can meet me there if you want."

I know the place she's talking about—a classic American diner with red vinyl booths and a menu that probably hasn't changed since the 1970s. I drove past it on my way to the cemetery this morning. "That sounds perfect."

"Actually, I was going to try to contact you anyway," she adds, and there's something in her tone that makes me pay closer attention. "Drew left you something. I've been trying to figure out how to get it to you."

The words hit me like a sucker punch. "He did?"

She nods, adjusting Tyler's position as he starts to get restless. "I was going to mail it, but I wasn't sure if you still had the same PO box in Taos. The one where we used to send Christmas cards."

"It's the same address, yeah, but since I'm here now..." I trail off, not sure how to finish that sentence. The idea that Drew left me something, that he was thinking about me even at the end, opens up a whole new realm of guilt and regret.

A gust of ocean wind blows a strand of auburn hair across Alma's face, and she tucks it behind her ear with her free hand. As I watch her, I'm struck again by how beautiful she is, even worn down by grief and exhaustion. She's always had the most expressive eyes—soulful when she's sad, sparkling when she's happy, fierce when she's protecting something she loves. Right now, they're guarded, careful, like she's not sure what to make of this unexpected encounter.

"I don't want to cut your visit short," she says, glancing back at Drew's headstone. "If you'd like to stay here a while longer, I understand. Take all the time you need."

I pick up the unopened beer cans from beside the blanket, suddenly feeling foolish for bringing alcohol to a cemetery in the first place. "Nah, I'm good. Drew never was much for conversation anyway, at least not with me. Not anymore."

That earns me a small smile, the first genuine one I've seen from her today. "I'm not going to take too long here. If you want, you can head to the diner first and I'll meet you there. Give you time to check your emails or whatever."

I shake my head. "I'll follow you there. Stay as long as you need to. This is important."

I make my way down the hill toward my rental car, tossing the beer cans into the trash bins near the cemetery entrance. There's a bench beneath the shade of a massive jacaranda tree, its purple blossoms scattered across the ground like confetti, but I walk past it. I need the safety and privacy of my car as all these memories come rushing back, threatening to overwhelm me.

After offering my condolences to Alma at Drew's funeral a year ago, I never thought I'd see her again. With Drew gone and everything that had happened in that hallway two months before he killed himself, there was no reason to keep in touch. There's an unspoken rule about getting too close to your best friend's widow—it's just something you don't do.

But that's not what's really bothering me as I sit in my rental car, watching Alma kneel in front of Drew's grave and trace his name with her finger. What's eating at me is the feeling that I'm an interloper here, that I know too much and not nearly enough at the same time.

Who am I to say that everything I thought I saw during that last visit pointed to a woman who was scared and possibly being hurt? So what if she answered my questions about whether things were okay with stammered yeses and furtive glances to make sure Drew wasn't close enough to hear? What if it had all been my imagination, my own guilty conscience projecting meaning onto innocent interactions?

But what if it hadn't been my imagination? What if my gut instinct was right, and she really wasn't safe around my best friend? What if Drew had become someone capable of hurting the woman he loved?

Yeah, right, Villier. Not that you did anything about it. You ran like a fucking coward because you were too ashamed to face how you really felt about her.

The sharp knock on my passenger window startles me from my dark thoughts, and I see Alma waving at me from outside the car, Tyler balanced on her hip.

"I'm ready," she says as I get out and follow her to her SUV parked a few spaces away. I hold open the rear door as she buckles Tyler into his car seat with the practiced efficiency of a mother who's done this a thousand times. Her hair catches the late morning sunlight, and for a moment she looks almost like her old self—the woman who used to laugh at Drew's terrible jokes and make him blush with her teasing.

"Look, Al," I say as she hands Tyler a purple octopus toy and double-checks his car seat buckles. "I'm sorry about what happened with Drew. That day when I came to visit and he lost it when he saw us talking—"

"You did what you could as a friend, Sawyer. That's all anyone could have done," she interrupts, but her voice is gentle now, tired. "You weren't the only one who tried to help him. His parents tried, his therapist at the VA tried, even some of the guys from your unit reached out. But Drew didn't want anyone's help. He was convinced he could handle it all on his own, that asking for help was somehow admitting defeat."

I could have done more, I want to tell her. *I could have fought harder, stood my ground, convinced him that nothing inappropriate was happening between us. I could have been a better friend.*

But I keep my mouth shut because, like she said, nothing I can say or do now will change the reality that Drew Thomas is dead.

"Are you ready for that coffee?" she asks as I close the car door, Tyler now happily occupied with his toys.

I nod, taking the hint that this conversation—the real one we need to have—will happen somewhere else, away from Drew's grave and the weight of everything we can't say here. "Lead the way."

CHAPTER TWO

Alma

As Sawyer follows me in his rental car through the winding streets that lead away from the cemetery, I catch glimpses of him in my rearview mirror and can't help but feel a knot of guilt tightening in my chest. What on earth am I doing, agreeing to have coffee with him? Sure, he was Drew's best friend once upon a time, but the last time they saw each other, they'd almost come to blows in our hallway. No wonder he made it crystal clear that day when I called him, desperate and afraid, that he didn't want anything to do with us anymore.

I should have gotten back in my car and driven home the moment I recognized him standing by Drew's grave, should have taken Tyler and left before this awkward reunion could unfold. But I didn't. And if I'm being honest with myself—brutally, painfully honest—part of me wanted to see him again. I never got the chance to speak to him during Drew's funeral, not with labor pains gripping me every hour and the chaos of military honors and final goodbyes.

But Sawyer's such a big part of Drew's past, and mine too, whether I want to admit it or not.

I'd met them both on the same night I got stood up on what was supposed to be my first real date in months. A friend from San Diego State, where I was grinding through my Master's in Early Childhood Education, had set me up with her cousin. It was meant to be a nice break from dealing with my mother, who'd just announced she was getting married to husband number five—a well-known Miami-based cosmetic surgeon—and needed my blessing. Not that she actually needed it; she would have married him with or without my approval. But at least this one lasted, since they're still married, still living in Miami, their artificially perfect smiles gracing the society pages of magazines she sends me religiously, as if I care about her latest charity gala or spa opening.

Sometimes she remembers to call on my birthday, but mostly she doesn't. She didn't attend my wedding to Drew, which I told myself was understandable because it was so last-minute, such a whirlwind of love and deployment sched-ules. But she couldn't make it to his funeral either, or to meet her first grandson. She'd had another procedure done to her face and couldn't be seen in public with bruising.

That's Mom for you, and it's something I learned to accept long ago. For as long as I can remember, her entire existence has revolved around whatever man she's with. Dad left us before I turned three, so I have no memories of him at all—just a faded photograph and child support checks that stopped coming when I was seven. What I do remember are the men who came after: Stepfather Number One through Number Three, each one bringing their own particular brand of disappointment. By the time Number Four came along, I was out of the house and supporting myself through college. After her announcement about Number Five, I figured it might be time to stop being such a hermit and maybe start my own love story.

Luckily for me, my friend's cousin never showed up that night.

Drew and Sawyer were members of a Marine sniper unit about to deploy to Afghanistan, enjoying their last few nights of freedom stateside. I remember catching Sawyer watching me from across the crowded bar as he nursed his beer, trying to appear disinterested but failing spectacularly. His intense gaze kept finding mine, and every time I looked his way, he'd quickly look somewhere else, like a teenager with his first crush.

But when I was about to leave—disappointed, embarrassed, and convinced that getting stood up was somehow a reflection of my worth—it wasn't Sawyer who came over to rescue my evening. It was Drew, with his easy smile and natural confidence, who slid into the empty chair across from me and said, "Well, whoever he is, he's an idiot for missing out on meeting you."

It became a running joke between the three of us over the years, how Sawyer would have made his move first if he weren't so damn shy, so caught up in his own head to take a chance. Drew used to tease him mercilessly about it, especially after a few beers.

But as quickly as the memory surfaces, I push it away, angry with myself for even entertaining such thoughts. How can I be so disloyal to Drew's memory? I loved him more than anything—we had so many wonderful years together, so many plans that will never come to fruition. Sure, I liked Sawyer too, but as a friend. He was always there for us, the steady presence in our lives who could make Drew laugh when nothing else could.

How was I supposed to know things would end the way they did? How could any of us have predicted that the war would follow Drew home, that it would slowly eat away at the man I married until there was nothing left but anger and pain and a desperation so deep it consumed everything?

I find a parking spot in front of Mel's Diner, the same place Drew and I used to come for late breakfast on lazy Sunday mornings when we were first married. By the time I turn off the engine, Sawyer is already jogging across the parking lot toward me, his limp barely noticeable now. When I struggle to unhook Tyler's carrier from its base—these things are more complicated than they should be—he's right there, offering to help.

"Here, let me get that," he says, and lifts the carrier with Tyler still sleeping inside like it weighs nothing at all. There's something so natural about the gesture, so easy, that for a moment I can almost pretend we're just old friends meeting for coffee, not two people carrying the weight of shared grief and unspoken regrets.

Inside the diner, we settle into a red vinyl booth near the window, Tyler's carrier balanced carefully on the bench beside me. The place hasn't changed much—same black-and-white checkered floor, same faded photographs of 1950s movie stars on the walls, same smell of coffee and bacon grease that's probably been here since the Eisenhower administration.

As Sawyer settles into the seat across from me, I find

myself studying his face and feeling a sharp pang of wistfulness. If Drew were here with us right now, we'd already be laughing over some ridiculous story he'd be telling, probably about one of his coworkers or something he'd seen on the news. Or he'd be playing with my hair, staring at me with those blue eyes until Sawyer would roll his eyes and tell us to get a room.

As friends, Drew and Sawyer were like night and day, perfectly complementary opposites. Drew was the all-American boy next door—blond hair that caught the light, sky-blue eyes that sparkled when he laughed, the kind of easy charm that made people gravitate toward him wherever he went. While Drew was outgoing and popular, always the center of attention at any gathering, Sawyer was the brooding introvert, the quiet Marine with thick dark hair and intense hazel-green eyes that seemed to see everything. Where Drew was lean and athletic, Sawyer was more solidly built—wide chest, narrow hips, arms marked with tattoos that told stories I never quite learned the full details of. One of them, some kind of intricate Celtic design, runs all the way down his right hand to his knuckles.

Even their preferences were opposite: Drew loved the ocean, could spend hours bodysurfing or just lying on the beach soaking up the sun. Sawyer preferred mountains and desert, wide open spaces where you could see for miles and the only sound was wind through sage brush.

Remembering that Sawyer's only here for a few hours before his flight back to New Mexico, I force myself to focus on the present moment, on the man sitting across from me who looks so different from the broken soldier who came back from Afghanistan years ago. He looks good—fit and tanned, with a confidence that wasn't there during those dark months at Walter Reed when none of us were sure he'd keep his leg. From what I've seen today, he barely walks with a limp anymore.

"So how are things with you?" I ask once the waitress—a tired-looking woman with kind eyes and sensible shoes—takes our order and disappears behind the counter. "I mean, really. Not just the polite answer."

"Busy," he replies, and there's something in his voice that suggests he prefers it that way. "Todd and I just completed the interior work on our latest eco-home before I left for this trip. It's finally ready for someone to live in."

"Are you planning to sell it?"

"Actually, we're thinking about renting it out, though I'd prefer a long-term tenant rather than vacation rentals. It's perfect for a small family—two bedrooms, open-plan living area, full kitchen. Solar panels provide all the power you need, so you're completely off-grid." He pauses, and for the first time since we sat down, his expression lightens with genuine enthusiasm. "You'd absolutely love it, Al. It comes with an indoor garden space where you can grow whatever you want year-round. Flowers, leafy greens, vegetables like kale and artichokes, even dwarf fruit trees. You always loved gardening, didn't you?"

I nod, touched that he remembered. "I do. But what would I know about living in an eco-home? It sounds complicated." Even though Drew and I were only renting that house in Torrance after he left the Marines, I'd trea-sured the small backyard space where I could plant salad greens and vegetables, using organic techniques I'd researched obsessively online. Gardening was my escape, my way of creating something beautiful when everything else felt chaotic.

"It's really not complicated at all. I could teach you how everything works in half an hour—there are instruction manuals, but honestly, maintenance is minimal. A few switches here and there, basic upkeep. That's about it." His expression grows more serious, the momentary lightness fading. "But anyway, let's talk about you. How are you and Tyler really doing?"

I shrug, suddenly feeling the weight of the past year settling on my shoulders like a heavy blanket. "We're okay. Could be better, but we're managing. Taking it one day at a time."

"And Drew's parents? I remember you mentioning some tension there."

My jaw tightens involuntarily. "We still don't see eye to eye on much. They mean well—I know they do—but sometimes they forget their boundaries. They'll make decisions about Tyler without consulting me first, like signing him up for activities or buying him things without asking what I think he needs." I can hear the frustration creeping into my voice and try to rein it in. "I understand he's their only connection to Drew now, but he's still my son first. Sometimes I feel like they're trying to turn him into a replacement for Drew, and that's not fair to any of us."

I pause, realizing how bitter I sound. "But what am I complaining about, really? It could be so much worse. At least Tyler has grandparents who love him and want to be involved in his life. Some kids don't even have that."

As Sawyer nods thoughtfully, his fingers wrapped around his coffee mug, I can almost feel the question he's building up to ask. The one we both know is coming, the real reason we're here having this conversation instead of just exchanging polite pleasantries at Drew's grave.

"I know we didn't get a chance to talk during Drew's funeral," he says after taking a sip of his coffee, his voice carefully measured. "But I need to understand what happened. When I came to visit that last time, I knew something was wrong. I could see it in Drew's behavior, in the way he was holding himself, but every time I tried to talk to him about it, he'd shut down or get angry. What was he like after his last deployment? What changed?"

I can feel Sawyer's gaze on me like a physical weight, and it's like he's seeing straight through every defense I've built up over the past year. The question I've been dreading, the conversation I've avoided having with everyone—his parents, the grief counselor, even myself most of the time.

"He was different," I say quietly, my eyes focused on the water glass in front of me rather than meeting Sawyer's intense stare.

"Different how?"

The words stick in my throat for a moment. How do you explain to someone that the man they knew and loved like a brother became someone else entirely? How do you describe watching someone you've built your entire life around slowly disappear, piece by piece, until you're living with a stranger who looks like your husband but sounds like someone else entirely?

"He was angry all the time," I finally manage. "Everything set him off—if I left dishes in the sink, if the neighbors were too loud, if his coffee wasn't hot enough. I couldn't do anything right, no matter how hard I tried. I started walking on eggshells around him, especially when he'd slip into one of his dark moods."

"What kind of moods?"

"The kind where he'd stare into space for hours at a time," I say slowly, the memories flooding back despite my efforts to keep them buried. "He'd be there physically, sitting right next to me on the couch or at the dinner table, but mentally he was somewhere else entirely. Somewhere I couldn't reach him. And he started forgetting things—simple things like appointments or conversations we'd had the day before. At first I thought he was just distracted, but it got worse."

"Was he self-medicating?"

The directness of the question catches me off guard, even though I should have expected it. Sawyer knows the signs—he's been there himself. "Beer mostly, but also whiskey. He developed a real love affair with Jameson." I can still see him sitting in his chair every evening, that amber bottle on the side table, the glass never quite empty. "He said it helped him sleep better than any of the medications the VA prescribed. Said the pills made him feel like a zombie, but the alcohol let him be himself."

Sawyer exhales sharply, shaking his head. "You should have called me earlier, Al. I mean, before that last conversation we had. I suspected something was wrong, but—"

"You were busy, Sawyer." The words come out more defensively than I intended. "You and Todd were building your business, and you'd gotten that job with Heath Kheiron. You had your own life to worry about." I start picking at a loose thread on the napkin in my hands, needing something to do with my fingers. "Besides, I think the change in routine affected Drew more than any of us realized. He loved being a Marine—loved the structure, the clear chain of command, the sense of purpose. Leading his men gave him something to focus on. But civilian life? He felt lost without all of that."

"I referred him to Trident Elite," Sawyer says quietly. "I thought if he could get into private security work, it might help with the transition."

"They didn't hire him." The rejection had been a devastating blow to Drew's already fragile ego, another reminder that his military service didn't automatically translate to civilian success.

"I heard about that. I'm sorry."

And he was angry with you for not pushing harder for his hiring, I almost add, but catch myself. *You had influence there —you knew Heath from when you were kids. Drew felt like you could have done more but chose not to.* One of the many resentments that had built up toward the end, though he'd only said it out loud once, during one of his darker moments when the whiskey had loosened his tongue.

If they're so fucking elite, why'd they hire a cripple like Sawyer to guard some billionaire when I'm obviously more qualified? I've served longer, and I sure as hell don't have shrapnel in my leg slowing me down if I need to run after the bad guys.

"What about therapy?" Sawyer asks, his deep voice pulling me back from that particular painful memory. "Was he getting treatment for PTSD through the VA?"

"He tried—he really did try at first. But he said therapy didn't do anything for him. He went through three different therapists in six months because he couldn't connect with any of them. He'd come home from sessions more frustrated than when he left." I can still remember those afternoons, watching him slam the front door and head straight for the liquor cabinet. "He said they didn't understand what he'd been through, that they'd never been to war, never had to make life-or-death decisions or watch their friends die. How could they possibly help him process something they'd never experienced themselves?"

Sawyer reaches across the table and covers my hands with his, and the warmth of his touch is unexpectedly comforting. His hazel-green eyes hold mine, steady and patient, giving me the strength to continue.

"They prescribed medications too, but Drew hated most of them. The ones that helped him sleep gave him nightmares —intense, violent ones where he'd wake up swinging and shouting. Sometimes he'd grab me in his sleep, thinking I was someone else." I can still feel those moments of terror, being jerked awake by his thrashing, not knowing if he'd recognize me or see me as a threat. "It was scary, Sawyer. Really scary."

The admission hangs between us, heavier than I expected. I've never said that out loud before—never told anyone how frightening those nights became, how I started sleeping in the guest room more often than not.

"The day he died," I continue, my voice beginning to crack despite my efforts to stay composed, "Drew texted me while I was at work. He told me he loved me and that he knew I'd be a good mother to our son. Just out of the blue, in the middle of a Tuesday afternoon." The memory of reading those words on my phone screen, the way my blood had turned cold with instant recognition that something was terribly wrong. "I knew immediately that something wasn't right. I rushed home, but the police were already there when

I arrived. Our neighbor had heard the gunshot and called 911."

The moment I finish speaking, the tears I've been holding back finally come. I pull my hands away from Sawyer's gentle grip and dab at my eyes with the napkin, angry at myself for crying in front of him. I've worked so hard to appear strong these past months, for Tyler's sake, for Drew's parents, for everyone who expects me to somehow hold it together because that's what military wives do—we endure, we adapt, we survive.

Even during Drew's funeral, when contractions were gripping me every hour and I could barely stand upright, I'd forced myself to stay composed through the military honors and the flag presentation and all those people offering condolences that felt hollow and useless.

"Alma, I'm so sorry," Sawyer says, and the genuine pain in his voice almost undoes me completely. "I wish I could have done more for him. After that day when I came to your house, when everything went wrong between us, he wouldn't take my calls anymore. I tried reaching out, but..."

"You tried, Sawyer. That's what matters." I take a shaky breath, trying to regain some semblance of control. "But nothing any of us did or didn't do is going to bring him back now."

"Did his parents know how bad his PTSD had gotten? Did they understand what you were dealing with?"

The question touches a nerve I didn't realize was still so raw. "Does it matter now whether they knew?"

I can hear the sharpness in my own voice and hate myself for it, but I can't seem to stop the words from coming. Drew was such a private person, especially about his struggles. He didn't want anyone to know about his problems—not his family, not his old friends from high school, not the community that had welcomed him home as a hero. To them, he was still the same Drew they'd always known, the hometown boy who'd joined the Marines and served his country with honor. He'd visit his old high school to talk to students about military service, always putting on that perfect facade of the successful veteran who'd transitioned seamlessly back to civilian life.

And that's exactly how Drew wanted it. He was determined to leave behind a legacy his family could be proud of, even though the demons he'd fought in the Afghan desert had followed him home and slowly transformed him into someone none of us recognized.

I'm equally determined to protect that legacy, even now. Even after everything that happened—the arguments behind closed doors that grew more frequent and more vicious, the broken furniture and holes punched in walls, the flashbacks that left him shaking and disoriented, and that terrible morning when he'd wrapped his hands around my throat and squeezed until I saw stars.

Because despite all of that, Drew was a good man at his core. He was a Marine who'd put his life on the line countless times to protect others, a husband who'd tried desperately to be the man he used to be, fighting a war inside his own mind that he was always destined to lose.

I want people to remember him as the hero he truly was —the son his parents adored, the amazing husband he could have been if the war hadn't broken something essential inside him. Not the tortured stranger who'd shared my bed those final months, the man who'd ultimately decided that everyone he loved would be better off without him.

Even though he's gone, I'll never break the promise I made to him in those final weeks, when he'd beg me through tears not to tell anyone how bad things had gotten. This secret is my burden to bear alone, the weight I'll carry to my own grave.

Because some truths are too heavy for anyone else to share, and some love is measured not in what you reveal, but in what you choose to protect.

CHAPTER THREE

TEN MINUTES LATER, I follow Alma back to her apartment a few miles away in San Pedro, surprised and deeply unsettled to find that it's located in one of the rougher parts of town. This isn't where Drew would have wanted his wife and son living—not with a car repair shop next door, the constant drone of an air compressor serving as background noise along with the angry whine of air ratchets that never seem to stop.

The knowledge that she's been forced to live like this because I wasn't there when she needed help sits like acid in my stomach. Drew would be rolling over in his grave if he knew his family had ended up here, in this industrial waste-land where the American dream goes to die.

When I step through her front door, it feels like I've entered a stranger's house, and the wrongness of it hits me like a physical blow. This sterile space is such a far cry from the homes she and Drew used to create together—places where every wall was covered with framed pictures of their adventures, where bookshelves overflowed with her poetry collections and his military histories, where you could feel the love in every carefully chosen detail.

Drew used to brag about how Alma could turn any drab military housing into a real home with just her touch. "She's got this gift," he'd tell me, eyes lighting up as he described her latest decorating project. "Takes these cookie-cutter places and makes them feel like they've been in our family for generations." He was right—Alma had always known how to transform any space with warm colors, handmade touches, and an intuitive understanding of what made a house feel like home.

But in this apartment with its off-white walls and impersonal rental furniture, I can barely find traces of the woman I knew. Other than Tyler's colorful toys scattered across the worn carpet, one lone framed photograph of her and Drew from their wedding day sitting next to Drew's carefully folded memorial flag in its triangular display case, and what looks like a poem torn from a book and hastily framed, there's nothing else that speaks to who she really is.

Is this what grief looks like when it strips away everything that used to matter? Or is this what happens when you're so busy just surviving that you forget how to live?

The thought that I could have prevented this—should have prevented this—makes my chest tighten with familiar self-loathing.

"I'll be right back," Alma says as I close the front door behind me, the sound echoing in the sparse room. "Could you keep an eye on Tyler for me? I just need to grab something from the bedroom."

"Of course," I reply, watching as she settles Tyler in his playpen with practiced efficiency before disappearing down the narrow hallway.

I turn my attention to Tyler, who's been banging away on some kind of piano toy with the focused determination that only toddlers possess. When he notices me watching, he stops and looks up at me with those impossibly blue eyes—Drew's eyes—and I feel something crack open in my chest. He pulls himself up on unsteady legs, gripping the playpen railing, and studies me with an intensity that's unsettling. It's like he's trying to figure out where I fit in his small world, whether I'm someone to be trusted or feared.

God, he looks so much like Drew it physically hurts. The same wheat-blond hair that catches the light, the same broad grin that used to make Drew's whole face light up, even the same stubborn set to his jaw that I remember from when we were kids and Drew was determined to prove some point or another.

This should be Drew sitting here, watching his son discover the world. Drew should be the one seeing Tyler's first steps, hearing his first words, teaching him how to throw a baseball or ride a bike. All those father-son moments that Drew used to dream about during our long nights on watch in Afghanistan, when he'd talk about the family he wanted to build with Alma when we got home.

Instead, it's me—the friend who failed him when he needed me most.

"Hey, little dude, how you doing?" I ask softly, my voice rougher than I intended.

Tyler responds with a delighted laugh and what sounds like "ba-ba" before he starts trying to climb over the railing with the fearless determination of someone who hasn't learned that the world can hurt you yet.

"Whoa there, Ty! Let's ask your mama first, okay?" I say

as he lifts one chubby leg, searching for a foothold against the mesh netting. "Hey, Al, is it okay if I hold Tyler?"

"Sure," comes her voice from the bedroom, and I turn back to Tyler with something that might almost be a smile.

"Looks like a jailbreak is definitely on the schedule, buddy."

Tyler shrieks with pure joy as I lift him from the playpen and carry him around the room like an airplane, the sound of his laughter filling the empty space and making it feel almost like a home. For these few moments, I can pretend this is normal—that I'm just Uncle Sawyer visiting his best friend's family, that Drew might walk through the door any second with takeout and terrible jokes.

When I finally settle on the couch with Tyler on the floor beside me, he immediately grabs onto my hand and stares up at me with those penetrating blue eyes that are so much like his father's it makes my throat close up. He should be looking at Drew like this, should be learning to trust his father's face, his father's voice. When Tyler reaches up with tiny fingers to touch my beard, I pretend to snap at his hand like a playful dog, and he erupts in giggles like it's the funniest thing he's ever seen.

Drew would have loved this. Would have spent hours making Tyler laugh just to hear that sound.

The guilt crashes over me in waves—guilt that I'm here experiencing these moments that should belong to my best friend, guilt that part of me is enjoying it, guilt that I'm sitting in his apartment with his wife and child while he's six feet underground because I wasn't there when he needed me most.

The front door suddenly swings open without warning,

and a young blond man strides in like he owns the place. He's wearing a dirty white t-shirt that looks like it hasn't been washed in days, torn jeans with holes in the knees, and flip-flops that have seen better years. Everything about him screams trouble, from his bloodshot eyes to the way he's carrying himself like he's looking for a fight.

My stomach drops and every protective instinct I've honed over years of combat and security work kicks into high gear. Is Alma seeing someone? Some loser who thinks he can just walk into her home whenever he wants?

"Who the fuck are you?" He glares at me as he slips keys into his back pocket, puffing out his chest like some kind of territorial animal. He can't be older than twenty-five, and something about his aggressive posture and dilated pupils suggests he's probably high on something. "Guess the bitch already found herself a replacement. Didn't take the slut long to move on, did it?"

The words hit me like a slap, and I instinctively pull Tyler closer to me, every muscle in my body coiling for action. Nobody—and I mean nobody—talks about Alma like that, especially not in front of her child.

From the hallway, Alma rushes out carrying a shoe box, her face flushed with anger and what looks like embarrass-ment. "Kevin, get out. Now."

Kevin. Drew's baby brother. I remember him now—the kid who was maybe sixteen when Drew and I deployed, all teenage bravado and hero worship for his big brother the Marine. But the intervening years haven't been kind to him, and whatever he's become bears little resemblance to the enthusiastic kid who used to pepper Drew with questions about military life.

After the way he just spoke to Alma, I don't care if he's the Pope himself—there's no way I'm letting him do whatever he wants while I'm here.

"You can't just walk in here anytime you feel like it, Kevin," Alma says with forced calm, though I can hear the steel beneath her words as she sets the box on the coffee table and gently takes Tyler from me. "If you want to see Tyler, you wait until I bring him to your parents' house tomorrow like we agreed. We've been over this."

"Oh, sure, listen to the woman who couldn't be there for my brother when he needed her most," Kevin scoffs, and the casual cruelty in his voice makes my hands clench into fists. "You left him, Alma. Abandoned him when things got tough. That's why he killed himself, and that makes you a first-class bitch in my book." He shoots a sideways glance at me, like a dog marking his territory. "I don't want the same shit happening to my nephew—you getting up and leaving him too when it gets inconvenient."

That's it. I've heard enough.

"That's enough, kid. You heard her. Get out." I grab Kevin by the arm and start dragging him toward the door, my grip probably harder than necessary but I'm past caring about his comfort.

"Get your fucking hands off me or I'll call the cops, man," he protests, struggling against my grip like the entitled little shit he clearly is. "You her new guy? Because let me tell you something, man—she's gonna leave you just like she left Drew. Left him cold and alone, and he killed himself because of her."

The words are like gasoline on a fire that's been burning in my gut since the moment he opened his mouth. "You don't have any idea what you're talking about, kid," I say through gritted teeth, fighting to keep my voice level for Tyler's sake. "Drew's suicide isn't Alma's fault. He had PTSD, and that's not something anyone can control as easily as your ignorant ass seems to think. So get your facts straight before you come in here spewing garbage."

"I don't care about your excuses," he spits, the words coming out in an angry rush. "If she'd just stayed with him instead of being a selfish bitch, he would still be alive today. She killed him just as sure as if she'd pulled the trigger herself."

The accusation hangs in the air like poison, and I can feel something dangerous rising in my chest. "You can tell yourself that lie all you want, but that's not how any of this works."

He scoffs with all the arrogance of someone who's never faced real hardship, never had to make life-or-death decisions, never watched friends die. "Yeah, right. Like you know how it works."

Like you know how it works?

The question detonates something inside me, and suddenly I'm seeing red. Who the fuck does this little punk think he is, standing here in his drug-addled ignorance, talking about things he can't even begin to comprehend?

"You want to know how it works?" I say, my voice dropping to that dangerous level that used to make enemy combatants think twice. "You close your eyes and all you see are the faces of the friends who didn't make it home. The brothers who went out on patrol one morning and came back in body bags. You see the people you had to kill—and yeah, some of them were women and children, but they were running at your position with RPGs and AK-47s, so it was either them or everyone in your unit."

Kevin's eyes are widening now, some of his bravado starting to crack as he realizes he might have bitten off more than he can chew.

"You want to know what your brother saw every time he closed his eyes? Every piece of trash on the side of the road that might be hiding an IED that could blow you and your buddies to pieces. Every shadow that might be hiding a sniper. Every civilian who might be carrying a suicide vest." I lean closer, making sure he understands exactly what kind of hell Drew lived through every single day. "Imagine carrying all of that around in your head for years, and then having some ignorant little shit who's never been further from home than the local dealer's house tell you it's all just an excuse."

"Alright, alright, man, I get it," Kevin stammers, his earlier aggression deflating like a punctured balloon. "Let me go. You don't have to be so dramatic about it. Jesus Christ, you're fucking crazy."

"Dramatic?" I shake my head in disbelief at his continued ignorance. "There's nothing dramatic about war, asshole. Nothing dramatic about watching your best friend slowly lose his mind because of what he saw and did over there. Your brother was a hero who served his country and paid a price for it that you'll never understand."

Kevin stares at me for a long moment, and I can see the wheels turning in his drug-addled brain. "I know who you are now," he says slowly. "You're Sawyer."

"So?"

"That's why you're here, isn't it?" His voice takes on a new edge, ugly and accusatory. "You waited until my brother was dead before you made your move on his wife. How long have you been sniffing around her, huh? Did you want her while Drew was still alive?"

The accusation hits closer to home than I want to admit, and the fact that there's a grain of truth in it makes it even worse. Because yes, I did have feelings for Alma while Drew was alive. Yes, I did want her in ways that made me hate myself. And yes, part of me is here now because I still want her, even though she belongs to Drew's memory and always will.

"Kevin, enough," Alma says, her voice cutting through the tension like a blade. "I've had it with your accusations and your disrespect. If you don't leave right now, I'm calling the police."

Kevin's jaw clenches as he glares at her with pure hatred. "Bitch—"

My fist connects with his jaw before he can finish the word, and he goes down hard on the concrete outside the door, yelping in pain and surprise. "Get the fuck out of here," I growl as he scrambles to his feet, one hand clutched to his face. "And don't come back. You hear me?"

His eyes are wide with shock and fear as he stares at me like he's seeing me clearly for the first time. "I'm calling the cops, man," he whines, backing away toward the stairs. "You fucking hit me."

"Go right ahead. Maybe they can teach you some manners while they're here." I slam the door and turn to face Alma, who's standing there with Tyler in her arms, her face pale and drawn.

The sight of her looking so fragile, so worn down by the constant battles she has to fight just to protect her son, makes something twist painfully in my chest. This isn't how it was supposed to be. Drew should be here defending his family, not leaving Alma to deal with his toxic little brother and the rest of the world alone.

"Why the hell does he have a key to your place, Al?" I ask, trying to keep the anger out of my voice because it's not directed at her.

Outside, I can hear Kevin shouting and cursing as he makes his way down the stairs, but I couldn't care less about his wounded pride. I'm still shaking with rage over the way he treated Alma, the casual cruelty with which he blamed her for Drew's death.

"I didn't give it to him," Alma replies wearily as she sets Tyler back on the floor. The little boy has stopped fussing, apparently unbothered by the drama, his attention already shifting to the box on the coffee table. "When Tyler and I first moved in here, I gave Drew's parents a spare key in case I locked myself out. A few months later when it actually happened, Kevin came over with the spare and apparently helped himself to a copy. 'Just in case,' he said."

I ball my hands into fists at my sides, fighting to control the protective rage that's coursing through my veins. "That's called breaking and entering, Al. It's a crime. Why didn't you call the police? Drew would never have stood for anyone treating you like this, not even family."

The truth is, I know Drew's parents were never thrilled about their son marrying Alma. To them, she was just another girl chasing Marines for the benefits and steady paycheck. It didn't matter that Alma was working toward her Master's degree when she met Drew, that she had dreams of opening her own preschool, that she was building a career and a future completely independent of any man. They saw what they wanted to see, and what they wanted to see was someone who wasn't good enough for their golden boy.

"But Drew's not here, is he?" she counters, and the simple statement hits me like a punch to the gut. "Besides, there's no point in calling the police now. I'm moving at the end of the month, and I'm definitely not giving anyone a spare key this time."

I look around the sparse apartment with new understanding. The lack of personal belongings, the temporary feel of everything—she's been packing, getting ready to start over somewhere else. "The end of the month is only a few days away. Where are all your moving boxes?"

"I rented this place furnished, so it's mostly just Tyler's things and my clothes," she explains, running a hand through her hair in a gesture that speaks to bone-deep exhaustion. "Everything from the house Drew and I shared is still in storage. Has been since..." She doesn't finish the sentence, but she doesn't need to.

"Where are you moving to?"

"I'm still looking. Turns out not many landlords are eager to rent to an unemployed widow with a toddler," she says with a bitter laugh that doesn't contain any real humor. "I mean, there are places available, but the decent ones cost more than I can afford on my current budget."

"California's not exactly known for being affordable." I almost tell her that this isn't like the Alma I used to know, the woman who had everything planned out months in advance, who never left anything to chance. But then what do I really know about her beyond the fact that she was the woman Drew fell for the night before we deployed, the one he married the moment we got back because he couldn't stand the thought of waiting another day to make her his wife?

He was crazy about her from the very beginning. It was love at first sight, the kind of instant, overwhelming connection that you don't argue with because it's bigger than logic or caution. I saw it happen that night at the bar, watched Drew's entire world shift on its axis the moment he looked into her eyes.

And I felt something shift in mine too, something I spent the next several years trying to bury and ignore.

But this broken, overwhelmed woman sitting across from me isn't the confident, vibrant person I remember. This is what grief and financial stress and constant harassment from Drew's family has done to her.

"So let me get this straight," I say, trying to keep the disbelief out of my voice. "You're moving out in less than a week, but you don't have a definite place lined up yet?"

"I have one more apartment to look at this afternoon—something temporary until I can find something better long-term that I can actually afford." She reaches for the box she'd set on the coffee table earlier and holds it out to me, clearly wanting to change the subject. "But don't worry about me, Sawyer. I'll figure it out. I always do. Anyway, this is what you came here for."

The dismissal stings more than it should, but I understand it. She doesn't want my pity or my help—she wants to maintain what's left of her dignity, to prove that she can handle whatever life throws at her without needing to be rescued. It's admirable and heartbreaking at the same time.

It takes me several seconds to accept the box from her, knowing there's so much more that needs to be said, so many ways I want to help that she'll never let me pursue. But I didn't come here to rescue her, no matter how much I might want to. I came here for whatever Drew left for me, whatever final message he wanted to send from beyond the grave.

"Thank you," I say quietly.

As I start to lift the lid, Alma reaches into her pocket and places something cool and metallic in my palm. "This fell out of the box when I was getting it down from the closet shelf. I didn't want to forget to give it to you."

The familiar weight of Drew's old compass settles in my hand, and suddenly the room seems to tilt around me. I recognize it immediately—the scratched brass surface, the cracked glass face, the way it sits just slightly off-balance because Drew dropped it during a firefight in our third month of deployment.

The sight of it hits me like a physical blow, and I have to close my eyes against the sudden rush of memories that threaten to overwhelm me. The Afghan desert stretches out behind my eyelids, brutal and unforgiving under the merciless sun. I can smell the dust and gunpowder, can hear the distant sound of enemy movement in the tree line to our west, can feel the familiar weight of my rifle and the adrenaline-soaked tension that came with knowing that any moment could be our last.

And then the boom when Smith stepped wrong, the earth-shaking explosion that changed everything, the chaos and screaming and blood that followed.

"Are you okay?" Alma's voice sounds distant, like it's coming from the other end of a long tunnel.

I force my eyes open and focus on the compass in my palm, grounding myself in the present moment. "Yeah, I'm fine. I just... I never expected to see this again." The words come out rougher than I intended, thick with emotions I can't quite name.

The last time I saw Drew holding this compass was the morning we got hit, just before we moved out to take our position for what would turn out to be our final mission. We were all on edge that day—a sniper's bullet had barely missed us the week before, close enough that the bark it tore from the tree between us had sprayed across Drew's face and left him shaken.

I can still hear Jonas's voice, dark with gallows humor as we all dropped to the ground: "Not today, motherfucker."

None of us knew how prophetic those words would turn out to be.

I turn my attention to the box in my lap and lift the lid with hands that aren't quite steady. Inside, carefully arranged like artifacts in a museum, are all the random souvenirs and keepsakes that we weren't supposed to take home but did anyway. A group photo of our unit taken when we first arrived in-country, all of us looking impossibly young and confident, followed by another picture taken just weeks before we were scheduled to rotate home—noticeably missing several faces.

I pick up each item and study it like I'm trying to decode some hidden message: pieces of shrapnel that nearly killed us, empty bullet casings from firefights that seemed to last forever, a creased map marked with positions we'd held and friends we'd lost, an Afghan afghani coin that Drew had picked up in a market in Kabul. These were the things that defined our time over there, the physical remnants of seven months that changed all of us in ways we're still trying to understand.

But beneath all of that, there's something else—the weight of promises made and broken, commitments that seemed so clear in the heat of combat but became impossibly complicated in the cold light of civilian life.

"Do you know why he left you the compass?" Alma asks as she settles Tyler on her lap, her voice soft with something that might be curiosity or might be understanding.

I clear my throat, my mouth suddenly dry as dust. In my mind, I can see Drew's ritual from that final morning, the way he'd rubbed the cracked glass face with his thumb before slipping it back into his breast pocket like a talisman. "It represents a promise we made to each other when we first deployed."

"What kind of promise?"

"To keep each other on the right course, no matter what happened." The words feel inadequate, failing to capture the gravity of what we'd sworn to each other in those early days when we still believed we were invincible. "To watch each other's backs, to make sure we both made it home in one piece."

But even as I say it, I know there was another promise that came with the compass, one I can't tell her about, one that's been haunting me since the moment I learned Drew was dead.

I've got a bad feeling about this mission, Villier. If anything happens to me out there, you know what you need to do, right?

Shut up, Thomas. Don't talk like that. We're going home in two weeks.

Just promise me, Sawyer. If something happens, if I don't make it back, you'll look after Alma. You'll make sure she's okay.

Nothing's going to happen. We're both going home.

Promise me.

Fine. I promise. But you're going to be the one taking care of her, not me.

How naive we'd been, thinking that the only threats we faced were the obvious ones—enemy bullets and roadside bombs and the thousand ways war could kill you in an instant. We never imagined that the real enemy would follow us home, would take up residence in Drew's mind and slowly eat away at everything that made him who he was.

I failed to keep both promises. I didn't keep Drew on the right course when he needed me most, and I sure as hell haven't been taking care of Alma the way I swore I would. Instead, I ran when things got complicated, when my own feelings threatened to compromise the simple clarity of friendship and duty.

"I should have been there for him, Al," I whisper, my voice breaking on the words as the full weight of my failure crashes over me. "I should have known how much he was hurting. Instead, I failed him. I fucking failed him when he needed me most."

The compass feels like it weighs a thousand pounds in my palm, a physical reminder of every way I let my best friend down. The guilt threatens to drown me, a black tide of self-recrimination and regret that I've been fighting since the moment I learned Drew was dead.

As the tears I've been holding back finally start to fall, I'm grateful that Alma doesn't try to offer empty platitudes or false comfort. Instead, with Tyler settled securely on her lap, she wraps her free arm around my bicep and leans her head against my shoulder in a gesture so simple and natural it nearly undoes me completely.

It's such a small thing, but it speaks volumes—a reminder of the bond the three of us used to share before everything got complicated, before I let my feelings for her turn friendship into something more dangerous and harder to navigate.

For just a moment, sitting there with her warm presence grounding me and Tyler's innocent chatter filling the silence, I can almost pretend that this is how things were supposed to turn out. That Drew is just in the other room, that we're all together the way we always planned to be, that the war never followed us home and love was simple and uncomplicated.

But the weight of the compass in my hand reminds me of the truth: Drew is gone, I failed to save him, and I'm here holding the woman I've loved for years while she grieves the man she actually chose to marry.

Some promises, once broken, can never be repaired. But maybe, if I'm lucky, I can find a way to honor at least part of what Drew asked of me, even if it means carrying this guilt for the rest of my life.

CHAPTER FOUR

Alma

SAWYER and I don't speak for several minutes and I'm grateful for the silence. There's something sacred about shared grief, about sitting in the wreckage of what used to be and acknowledging that some losses are too deep for words. The weight of his head against my shoulder, the way his breathing gradually steadies, the compass still clutched in his trembling hand—all of it feels like a prayer for Drew, a moment of communion with the man we both loved and lost.

I've rehashed Drew's death in my head countless times over the past year, asking the same unanswerable questions until they've worn grooves in my mind. Why didn't he reach out? Why wasn't love enough to keep him here? What could I have done differently? But sitting here with Sawyer, feeling his pain mix with mine, I realize that maybe the questions aren't meant to have answers. Maybe the only thing we can do is hope that Drew found peace in the end, and that someday, we will too.

Tyler starts pulling on my shirt and making his hungry sounds—those insistent little whimpers that mean nursing time is non-negotiable. I lift my head from Sawyer's shoulder, immediately missing the solid warmth of him. "Do you need to leave right away? I have to nurse Tyler."

Sawyer shakes his head, wiping at his eyes with the back of his hand in a gesture so achingly vulnerable it makes my heart clench. "My flight isn't for a few hours. But if you'd rather I leave..."

"No, of course not." The words come out more urgently than I intended, revealing how much I don't want him to go. How long has it been since I had an adult conversation that wasn't about Tyler's schedule or Drew's family's latest demand? "But I need to nurse him and get him down for his nap. If you can stay, that would be wonderful. I've got water and juice in the fridge, some fruit too."

He manages a smile that doesn't quite reach his eyes. "Go do what you need to do, Al. I'll be fine here."

As I make my way to the nursery with Tyler, I can't help but notice how safe I feel with Sawyer here. He didn't have to defend me against Kevin—hell, most people would have just stood there awkwardly and pretended not to notice the family drama. But Sawyer stepped in without hesitation, protecting Tyler and me like we were his responsibility. After a year of being blamed for Drew's death by his family, of feeling like I'm drowning in guilt and isolation, Sawyer's fierce defense means more to me than he could possibly know.

In the dim nursery, I settle into the rocking chair that's one of the few pieces I kept from the house Drew and I shared. Tyler latches on immediately, his tiny fist curling against my chest as he nurses with the single-minded focus that only babies possess. These quiet moments are when I miss Drew most acutely—not the angry, broken man he became at the end, but the Drew who used to talk about watching me nurse our children, who would trace patterns on my belly when I was pregnant and whisper stories to Tyler before he was born.

But they're also the moments when I feel most like myself, most connected to the fierce maternal love that's kept me going through the darkest times. Tyler doesn't care that his father is gone or that his grandmother thinks I'm a terrible mother or that we're living in a barely-habitable apartment next to a car repair shop. He just knows that I'm here, that I'm his source of comfort and nourishment and safety. And somehow, that's enough to make me feel like maybe I can figure out the rest.

Half an hour later, I tiptoe out of the nursery and find Sawyer standing in front of the entertainment center, holding the framed copy of "Invictus" that I've carried with me through every move since college. His expression is distant, thoughtful, like he's trying to solve some complex equation in his head.

Besides our wedding photo and Drew's memorial flag, that poem is one of the few personal items I couldn't bear to put in storage. "I am the master of my fate, I am the captain of my soul"—words that used to give me strength but now feel like a cruel joke. How can I be the master of anything when every choice I make seems to lead to more pain, more judgment, more impossible situations?

Sawyer turns when he hears me enter the living room, and there's something different in his face—an energy, an intensity that wasn't there before. "I have an idea," he announces. "It's completely insane, but hear me out."

"What is it?" I settle onto the couch, suddenly aware of how quiet the apartment feels without Tyler's chatter.

"You and Tyler should come stay in the rammed earth house Todd and I just finished. You wouldn't need to buy anything—it's fully furnished and ready for someone to make it home."

I stare at him, certain I've misheard. "You mean move to New Mexico? Sawyer, I can't do that."

"Why not?"

The question is so simple, so direct, that it catches me off guard. Why not? Because it's crazy? Because it's running away? Because it would mean leaving behind everything familiar, even if familiar has become synonymous with miserable?

"What about Drew's parents?" I finally manage. "Tyler is their only connection to him. They'd be devastated if I took him away. And I'm not sure it's safe to raise a child in the middle of nowhere."

Sawyer moves to the couch and sits beside me, close enough that I can smell his cologne—something woody and clean that reminds me of the outdoors. "Why wouldn't it be safe? It's a real community, Al, just off-grid. Sustainable living doesn't mean primitive living. These homes have everything you need—running water, electricity from solar panels, internet, the works."

He leans forward, his enthusiasm growing as he talks. "I've seen families thrive out there. Some discover it's not for them and move on, but others find exactly what they were looking for. Todd and I live close by, and I could introduce you to my friends Dax and Harlow. They have twins—Dax

Jr. and Anita Pearl—who are about a year and a half. They'd be perfect playmates for Tyler."

I study his face, looking for signs that this is some elaborate joke or pity offer. But his hazel eyes are completely serious, almost urgent. "You really mean this."

"I do." He runs a hand through his hair, a nervous gesture I remember from years ago. "Look, Al, you don't have a job here, and in a few days you won't have a place to live. The only family you have is Drew's, and from what I've seen today, that relationship is pretty toxic. What's really keeping you here?"

The question hits harder than I expected because the honest answer is: nothing. Nothing except fear and inertia and the terrible weight of knowing that leaving would feel like abandoning Drew somehow.

"We don't get along," I admit, thinking of Kevin's cruel words, of Frank and Doreen's constant criticism disguised as concern.

"What about friends?"

"Most of my close friends were Marine wives back when we lived near Camp Pendleton. We keep in touch through social media, but it's not the same. Here..." I pause, realizing how pathetic this sounds. "The only people I really know are other parents from the library story time and the park where I take Tyler. That's it."

A particularly loud burst of compressed air from the shop next door punctuates my words, and Sawyer waits for the noise to die down before continuing. "So think of it as a fresh start. New surroundings, new experiences, new friends. Definitely no industrial soundtrack."

I can't help but laugh at that. "You make it sound so simple."

"Because in many ways, it is."

"What about you?" The question slips out before I can stop it, revealing more about my thought process than I intended.

"What about me?"

Heat creeps up my neck as I realize how that sounded. "I mean, what would your girlfriend think about this arrangement? Wouldn't it be awkward?"

Sawyer's eyes narrow slightly as he studies my face. "Even if I had a girlfriend, which I don't, this wouldn't affect my relationship with her. You'd be renting a completely separate house."

"Are you still seeing that massage therapist? Sage?" The name tastes bitter on my tongue, though I can't quite analyze why. "I remember you mentioning her to Drew. He said she helped you with your recovery, though he was never interested in trying alternative therapies himself."

"We're not together anymore," Sawyer says quietly. "Haven't been for over a year. Are you trying to change the subject, Al?"

I shake my head quickly, embarrassed to be caught deflecting. "No, not exactly. I just don't want to impose on you or complicate your life if I decide to do this."

"You wouldn't be imposing at all."

I blow out a long breath, realizing I've run out of reasonable objections. "So hypothetically, if I said yes, how soon would I need to move into this house?"

"Hypothetically," Sawyer says with the hint of a smile, "how soon do you need to be out of here?"

"Yesterday," I reply, and another blast of air from the repair shop perfectly punctuates my point, making us both laugh.

"How long is the drive? I can't fly with my stuff—it would cost a fortune, and I can't afford it anyway."

"About thirteen or fourteen hours, depending on traffic and how many stops you make. Most people split it up, spend the night in Flagstaff or somewhere similar." He pauses, then adds, "But I wouldn't let you make that drive alone with Tyler. We could go together, rent a trailer for your things. Your SUV has a hitch, right?"

The mention of the hitch brings back a flood of memories —Drew installing it himself the weekend after we bought the SUV, so excited about all the camping trips we were going to take. We used it exactly twice before his final deployment, and never again after he came back changed.

"Yes, it does," I manage.

"I can help you arrange the trailer rental and get everything packed," Sawyer continues. "But don't make this decision right now, Alma. Think it over tonight. Consider all the pros and cons. This is a big change."

"How long do I have before you need to rent the house to someone else?"

"Maybe a week? But honestly, you don't have that luxury. You need a place to live in four days."

I chew my lower lip, a nervous habit I developed during Drew's worst episodes. The idea of starting over somewhere completely new is simultaneously terrifying and exhilarating. When was the last time I felt excited about anything? When was the last time I looked forward to tomorrow instead of just enduring it?

"I hate the idea of you missing your flight just to drive back here with me," I say. "I could think about it tonight and call you in the morning."

"Flights can be changed," he says simply. "I'm in no hurry to get back, and this is important." He pulls out his phone and starts tapping the screen. "Let me send you some photos of the house so you can see what you'd be getting into. If you have questions, call me. If you decide yes and I'm still in town, I'll help you pack and we can drive out together."

My phone starts buzzing with incoming photos, each one more intriguing than the last. "I should probably still check out that last apartment this afternoon, just to be thorough."

"Of course," Sawyer says, though something in his expression suggests he already knows what my decision will be. "Check it out, then let me know. You know where to find me, Al."

After he leaves, taking with him the sense of safety and possibility that had briefly filled the apartment, I sit in the sudden quiet and scroll through the photos he sent. Each image seems to whisper promises of a different life: Adobe walls that curve like embracing arms. Skylights that would flood the space with natural light. An indoor garden where I could grow fresh vegetables year-round. Wide open spaces where Tyler could run and play without the constant noise of traffic and machinery.

But it's more than just the house—it's what it represents. A chance to start over somewhere no one knows my story, where I'm not "the widow who couldn't save her husband" or "the woman who drove a war hero to suicide." A place where Tyler could grow up surrounded by mountains and sky instead of concrete and exhaust fumes.

Two hours later, as I'm getting Tyler ready for our appointment to see the last apartment, Frank and Doreen arrive in their silver Mercedes SUV. I see them through the window and my stomach immediately knots with dread. Doreen emerges first, her perfectly coiffed blonde hair and immaculate makeup making her look like she's heading to a charity luncheon rather than visiting her grandson in this shabby neighborhood.

The annoyance on her face is evident even from a distance. "Kevin said Sawyer assaulted him," she announces before I can even greet them properly. "Is that true?"

I nod, settling Tyler more securely on my hip. "Kevin was extremely rude to both Sawyer and me. When I asked him to leave and he refused, Sawyer helped him find the door."

"He didn't need to put his hands on our son," Frank says, his mouth set in that thin line that means he's building up to a lecture. At sixty, Frank Thomas still carries himself like the successful defense contractor he is, all rigid posture and barely controlled authority. "Kevin was just visiting his nephew."

"Visiting?" I shut the car door harder than necessary and turn to face them. "By using a key I never gave him to walk into my apartment whenever he feels like it? I've told him repeatedly that he can't do that, but he ignores me every time."

"Where are you going?" Doreen interrupts, clearly not interested in discussing Kevin's boundary issues. "We came to see our grandson. Are we not allowed to visit now?"

"Of course you can see him. But I have an appointment in ten minutes, and I can't be late." I check my phone, though

I already know the time. "I'm bringing Tyler over tomorrow afternoon like we planned."

"We could watch him while you go to this appointment," Doreen suggests, her voice taking on that hopeful tone that somehow manages to sound manipulative. "It would save you from dragging him around town."

"I'll bring him tomorrow as scheduled," I repeat firmly. We've been through this dance too many times. They used to drop by whenever they wanted until I finally insisted on a schedule that actually worked for me. But even that arrangement fell apart after they took Tyler to a play center without asking my permission and kept him three hours longer than we'd agreed. There was also that suspicious moment when I caught Doreen quickly closing her laptop after I glimpsed what looked like a search for California custody laws.

"Kevin tells us you still haven't found a place to live," Frank says, and there's something in his tone that puts me on edge.

"I haven't made a final decision yet." It's not exactly a lie, but it's not the whole truth either.

"Why don't you and Tyler move in with us?" Doreen asks, as if the idea just occurred to her, though I suspect they've been planning this conversation. "You could have Drew's old room, and we could convert the guest room into Tyler's nursery. It would be perfect."

"It's what Drew would have wanted," Frank adds, playing the guilt card with practiced ease.

"That way you wouldn't be alone, and we could help with Tyler while you go back to work," Doreen continues. "Your teaching credentials are still current, aren't they?"

The question irritates me because they already know the

answer. Ever since Drew died, they've questioned every decision I've made—my choice to stay home with Tyler instead of rushing back to work, my decision to breastfeed for a full year, even my preference for natural parenting methods over their more rigid approach. With the two-year suicide clause still in effect on Drew's life insurance, every dollar matters, but I refuse to become financially dependent on Frank and Doreen. That would give them even more control over my life and Tyler's.

"I really need to go," I say, glancing at my phone again. "I'll see you tomorrow at noon with Tyler."

They exchange one of their loaded looks but don't argue further. I drive away watching them in my rearview mirror until I turn at the busy intersection, feeling like I've just escaped something that was slowly suffocating me.

Ten minutes later, I park in the driveway of what can only generously be called a house. The single-story building squats behind a chain-link fence, its paint peeling in long strips that flutter in the breeze like dying skin. The front yard is littered with beer cans and cigarette butts, the grass brown and patchy where it exists at all. Even from inside my car, I can smell something unpleasant—garbage, maybe, or sewage.

I grip the steering wheel and stare at the garage door, one of its windows covered with duct tape that's started to peel at the corners. In the back seat, Tyler babbles happily to his toy animals, blissfully unaware that we're considering calling this place home. I look around at the broken fence, the house next door with its cracked windows and security bars, the general air of defeat that hangs over the entire street like smog.

What the hell am I doing here?

This isn't a home—it's a place where dreams go to die. It's

where I'd bring my son to live because I'm too scared to take a chance on something better, too paralyzed by fear and guilt to choose hope over safety.

I pull out my phone and scroll through Sawyer's photos again, seeing them with new eyes after witnessing the alternative. The first image shows a graceful dome rising from the high desert like something from a science fiction movie, but in the best possible way. It's surrounded by endless sagebrush and backed by the dramatic peaks of the Sangre de Cristo mountains, their snow-covered summits gleaming in the clear light.

The next photo is taken from the doorway, showing a living space that manages to be both rustic and sophisticated. Colorful mosaic tiles flow across the floor like a frozen river, and to the left, an indoor garden thrives behind a wall of windows. I can clearly see kale and Brussels sprouts, artichokes and what might be a small citrus tree. It's not just a garden—it's a promise that life can flourish even in the harshest environments.

I look up at the house in front of me, then back at my phone. The contrast is so stark it's almost comical. Here I am, sitting in a neighborhood that looks like it's been forgotten by hope itself, staring at photos of a place where I could watch Tyler grow up surrounded by beauty and possibility.

For the past year, I've been in survival mode, just trying to get through each day without completely falling apart. I've made decisions based on fear and obligation, staying in Los Angeles because it felt like what I was supposed to do, like leaving would somehow dishonor Drew's memory. But what if staying is actually the betrayal? What if clinging to a life that makes us both miserable is the real disservice to everything Drew fought for?

I think about the poem Sawyer was holding earlier, the words that have sustained me through dark moments: "I am the master of my fate, I am the captain of my soul." When was the last time I acted like the captain of anything? When did I stop making choices based on what I wanted and start making them based on what other people expected?

Tyler makes a happy sound from the backseat, and I turn to see him grinning at me with pure, uncomplicated joy. He doesn't care where we live as long as we're together. He doesn't need the approval of his grandparents or the familiar streets of San Pedro. He needs a mother who's strong enough to choose hope over fear, adventure over safety, possibility over the known quantity of misery.

I think about Sawyer's offer—not just the house, but what it represents. A chance to start over in a place where no one knows my story, where Tyler can grow up surrounded by people who choose to live differently, who prioritize sustainability and community over material success. A place where I could rediscover who I am when I'm not defined by loss and guilt and the weight of other people's expectations.

The decision crystallizes in my mind with sudden, startling clarity. I don't need to see this apartment because I already know it's not what I want for Tyler or myself. What I want is a new beginning, a chance to write a different story than the one I've been trapped in for the past year.

I want to wake up to mountain views instead of the sound of air compressors. I want Tyler to play in gardens instead of avoiding broken glass on sidewalks. I want to remember what it feels like to look forward to tomorrow instead of just enduring it.

For the first time in months, I feel something that might actually be excitement flickering to life in my chest. It's fragile and uncertain, but it's real. And maybe that's enough to build a new life on—one choice at a time, one day at a time, one mile at a time toward something better.

I start the car and pull away from the house without looking back, my mind already racing ahead to everything I'll need to do to make this impossible, wonderful, terrifying dream a reality.

CHAPTER FIVE

Sawyer

It's been two days since Alma surprised me with her decision to move to Taos, and I'm still processing the magnitude of what's happening. When I made that impulsive offer for her to rent the rammed earth house, part of me expected her to politely decline after a day or two of consideration. But she didn't. She called me that very evening, her voice shaking with nervous energy, and said yes to completely upturning her life based on photos from a stranger's phone.

I'm glad she decided to take the leap, though. She's committed to giving it a try for three months, which feels like a reasonable trial period. At this point, anything has to be better than living next to that damn car repair shop, constantly looking over her shoulder for Kevin's next uninvited appearance.

After returning my rental car, I take a cab back to Alma's apartment through the early morning Los Angeles traffic. These past two days have been a whirlwind of packing boxes and making arrangements while Tyler spent extended visits with his grandparents. Tomorrow marks the beginning of my next assignment-free period—nearly three weeks before Blackwater Ridge Security needs me again. It's one of the unexpected perks of working part-time for the company that Garrett Morrison, an old Army Ranger buddy, built from the ground up after his own military service ended.

Garrett and I first met during a family vacation at Lake Winnipesaukee when we were kids, long before either of us knew we'd end up in the military. Years later, when our paths crossed again during a joint training exercise, we discovered we'd both been shaped by similar experiences and were dealing with similar demons. When he started Blackwater Ridge after leaving the Rangers, he reached out to offer me work that actually meant something—protecting people who were making a difference in the world, rather than just anyone with enough money to pay.

Sure, the part-time schedule means less money than I could make elsewhere, but I don't need much to be happy. Out there in Taos, living off the grid, I have almost everything I need for a simple, meaningful life.

Almost.

I arrive at Alma's apartment at eight sharp and find her loading the last of her bags and a cooler into the SUV. Tyler is already secured in his car seat, clapping his hands and babbling excitedly when he sees me approach. The sight of his pure, uncomplicated joy makes my chest tight with emotion.

"Hey there, little man," I murmur, leaning down to press a gentle kiss to his forehead. His tiny hand immediately reaches for my beard, and I can't help but smile at his fearless curiosity about the world around him.

I help Alma arrange the remaining bags in the cargo area

alongside my own duffel bag, trying not to notice how her fingers brush mine when we both reach for the same handle, trying not to think about how this simple domestic moment feels more natural than it should.

"You excited yet?" I ask as she tucks Tyler's overstuffed diaper bag into the space behind the driver's seat.

"Are you kidding? I'm so excited I'm literally shaking!" She turns to face me fully, and I'm struck by how beautiful she looks in the morning light. She's wearing a simple blue t-shirt and dark yoga pants, her auburn hair pulled back in a loose bun that makes her look younger, more carefree than I've seen her since Drew's funeral. Even without makeup, she radiates a kind of nervous energy that's infectious. "I barely slept last night—kept going over lists in my head, making sure I hadn't forgotten anything important."

But then her smile fades, replaced by something more complex, more bittersweet. Her brow furrows as she looks past me toward the street. "Tyler and I visited Drew yesterday, and we stayed for a long time. I told him what we were doing, explained that we wouldn't be able to visit his grave for a while." She sighs, wrapping her arms around herself like she's trying to hold something together. "I know he's been gone for over a year, but I got used to those weekly visits. They were... grounding, I guess. A way to feel connected to him."

The vulnerability in her admission catches me off guard. "You don't have to do this, you know," I say quietly. "If you're having doubts, if leaving feels like you're abandoning him somehow, we can figure out something else."

"No, that's not it." She shakes her head quickly, her hands rubbing nervously along her thighs. "I know I can't keep living in the past, blaming myself for what happened, staying frozen in place because moving forward feels like betrayal. Drew wouldn't want that for Tyler or me. He'd want us to choose life, to choose hope, even when it's scary."

Her words hit something deep in my chest, a recognition of the courage it takes to make this kind of choice. "You're doing the right thing, Al."

"I hope so." She takes a deep breath, squaring her shoulders like she's preparing for battle. "Anyway, I need to do one final check of the apartment and leave the keys for the landlord."

While Alma disappears back into the building for her last walk-through, I turn my attention to the trailer hitch, checking the connection and lock mechanism one more time. I'd already inspected everything thoroughly last night after loading Tyler's disassembled crib and changing table, but it doesn't hurt to be cautious. The last thing we need is mechanical problems on a fourteen-hour drive across the desert.

The repetitive task also gives me something to focus on besides the way my heart rate picks up every time Alma smiles, or how right it felt to help her pack up her life, or the dangerous fantasy that's been building in the back of my mind about what it might be like if this move meant something more than just helping out Drew's widow.

When she emerges from the apartment for the final time, keys in hand, there's something definitive about the way she closes the door behind her. Like she's not just leaving a place, but closing a chapter.

"That's it," she announces, walking back to the SUV with a determined stride. "I left a message for the landlady that the keys are on the kitchen counter. Oh, and there are sandwiches in the cooler—I made them with whatever was left in the refrigerator so nothing would go to waste. Egg salad, ham and cheese, roast beef. There's also pasta salad, some fruit, and plenty of water for the road."

"That's perfect. Thank you." The thoughtfulness of it, the way she's taken care of every detail, reminds me of the woman Drew used to describe—someone who could turn any situation into something warmer, more comfortable.

She laughs, a sound that's lighter than any I've heard from her in years. "That's what happens when you've got a refrigerator to empty and a compulsive need to be prepared for everything." She pauses, covering her mouth with both hands in a gesture of disbelief before letting them fall. "God, Sawyer, I still can't believe I'm actually doing this. Part of me keeps waiting to wake up and realize this is all some elaborate dream."

"If you're having second thoughts—"

"And waste all those sandwiches and the hours of packing we did? Absolutely not!" Her eyes sparkle with something that might actually be excitement. "It's surreal, that's all. But it's also the first real adventure I've chosen for myself in... I can't even remember how long. Tyler and I are ready for something new."

She checks Tyler's seatbelt one more time and hands him a bright yellow plastic giraffe that immediately goes straight to his mouth. "So what's our route? I know it's a long drive, but I've never actually done it before."

I pull the folded map from my backpack and spread it across the SUV's hood. As Alma steps closer to look, I catch the faint scent of roses in her hair—probably from whatever shampoo she uses—and have to consciously focus on the red and blue lines crisscrossing the paper in front of me.

"We'll take I-15 North to Barstow, then pick up I-40 East all the way to Albuquerque," I trace the route with my finger, hyperaware of how close she's standing. "From there, we head north to Santa Fe and then up to Taos. It's mostly highway driving, pretty straightforward."

"Where are we stopping for the night?"

I fold the map and hand it to her, our fingers brushing briefly in the exchange. "Flagstaff. I made reservations at a hotel." When her eyebrows rise slightly, I quickly add, "Separate rooms, obviously."

"Oh, okay." She tucks the map between the center console and passenger seat, her cheeks slightly pink. "I can take a turn driving if you want. I'm used to long road trips from when Drew and I would drive up to visit his family."

"You don't have to worry about that. I actually enjoy long drives—gives me time to think." I pause, remembering something. "If we didn't have the trailer, we could even make a detour down to Sedona, check out the red rocks. But with Tyler and all our stuff, it's better to stick to the main route."

"Have you been to Sedona before?"

"A few times, yeah."

Something in my tone must give me away because her expression becomes more curious. "Oh, that's right. I remember Drew mentioning that you were seeing someone there for a while. Wasn't that where you went for some kind of alternative therapy?"

The question makes me uncomfortable, stirring up memories I'd rather leave buried. "That was years ago," I mutter, hoping she'll let it drop.

But Alma has always been perceptive, and I can see her putting pieces together. The truth is, Sage was a big part of my recovery after Afghanistan—and Iraq before that. She practiced some kind of deep tissue bodywork combined with what she called somatic therapy, helping people release trauma that had gotten stuck in their bodies. The sessions were brutal, like being put through an emotional meat grinder while lying on her massage table, often leaving me raw and shaken for days afterward.

But it worked. Over the course of ten sessions, she helped me process things that traditional therapy hadn't even touched. Combined with the tai chi and yoga practices she recommended, I went from barely being able to walk without pain to functioning almost normally. I was even able to stop taking most of the medications the VA had prescribed.

Drew had dismissed it all as "woo-woo medicine" and "expensive nonsense," but I knew better. Sometimes the unconventional approaches are the only ones that work, especially when you're dealing with wounds that go deeper than flesh and bone.

The personal relationship that developed between Sage and me afterward was complicated—two people with their own trauma trying to heal each other. It lasted about a year before we both realized we were better as healer and patient than as lovers. Last I heard, she'd moved to Los Angeles and was working with musicians and other high-profile clients, but I haven't looked her up. Some chapters are better left closed.

A silver Toyota sedan pulls up behind our trailer just as Alma slides into the passenger seat, interrupting my brooding thoughts about the past. She immediately tenses, biting her lower lip—a nervous habit I remember from years ago.

"Oh, great," she mutters under her breath, already getting back out of the car. "It's Drew's parents. Can you keep an eye on Tyler for me?"

"Of course." I've only met Frank and Doreen Thomas twice—once at a barbecue when Drew and Alma were still newlyweds, and again at Drew's funeral. They're a successful, well-dressed couple who've always struck me as people accustomed to getting their way. Frank runs a defense contracting firm, and Doreen owns an upscale flower shop in Palos Verdes. Both of them have the kind of polished confidence that comes from never having to worry about money or social status.

They also made it clear from the beginning that they didn't think Alma was quite good enough for their son.

As Frank and Doreen emerge from their sedan, Alma moves to intercept them before they can get too close to Tyler. I can see the tension in her shoulders, the way she's bracing herself for conflict.

"This is not right, Alma," Doreen announces without preamble, her voice carrying the authority of someone who's used to being obeyed. She's dressed in a tailored beige pantsuit that probably costs more than most people make in a month, her silver hair perfectly styled despite the early hour. "You cannot just take our grandson away from us like this. I thought we'd talked sense into you last night."

"I'm doing what's best for Tyler and me," Alma replies, her voice steady despite the obvious stress.

"Best?" Doreen's voice rises, drawing stares from a few

early morning joggers. "By dragging him to the middle of nowhere? Away from his family, from everything he knows?"

"I am his family," Alma says with quiet firmness. "I'm his mother. And this isn't forever—you're welcome to visit us in Taos anytime."

Frank steps forward, trying to project the same commanding presence that probably serves him well in business meetings. "Come on, Alma. You made this decision two days ago. Two days! That's not enough time to think through something this important. If you needed to move somewhere better, we could have helped you find a nice place here in California. If the problem was Kevin's behavior—"

"Kevin isn't the reason I'm leaving, Frank." Alma's patience is clearly wearing thin. "Look, I understand you're upset about the short notice, but Tyler and I are leaving today. You have our new address, you have my phone number. Nothing's stopping you from staying in touch."

"You've been involved with him for a while now, haven't you?" Doreen points directly at me, her voice dripping with accusation. "That's what this is really about. First you chased after our son, and now you're running off with his best friend. I bet you two were carrying on behind Drew's back—"

"That's enough." The words come out harder than I intended, cutting through Doreen's vitriol like a blade. I step away from the SUV, putting myself between her and Alma. "I understand you're upset about losing easy access to your grandson, but you're way out of line."

Both Frank and Doreen seem startled by my intervention, as if they'd forgotten I was there. Behind me, I can hear Tyler starting to fuss, probably picking up on the adult tension surrounding him.

"Drew was my friend," I continue, keeping my voice level but firm. "He saved my life in Afghanistan, and I'll never forget that debt. I would never do anything to betray his trust or dishonor his memory."

"Dishonor his memory?" Frank's face is reddening with anger. "That's exactly what you're doing! You're taking our grandson away from us, putting some crazy idea in Alma's head about living like a hermit in the desert. She doesn't know what she's doing—if she did, Drew would still be alive."

The accusation hangs in the air like poison, and I see Alma flinch as if she's been physically struck. This is clearly not the first time they've blamed her for Drew's suicide, and the casual cruelty of it makes my hands clench into fists.

"Drew's death is not her fault," I say, my voice dropping to a dangerous level. "PTSD and survivor's guilt are real things that real soldiers deal with every day. Alma did every-thing she could to help him, and blaming her for his illness is not only wrong, it's cruel."

"I'm done here." Frank shakes his head in disgust and turns toward his wife. "Get in the car, Doreen. There's nothing more we can do."

As they leave without saying goodbye to Tyler or offering any kind of civil farewell, Alma stands beside me with her son in her arms, blinking back tears. The morning sun catches the moisture in her eyes, and I have to resist the urge to pull them both into a protective embrace.

"I understand where they're coming from," she says quietly, her voice thick with emotion. "Tyler is their only connection to Drew, and I'm taking him away. In their minds, I'm being selfish."

"You're being a good mother," I correct her. "You're

making hard choices to build a better life for your son. That's not selfish—that's exactly what Drew would want you to do."

She looks up at me with those dark eyes that seem to see straight through all my carefully constructed defenses. "But what if it doesn't work out, Sawyer? What if I'm making a huge mistake and dragging Tyler into something that's wrong for both of us?"

The question hits me at a deep level because I recognize the fear behind it. I remember asking myself the same thing when I was living in that beat-up camper van, learning to build my first rammed earth house with nothing but YouTube videos and stubborn determination. This was before Garrett offered me work with Blackwater Ridge, back when I was still waking up screaming from nightmares about Smith and Jonas, still wondering why I'd been spared when better men had died.

I reach for her free hand, covering it with both of mine. Her skin is soft and warm, and she doesn't pull away. "But what if it does work out, Al? What if this is exactly what you and Tyler need—a chance to start fresh, to build something beautiful from scratch?"

She studies my face for a long moment, searching for something I hope she finds there. Tyler chooses that moment to reach for me, his chubby arms extending in the universal toddler gesture for "pick me up," and without thinking, I take him from Alma's arms. He settles against my chest like he belongs there, his small hand fisting in my shirt.

"You really think we can do this?" Alma asks, her voice small but hopeful.

Looking down at Tyler's trusting face, then back at the woman who's brave enough to risk everything for the chance at something better, I feel something shift in my chest—a recognition that maybe this isn't just about helping Drew's widow anymore. Maybe this is about all of us finding our way to something that looks like family, even if it's not the family any of us originally planned.

"I think you're the strongest person I know," I tell her honestly. "And I think Tyler's lucky to have a mother who's willing to fight for his future instead of just accepting whatever life hands them."

She smiles then, the first truly radiant expression I've seen from her all morning. "Well then, I guess we better get going before I lose my nerve."

As we load into the SUV—Tyler secure in his car seat, Alma checking her seatbelt, me adjusting the mirrors—I can't shake the feeling that we're not just starting a road trip. We're beginning something entirely new, something that could change all our lives in ways we can't yet imagine.

The engine turns over smoothly, the trailer settles into position behind us, and the road stretches ahead like a promise of possibilities yet to be discovered.

CHAPTER SIX

Alma

THE DRIVE OUT of LA is the usual bumper-to-bumper nightmare, but by the time we merge onto I-15, the road opens up like a promise of freedom. Tyler laughs and babbles happily as he watches the world blur past his window, pointing at passing trucks and clapping his hands like he knows we're heading somewhere magical. His pure joy is exactly the balm I need after the brutal confrontation with Drew's parents, and I'm grateful that Sawyer doesn't try to fill the silence with empty reassurances or force me to process what just happened.

Instead, he lets me sit with my thoughts while the desert landscape gradually replaces the urban sprawl, the mountains rising in the distance like ancient guardians welcoming us toward our new life.

At Barstow Station, we find an empty booth tucked away in the back of the old train car that serves as the restaurant's dining room. The vintage atmosphere is charming in a kitschy way, and I'm able to nurse Tyler discreetly while Sawyer disappears to gather supplies for the rest of our journey. When he returns, his arms are loaded with bottles of juice and water, various snacks, and something small that makes him grin like a kid.

"I got this for Tyler," he says, sliding into the booth across from me and holding up a shiny pressed penny. "Figured I'd make sure he has a souvenir from each stop on his first cross-country road trip." He slips the penny into the first slot of a vinyl collector's book and hands it to me with an expression so tender it makes my chest tight. "I know he won't remember this trip, but..."

"I'll remember," I say softly, tucking the penny book into Tyler's diaper bag like it's something precious. "Does that count?"

Sawyer doesn't answer immediately, but I catch the way his cheeks flush beneath his beard as he takes a long sip of water, and something warm unfurls in my stomach at the sight.

From Barstow, we settle into the rhythm of the open road. I move to the backseat to be closer to Tyler, entertaining him with the collection of toys and books I'd carefully selected for the journey. It becomes a kind of game—me catching Sawyer's eyes in the rearview mirror as he glances back to check on us, him catching me watching the confident way his hands grip the steering wheel or the way he absently taps along to the music.

It's harmless flirtation, I tell myself. Just the forced intimacy of travel, the way being in close quarters can make anyone seem more attractive than they really are. I've never met any of Sawyer's girlfriends, though I remember Drew showing me a photo once—a petite woman with a pixie haircut who Drew had described as "some kind of New Age yoga instructor who thinks she can fix everyone with crystals and deep breathing." At the time, I'd been mildly curious about what kind of woman could capture Sawyer's attention, but I'd pushed the thought away as inappropriate.

Now, watching him navigate the highway with easy competence while humming along to Dave Matthews, I find myself wondering what happened to that relationship, why he's apparently single now, whether he's the kind of man who prefers casual dating or something more serious.

Stop it, I tell myself firmly. *You have no business wondering about Sawyer's love life.*

"You sure you don't want me to take over driving for a while?" I ask when I catch him looking at me again in the mirror, his gaze lingering a beat too long before returning to the road.

"Nah, I'm good. Feel free to take a nap if you want, Al. I've got this covered." He reaches for the radio dial with one hand. "You don't mind country music, do you?"

So far our playlist has been an eclectic mix of Phish, Dave Matthews, and some indie rock I don't recognize. "I never would have pegged you as a country music fan, Sawyer."

"I'm cycling through everything on my phone, and I think country's up next in the rotation. Figure Tyler probably wouldn't appreciate my death metal collection."

I laugh despite myself. "I know I wouldn't appreciate it with him in the car, but country's fine."

"Country it is, then." His grin in the rearview mirror is warm and genuine, the kind that crinkles the corners of his eyes and makes him look younger, less burdened.

By the time Kip Moore's "Bittersweet Company" fills the

car with its melancholy melody, Tyler has succumbed to the gentle motion of the road and fallen asleep in his car seat. I prop one of the neck pillows I'd brought against the window and let my own eyes drift closed, lulled by the steady hum of tires on asphalt and the surprisingly soothing sound of Sawyer's voice humming along to the music.

When I wake up, Tyler is awake and contentedly kicking at one of his stuffed animals, making those happy baby sounds that never fail to make me smile. Sawyer glances at me in the mirror, and there's something soft in his expression that makes my pulse quicken.

"Are we there yet?" I ask, stretching to work out the kinks in my neck and shoulders.

"Almost. Maybe ten more minutes."

"Thank God." I look over at Tyler, who seems perfectly content but is making that concentrated face that every parent learns to recognize. "Uh-oh. I think Tyler had a blowout."

"Make that eight minutes," Sawyer says, pressing harder on the gas pedal. "You might want to crack a window."

We make it to Flagstaff in seven minutes flat. While Sawyer fills up the gas tank, I find the family restroom and spend fifteen minutes dealing with the aftermath of what can only be described as a diaper catastrophe. When I finally emerge, Sawyer has moved the SUV to a parking spot with all the windows rolled down, and he's standing outside looking like he's trying not to laugh.

"That bad, huh?" I ask, unable to suppress my own giggles.

"Let's just say I have a whole new respect for parenthood," he says with a grin. "And for industrial-strength air fresheners."

"Well, I need to stretch my legs after that ordeal, and Tyler's getting restless. Any suggestions?"

"I could use some movement too," he says, rolling his shoulders and stretching his neck in a way that draws my attention to the strong line of his throat. "It's still early enough that we could walk around downtown, check out some of the Route 66 shops, grab dinner somewhere."

"That sounds perfect." I secure Tyler in his stroller, grateful for the chance to move around after hours of sitting. "Lead the way."

Downtown Flagstaff has that charming, slightly touristy feel of a town that knows it's a waystation for travelers but has managed to maintain its own identity. We park along Aspen Avenue and wander slowly past shops and restaurants, taking our time and letting Tyler point excitedly at everything that catches his attention—dogs, colorful signs, other children.

I wish we had more time to really explore, to duck into the vintage shops and art galleries that line the street, but this is just a stopover on our way to something bigger. Still, there's something peaceful about walking beside Sawyer as he pushes Tyler's stroller, the three of us moving through the late afternoon like we're a family instead of two people bound together by grief and circumstance.

We find a local pizzeria that looks family-friendly and settle into a booth near the window. Tyler sits in a high chair between us, happily demolishing Cheerios while Sawyer tells me about his journey into sustainable building.

"I learned mostly by attending workshops and making a lot of expensive mistakes," he says, tearing off a piece of pizza for Tyler to gnaw on. "But when I met Dax Drexel—he's a master woodworker who lives in the community—everything clicked. We spent almost three years building his place, the Pearl. It's this incredible 6,000-square-foot home that he used to rent out for workshops before he got married."

"His wife left New York to live off the grid?" The idea seems simultaneously romantic and terrifying.

"Harlow's a transplant surgeon, or was. A lot of people leave big cities for Taos—doctors, teachers, business owners, artists. It's like a regular slice of Americana, just completely self-sufficient."

"Does she still practice medicine?"

"Not surgery, but she keeps her license current. They fly back to New York every few months because Dax's father lives there, and Harlow still owns half of a private practice with a colleague." Sawyer pauses when Tyler interrupts by offering him a soggy Cheerio, which Sawyer accepts with appropriate gravitas before Tyler changes his mind and pops it into his own mouth instead.

"When they're out of town, Todd and I maintain the Pearl for them. They're excited to meet you and Tyler—Harlow especially. She doesn't get many opportunities to hang out with other women our age."

"I'm glad to hear that. I was worried I wouldn't know anyone besides you." The admission feels more vulnerable than I intended.

"Is that a problem?" There's something careful in his voice, like he's trying not to read too much into my words.

"No, but Tyler needs playmates. Kids his own age." I focus on wiping Tyler's face to avoid meeting Sawyer's eyes.

"Well, now I'm hurt," he says with exaggerated sadness, making a pouty face that delights Tyler. "I was hoping to be his favorite playmate."

"You're definitely in the running," I say, and the smile he gives me in return makes my stomach flutter in a way that's both thrilling and dangerous.

"I really hope this move works out for you and Tyler, Alma. You're taking a huge leap of faith."

"It worked out for you," I point out. "I remember when you came back from Afghanistan—you were in rough shape. All those surgeries on your leg, constantly in pain. Then you disappeared to New Mexico, and the next time we saw you, you looked like a completely different person."

Sawyer is quiet for a moment, his fingers absently tracing patterns on the table. "I wouldn't go that far, but leaving LA definitely helped. Even Todd's Hollywood mansion couldn't make me want to stay, though for a while there I thought it was the ocean air that was making my leg hurt worse."

"Was it?"

He taps his temple. "No, it was all up here. The pain was real, but it was coming from trauma, not tissue damage. I was taking seven different medications just to get through each day—one to help me sleep, another to deal with the nightmares, another for the physical pain. When I realized I couldn't function without popping pills every few hours, I knew I had to find some kind of reset button."

The parallels to Drew's situation hit me like a physical blow. "That sounds exactly like Drew. By the end, he was taking eight different medications and could barely leave the house. The side effects were almost worse than the original problems."

"I'm sorry, Al. I wish you'd felt like you could tell me what was happening."

"I figured if he'd seen you go through it successfully, he would have reached out to you on his own."

"He didn't, but if he had, I would have shared what worked for me." Sawyer sets down his water bottle and meets my eyes directly. "Would you like to know what helped?"

"Please."

"It started with a yoga class at the VA. I hated admitting I needed help with anything, but the instructor was this gruff ex-Marine who made it clear that yoga wasn't about crystals and meditation—it was about reclaiming your body from trauma." He pauses, his Adam's apple bobbing as he swallows. "That's when I decided to leave everything behind and take a road trip. Todd wasn't happy—he'd just bought this incredible house near Chateau Marmont, paid a fortune for it. He could literally walk to any hot club in Hollywood, and he wanted to keep an eye on his little brother to make sure I didn't..." He trails off, but I understand what he's not saying.

"So he could tell you were struggling?"

"Oh yeah. He's my older brother—he sees everything. I did a decent job hiding it from everyone else, but Todd knew I was in trouble. Being around his crowd wasn't helping either. All that Hollywood excess—the drinking, the drugs, the meaningless hookups. It was exciting for a while, but it was also making everything worse."

"And so you took that road trip."

"And ended up in New Mexico. Santa Fe first, where I found a brochure about sustainable building. Someone was offering a workshop for people willing to do manual labor in exchange for hands-on training. It sounded perfect—hard work, learning something useful, being part of something bigger than myself."

"And you've been there ever since."

"Ever since," he confirms with a shrug. "But don't get me wrong—building sustainable homes was just part of it. There was a lot of other work involved, more... alternative approaches."

"How alternative are we talking? Building houses replaced your need for seven medications?"

"I still take one when I absolutely have to, but that's it. As for alternative..." He grins sheepishly. "Bodywork, meditation, different types of yoga, qi gong, acupuncture. You name it, I probably tried it. Some things stuck, others didn't. I'm not saying I'm completely healed, but I'm functional in a way I never thought I'd be again."

"I'm happy you found what worked for you, Sawyer." I lift Tyler from his high chair and settle him in my lap, wishing desperately that Drew had been open to trying something, anything that might have helped him find a different path.

By the time we make it to the hotel an hour later, Tyler is in full meltdown mode—cranky, tired, and hungry despite having eaten at the restaurant. Sawyer helps carry my bags up to my room and efficiently sets up Tyler's portable crib while I try to soothe my increasingly agitated son.

"I'm right across the hall," Sawyer says as I walk him to the door, Tyler finally calm in my arms with his beloved purple octopus clutched against his chest. "If you need anything—anything at all—just holler. Or call."

"I will." He opens the door but doesn't step through it, lingering in the threshold in a way that makes the air between us feel charged with possibility. He's standing close enough that I can smell his cologne mixed with something that's purely him—woodsy and clean and masculine in a way that makes my heart race.

Almost without thinking, I reach out and touch his forearm, just a brief contact, but electricity shoots through me at the simple connection. "So what are your plans for the evening? Meeting up with friends in the area?"

"No friends here," he says, his voice slightly rougher than usual. "I'll probably hit the hotel gym, try to work out some of these road knots."

I tilt my head toward Tyler, who's fighting sleep in my arms, and decide to be playful for once instead of cautious. After all the heavy conversation about PTSD and medication and recovery, I want to end the evening on a lighter note. "Well, I've got a hot date with a blond tonight. Bath time, story time, then bed. You'd probably be jealous."

"I absolutely am," Sawyer says, and his laugh is warm and genuine. "Though I hope you don't limit yourself to blonds exclusively. I hear brunettes can be way more fun."

The flirtation in his voice makes my breath catch, and suddenly the space between us feels charged with something dangerous and thrilling. Everything about Sawyer reminds me of those classic movie heroes—brooding and intense like Humphrey Bogart, but with a gentleness that Bogart never quite managed. His scent, his presence, the way he's looking at me like I'm something precious and fragile—it all combines to remind me how long it's been since I've been close to a man, since I've felt desired instead of just tolerated.

"That's what I've heard too," I say, biting my lower lip in a gesture that feels both innocent and provocative. "Maybe I should give it a try sometime."

"You should, Al." His voice has dropped to barely above a whisper, and I watch his gaze flicker to my mouth before returning to my eyes. "You definitely won't regret it."

"You sound pretty confident about that, Mr. Villier."

"Damn right I am," he murmurs, and suddenly he's leaning closer, close enough that I can feel the warmth radiating from his skin, close enough that I could count his eyelashes if I wanted to. My body responds without conscious thought, swaying toward him like a magnet finding true north.

For a heartbeat, we're suspended in that space between intention and action, the air around us thick with possibility. I can feel myself leaning into him, drawn by something I've been trying to ignore for longer than I want to admit.

And then the memory hits me like cold water—another doorway, another moment of standing too close to Sawyer while my husband was just down the hall. The day Drew caught us in what looked like an intimate moment, the day that changed everything between the three of us and set in motion the chain of events that led to Drew's death.

I pull back abruptly, stumbling slightly as reality crashes over me. "I have to go. Thank you for all your help today."

I close the door harder than necessary and immediately turn the deadbolt, leaning against the wood as my heart pounds against my ribs. Tyler stirs in my arms, picking up on my agitation, and I force myself to breathe slowly and evenly until he settles again.

Get a hold of yourself, Alma. He's Drew's best friend. He's completely off-limits.

But even as I try to rationalize away what just happened, I can still feel the ghost of Sawyer's presence, can still smell his cologne lingering in the air, can still remember the way his eyes had darkened when I bit my lip.

I hurry to the bathroom and start running water for Tyler's bath, desperate for the distraction of routine. But as I help my son splash in the warm water, my mind keeps circling back to all the ways I failed Drew when he needed me most. Maybe his parents and Kevin are right—maybe if I'd stayed instead of leaving when things got difficult, he'd still be alive. Maybe I wouldn't be running halfway across the country, fleeing the ghosts of my failures as a wife and mother.

Why else would I have settled for that terrible apartment next to the car repair shop? I'd been too afraid to move somewhere better, too worried about what people would say about the widow who couldn't save her war hero husband. I'd let fear and shame govern every decision, choosing the path of least resistance instead of fighting for the life Tyler and I deserved.

But that's over now. I've finally woken up, and here I am hundreds of miles from where I used to be, looking for a second chance at happiness.

I just can't allow myself to find that happiness in Sawyer. Not him. Not my husband's best friend, no matter how much my traitorous heart wants something that can never be.

As I lift Tyler from the bath and wrap him in a fluffy hotel towel, I make myself a promise: I'll build a new life in

Taos, I'll give my son the future he deserves, but I won't complicate things by wanting something I can never have.

Even if that something is standing right across the hall, probably thinking about me the same way I'm thinking about him.

Especially then.

CHAPTER SEVEN

Sawyer

ALMA IS ALREADY PACKED and ready to go when I find her in the hotel restaurant the next morning, Tyler contentedly eating pieces of banana in his high chair while she nurses a cup of coffee that looks like it's gone cold. The careful distance she maintains when she sees me approach tells me everything I need to know about how she's processing what almost happened between us last night.

We keep our conversation determinedly neutral—the weather, the remaining drive time, anything that doesn't require us to acknowledge the elephant in the room. She asks about road conditions. I mention the forecast looks good. Tyler babbles happily, oblivious to the tension crackling between the adults.

On the road, the silence stretches between us like a taut wire. I keep my eyes fixed on the asphalt ahead while Alma stares out the passenger window at the endless expanse of desert, occasionally consulting the map to track our progress through small New Mexican towns. She's not looking my way if she can help it, and I can't blame her.

The weight of my own stupidity sits heavy in my chest. Drew hasn't even been dead a full year, and here I am making moves on his wife. What the hell was I thinking last night? Why couldn't I have just helped her find a decent apartment back in LA and walked away? I could have fulfilled my promise to Drew, kept my distance, and maintained whatever was left of my honor.

Promise kept. End of story.

But instead, I had to complicate everything. I asked Alma to uproot her entire life and move to a place where she doesn't know anyone except me. Was I helping her, or was I maneuvering her into a situation where I'd be the only familiar face, the only source of support? The thought makes me sick.

For the first four hours, Alma sits in the backseat with Tyler, completely absorbed in entertaining him with an arsenal of toys—hand puppets, cloth books, stuffed animals that sing when you squeeze them. I find myself stealing glances in the rearview mirror, watching how she becomes completely present with him, using different voices for each character, singing nursery rhymes with genuine enthusiasm even when her voice cracks from overuse.

I'd always known she was good with children—she'd been teaching kindergarten when Drew left the Marines—but witnessing her maternal instincts in action is something else entirely. The way she anticipates Tyler's needs, how she can calm his fussing with just a change in her tone, the pure love that radiates from her when she looks at him—it's beautiful and heartbreaking and makes me ache for things I have no right to want.

We stop for gas and lunch in Thoreau, New Mexico, a

tiny town that seems to exist solely to serve travelers on their way to somewhere else. Despite the awkwardness between us, I don't forget my promise about the pressed penny collection. I find the machine outside the gas station and crank out another one—a roadrunner this time, appropriate for the desert landscape surrounding us. That makes five coins since we started the collection in Barstow.

When we get back on the road, Alma moves to the front passenger seat, adjusting a clip-on mirror on the sun visor so she can keep an eye on Tyler. From here, it's about four hours to Taos—four more hours of this suffocating tension, four more hours of pretending that everything is normal when we both know it's not.

We manage some stilted conversation about music preferences before she falls quiet again, eventually propping her bare feet on the dashboard and leaning back in her seat. Her toenails are painted a soft pink that makes me think of desert sunrises, and I have to force myself to focus on the road instead of the graceful curve of her ankles.

Before long, she's asleep, her breathing deep and even, one hand curled against her cheek like a child. The steady rhythm of tires on asphalt creates a hypnotic backdrop, and for the first time all day, I allow myself to relax slightly. Tyler's content in his car seat, Alma's finally at peace, and we're making good time toward our destination.

That's when everything goes to hell.

The explosion shatters the cocoon of calm like a sledgehammer through glass.

My brain doesn't register "tire blowout"—it registers "IED." The deafening bang reverberates through my bones, followed immediately by the acrid smell of burning rubber that my traumatized mind interprets as something far more sinister. Smoke billows in the side mirror, debris scattering across the highway like deadly shrapnel, and suddenly I'm not on Interstate 40 anymore.

I'm back in the Afghan mountains, twenty-three years old and watching my world explode.

The SUV lurches violently to the right as the blown tire tries to drag us off the road. The trailer whips behind us like a wounded animal, metal screaming against metal in a sound that transforms into the distinctive whistle of incoming mortars. A car horn blares—long and angry—as another vehicle swerves to avoid our careening trailer, and the sound becomes the desperate shouts of Marines calling for cover.

My hands clamp around the steering wheel with white-knuckled desperation, every tendon standing out like steel cables under strain. I can feel the phantom weight of my rifle, can taste copper and fear on my tongue, can smell the distinctive cocktail of cordite and blood that meant someone wasn't going home.

The highway dissolves beneath my eyes, replaced by sun-bleached Afghan dirt and rocky outcroppings where snipers could hide. My breath comes in sharp, shallow bursts, each inhale pulling in dust and death instead of desert air.

And Smith—God, Smith is about to step on that pressure plate, about to take that fatal step that will scatter his pieces across fifty yards of hostile terrain.

"CONTACT LEFT! IED! GET DOWN!"

The words tear from my throat with the force of muscle memory, my body moving before my conscious mind can catch up. Pure instinct takes over—the kind drilled into

Marines through countless hours of training, the kind that keeps you alive when thinking takes too long.

I lunge across the center console, my entire world narrowing to a single imperative: protect the team. In my fractured reality, I'm shielding my squad from the secondary explosion that always follows, from the sniper fire I know is coming, from the chaos that kills more soldiers than the initial blast ever does.

The phantom pain in my leg blazes to life—the exact spot where shrapnel tore through muscle and bone, where Drew's tourniquets kept me from bleeding out in that cursed valley. I can hear Drew's voice as clearly as if he's sitting beside me: "I got you, brother, I got you, just stay with me," but Drew's dead and I failed him and I can't save anyone and—

"Sawyer. Sawyer, look at me."

The voice cuts through the chaos like a lifeline thrown to a drowning man. Soft. Feminine. Wrong for a combat zone, but right in a way that makes my fractured mind scramble for purchase in the present moment.

My eyes snap into focus, and I'm hovering over Alma like a shield, my body caging her against the passenger seat, protecting her from threats only I can see. The desert heat evaporates, replaced by the cool blast of air conditioning. The smell of blood and cordite fades, overwhelmed by the synthetic pine scent of the air freshener hanging from the rearview mirror.

"It's okay," Alma says, her voice steady and sure, each word pulling me back from the precipice. "We're okay, Sawyer. It was just a blown tire. We're safe. Tyler's safe. You kept us safe."

I'm half-sprawled across her seat, my arms braced on

either side of her shoulders, my chest heaving like I've just finished a marathon in full gear. My heart is hammering so hard I'm surprised it doesn't burst through my ribs, and every nerve ending in my body is firing at once, hyper-alert to threats that exist only in my traumatized memory.

But Alma's eyes hold mine, dark and patient and infinitely calm, anchoring me to reality with the weight of her unwavering gaze. Her hands come up to rest against my chest —not pushing me away, just grounding me, letting me feel the steady rhythm of her breathing, the warmth of her palms through my shirt.

Tyler's confused whimper from the backseat snaps the final thread connecting me to the past, and present reality crashes back with brutal clarity. I'm not in Afghanistan. I'm on a highway in New Mexico with my dead best friend's wife and child, and I just completely lost my shit over a blown tire.

"How's Tyler?" I gasp, my voice raw from shouting. My heart is still trying to punch its way out of my chest, and I'm hyperaware of every point where Alma's body touches mine —her palms against my chest, the whisper of her breath against my throat, the scent of her shampoo cutting through the lingering phantom smells of war. "Is he hurt? Why isn't he crying?"

"Tyler's fine," she assures me, her voice gentle but certain. "He was startled by the noise, but he's okay. Look."

I force myself to turn and check the backseat, relief flooding through me at the sight of Tyler happily sucking on a fruit pouch, his eyes wide with curiosity rather than fear. He's watching us with the unconcerned interest of a child who trusts the adults to handle whatever's happening.

The relief makes me dizzy, and I finally notice how intimately close I am to Alma—close enough to count the flecks of gold in her brown eyes, to see the faint scar above her upper lip that I'd never noticed before, to feel the rapid rise and fall of her chest as adrenaline courses through both our systems.

I should move. I should put distance between us before this situation gets any more complicated than it already is. But her hands are still pressed against my chest, and she's not pushing me away, and there's something in her eyes that looks like concern mixed with something deeper, something that makes my breath catch for entirely different reasons.

"Sorry," I mumble, fumbling for the glove compartment where I keep my emergency medication. My hands shake as I dry-swallow a Metoprolol—a beta-blocker for acute PTSD symptoms that I haven't needed in over two years. The bitter taste reminds me of all the ways I'm still broken, still dangerous to the people I care about.

The irony isn't lost on me that the last time I took one of these was after that confrontation with Drew in their hallway, when I realized I might have to choose between my loyalty to my best friend and protecting his family from his deteriorating mental state.

I am the master of my fate, I am the captain of my soul.

I repeat the lines from Henley's poem like a mantra, using the familiar words to rebuild the walls in my mind, to stuff the demons back into their cages where they belong. I take slow, measured breaths, feeling the medication begin to dull the sharp edges of panic.

"That's better," I say, my voice slightly steadier as I check on Tyler again in the mirror. He's moved on from his fruit pouch to a teething ring, completely unfazed by the adults' drama. When I look back at Alma, I notice details I've been trying not to see for months—the thick sweep of her eyelashes, the way her lips part slightly when she's concentrating, the graceful line of her throat.

"Well, that blown tire and your NASCAR-worthy defensive driving definitely got my heart rate up," she says with a shaky laugh, trying to inject some levity into the moment. "I think I aged about five years in thirty seconds."

Her attempt at humor breaks something loose in my chest, and I find myself laughing too—the kind of raw, slightly hysterical laughter that comes after surviving something that could have gone very wrong. The sound mingles with the rush of passing traffic, chasing away the last echoes of phantom gunfire in my head.

But as our laughter fades, something else takes its place—an electric awareness that makes every nerve ending sing with dangerous possibility. Maybe it's the adrenaline still flooding our systems, or the way we're both breathing hard, or how my hands are still braced on either side of her shoulders, trapping her beneath me in a way that should feel threatening but somehow doesn't.

Her eyes drop to my mouth, then flick back up to meet mine, and I can see the exact moment she realizes what's about to happen. What's been building between us since that moment in the hotel doorway, maybe even since that day in her hallway over a year ago.

The kiss explodes between us like the tire—sudden and violent and completely inevitable. My hands slide up to cradle her face like she's something precious and fragile, while her fingers find the nape of my neck, sending electricity shooting down my spine. She tastes like coffee and fear and something I've been denying myself for longer than I care to admit.

For a heartbeat, maybe two, the world narrows to this—the soft warmth of her mouth, the way she melts into me like she belongs there, the sound she makes against my lips that's part surprise, part surrender. My entire universe contracts to the feel of her, the taste of her, the way she fits against me like we were designed for this moment.

Then reality crashes back like a freight train.

Drew's wife. Your best friend's wife. What the fuck are you doing?

We break apart like we've been electrocuted, staring at each other with matching expressions of horror and want and desperate confusion. The ghost of Drew seems to materialize between us, and all I can hear is his voice from that terrible night: "I see how you look at her, brother. Don't think I don't know."

"I need to... I'm going to change the tire," I stammer, practically falling out of the SUV in my haste to escape the suffocating intimacy of the moment. The roar of passing cars on the interstate drowns out everything except the accusatory loop playing in my head: *What the hell were you thinking? What the hell were you thinking?*

But even as guilt claws at my chest with razor-sharp talons, I can still feel the phantom press of her lips against mine, can still taste her on my tongue, can still remember the way she'd responded like she'd been waiting for this as long as I had.

A truck pulls over about fifty yards ahead of us, its hazard lights blinking. I straighten my shoulders instinctively when I spot the driver's military bearing—even in civilian clothes, you can always tell. It's in the way he carries himself, how his eyes automatically scan the environment for threats before focusing on the immediate situation.

"You folks alright?" he calls out as he approaches, and I give him a thumbs up, trying to hide the fact that my hands are still shaking.

"Yeah, we're good. Just a blowout."

His wife—a kind-faced woman with graying hair—hurries toward Alma and Tyler. "Oh honey, are you okay? We saw the debris scattered all over the road back there and were worried someone might have gotten hurt."

"We're fine, thank you," Alma says, but I can hear the slight tremor in her voice that suggests she's still processing everything that just happened—the tire, my episode, the kiss that changed everything between us.

"You got a spare?" the man asks, reaching me. That's when I spot it—the Marine Corps tattoo on his forearm, the familiar eagle, globe, and anchor that marks him as one of us. The tension in my shoulders eases fractionally.

"Full-size spare in the back," Alma calls out. "I had the pressure checked before we left California."

The Marine extends his hand with the kind of firm grip that speaks to shared experience. "Willy Castellano. Hell of some defensive driving back there, brother."

I blink in surprise. "How did you—"

"The way you controlled that swerve when the tire went." He taps his temple with a knowing look. "Plus that thousand-yard stare you're sporting. Been there myself, Marine."

His voice drops so only I can hear: "Sand or mountains?"

"Mountains," I manage, grateful that I don't have to explain. "Afghanistan. You?"

"Desert Shield and Iraqi Freedom. Two tours." He moves toward the back of the SUV, his voice remaining low and confidential. "First time something like this has taken you back?"

I hesitate, then nod. There's no point in lying to someone who clearly understands the territory.

"Lisa!" he calls to his wife. "Why don't you take the lady and the little one to our truck? Air conditioning's running, and it's got to be more comfortable than standing out here in the heat."

As they walk away, Willy turns back to me with the kind of direct gaze that cuts through bullshit. "Had my first major episode at a Fourth of July barbecue. Started hitting the deck every time someone set off a firecracker. Scared the hell out of my kids, embarrassed my wife. Thought I was losing my mind."

We work on loosening the lug nuts together, the familiar routine of manual labor helping to ground me in the present moment. "How'd you get through it?" I ask finally.

"Got help. Real help, not just pills and platitudes. Learned my triggers, developed coping strategies, found people who understood what I was going through." He glances meaningfully toward the truck where Alma sits with Tyler and his wife. "But the hardest part? Learning to let people love you through it. Sometimes the people who want to help most are the ones we push away hardest, because we're so afraid of being a burden."

I think about Drew, about that night in the hallway when I tried to help and ended up making everything worse. About how my attempt to protect Alma from her husband's deteriorating mental state had driven a wedge between Drew and me that never healed. "It's complicated," I mutter.

"Isn't it always?" He starts working the tire iron with practiced efficiency. "But here's what I learned in twenty years of marriage and fifteen years of dealing with PTSD—the guilt's usually the worst part. Survivor's guilt, guilt about wanting things we think we shouldn't want, guilt about being alive when others aren't."

My chest tightens at how precisely his words hit their target. "How do you deal with that?"

"By remembering what we fought for in the first place." He looks me straight in the eye with the kind of unwavering intensity that only comes from hard-won wisdom. "The right to live, Marine. The right to love. The right to be happy. The right to build something good out of the wreckage."

He pauses, rolling the damaged tire away from the SUV. "Our brothers who didn't make it home—they didn't die so we could spend the rest of our lives punishing ourselves for surviving. They died so we could have the chance to live fully, to love deeply, to find whatever happiness this fucked-up world has to offer."

Forty-five minutes later, we're back on the road with a new tire and Willy's business card tucked into my wallet. As I watch his truck disappear into the heat shimmer ahead of us, his words echo in my head like a bell that can't be un-rung.

But when I get back in the SUV, Alma has moved to the backseat with Tyler, and the message is clear. There are no more glances in the rearview mirror, no more casual conversation. She's created as much physical distance as the confines of the vehicle allow, and I can't blame her for it.

We don't talk for the rest of the drive, not even during our stop in Albuquerque for gas and snacks. The silence stretches between us like a gulf that grows wider with each passing mile, filled with everything we can't say, everything we shouldn't want, everything that changed in those few seconds when the world exploded and we found ourselves kissing like our lives depended on it.

By the time we reach Taos, darkness has fallen over the high desert like a protective blanket. The lights of the town twinkle in the valley below us, but it's too late and we're all too emotionally wrung out to make the final push to the rammed earth house. I make the executive decision to get them rooms at La Fonda Hotel for the night—separate rooms, naturally—and promise to pick them up in the morning for the grand tour of their new temporary home.

But as I make my way back to the SUV after helping them get settled, Willy's words keep cycling through my head like a song I can't shake: *The right to live. The right to love. The right to be happy.*

I know we'll have to talk about what happened—the episode, the kiss, the way everything between us shifted in the space of a few heartbeats. But not tonight. Tonight, we all need time to process, to figure out what comes next, to decide whether we're brave enough to face the truth that's been building between us since that day in her hallway.

The truth that maybe some promises to the dead have to be weighed against the possibilities of the living.

The truth that maybe Drew would want us to choose happiness over guilt, love over loyalty to his memory.

The truth that maybe, just maybe, we deserve a chance to find out what could grow in the space between survival and actually living.

CHAPTER EIGHT

Alma

DREW'S HANDS are already around my neck before I can stop him. I open my mouth to scream but no sound comes out. I will myself to move but I can't—I'm frozen in place as his fingers tighten like a vise, cutting off my air, cutting off my voice, cutting off everything except the terror that floods my system like ice water.

I bolt upright in the hotel bed, a scream trapped in my throat like a bird beating against glass. It's just a dream, Alma. He's dead. He can't hurt you anymore.

But I look around the room anyway, my heart hammering against my ribs as I scan every shadow, every corner where danger might hide. Next to the bed, in the portable crib the hotel staff brought up, Tyler sleeps peacefully, his tiny chest rising and falling with the steady rhythm of complete trust. He's oblivious to his mother's panic, safe in the cocoon of childhood where monsters only exist in storybooks.

I take slow, measured breaths, letting my gaze wander around the unfamiliar hotel room until the digital clock comes into focus: 3:17 AM, the numbers glowing red in the semi-darkness like accusing eyes. I wonder when the dreams will finally stop, when my subconscious will finally release its death grip on the past and allow me to move forward into whatever future I'm trying to build.

After all, wasn't that why I'd chosen that terrible apartment next to the car repair shop? I'd allowed my guilt and apathy to make decisions for me after Drew's death, letting the weight of what I couldn't save dictate every choice I made. I'd always prided myself on being resilient, someone who could pick herself up and move forward when life knocked her down. But Drew's death—and the complicated grief that came with it—had been different. The guilt was so much worse because part of me, the part I could never admit out loud, had felt relief when it was over.

Relief that I didn't have to walk on eggshells anymore. Relief that Tyler would never have to see his father in one of those dark rages. Relief that I could finally stop pretending everything was fine when everything was falling apart.

That relief made the guilt unbearable.

But things are different now. I'm taking control of my life instead of letting fear and shame drive me into hiding. This time, I'm determined not to let grief win, not to let the past poison whatever chances I have at building something better for Tyler and myself.

I lie back down on the pillow and close my eyes, willing sleep to return. But instead of dreams, what comes is the memory of yesterday's kiss—the way it exploded between Sawyer and me like something that had been building pressure for months, maybe years, and finally found its release.

Neither of us has mentioned it, as if acknowledging what happened might make it more real, more complicated than it already is. We're walking around it like it's a landmine that might detonate if we look at it too directly. But ignoring it doesn't make it disappear. If anything, the silence makes it loom larger, filling the space between us with unspoken questions and dangerous possibilities.

How do you bring up something like that? "Oh, by the way, about that kiss that turned my world upside down..."

I sigh, tracing my upper lip with my fingertip, still able to feel the ghost of his mouth on mine. My lips tingle as I remember how the entire world seemed to fall away the moment we touched—no past, no guilt, no complicated loyalties, just the pure electric connection of two people who'd been circling each other for longer than either wanted to admit.

It was quick and unexpected, over almost before it began. But in that brief moment, I caught a glimpse of what my world could be like again—a world where I could love and be loved in return, where I could be more than just a widow defined by loss and regret.

I deserve that, don't I? The right to happiness, to love, to a future that isn't held hostage by the past?

The questions follow me into restless sleep, and when morning finally comes, I still don't have any answers.

The next morning, Sawyer arrives at the hotel looking more relaxed than I've seen him since we left California. He's wearing a white t-shirt layered under a denim shirt and cargo pants, and maybe it's the high desert light or the mountain air, but even the worry lines that usually bracket his eyes seem softer. The awkwardness from yesterday has receded enough that we can actually look at each other without immediately thinking about what happened on the side of that highway.

We're talking like the kiss never happened, which is probably for the best. I can agonize over what it meant later—right now, I just want to see my new home and start figuring out how to build a life here.

As we step out of the hotel's front doors, which face directly onto Taos Plaza, I'm struck by an immediate sense of peace that I can't quite explain. The energy here is different from anywhere I've ever lived—calmer, more grounded, like the mountains themselves are emanating some kind of ancient serenity. For one thing, there's no traffic noise, no constant urban hum that follows you everywhere in Los Angeles.

"Would you like a quick tour of the town first?" Sawyer asks as he loads my overnight bag into the SUV, which looks strange without its trailer. "We should probably stop for groceries too. There's nothing out at the community as far as shopping goes, so we'll need to stock you up on basics here."

"Tour first, then groceries," I say, securing Tyler in his car seat. He babbles happily, pointing at everything that catches his attention—the adobe buildings, the colorful prayer flags strung between trees, a dog walking past with its owner.

"Perfect. I need to pick up supplies anyway, and it'll be a good way to get you oriented to the town."

We begin at Taos Plaza, right outside the hotel, and I'm stunned by the endless expanse of sky overhead—thick white clouds set against the deepest blue I've ever seen, like something from a postcard that's been oversaturated for effect.

Except this is real. The air smells clean and thin, carrying scents of pine and sage and something indefinable that might just be possibility.

"This place is so beautiful," I say as we cross the street with Tyler snug in the baby carrier against my chest. "And eclectic. I can't believe I missed all this when we drove in last night. What's this architecture called? Adobe?"

"That's right. Adobe is a mixture of mud, straw, and water—basically the same building material people have been using here for over a thousand years. The style is called Pueblo Revival, and it's a blend of three cultures." Sawyer stops in the middle of the plaza, gesturing for me to turn around and take in the full view. "Native American pueblos that were here long before anyone else, Spanish colonial influences from when this was part of Mexico, and Anglo-American adaptations that came later. The name Taos itself comes from the Tiwa word meaning 'place of red willows.'"

"Place of red willows," I repeat, liking the sound of it. "That's beautiful."

As we wander around the plaza, we pause frequently to take pictures. Some are of the architecture, some of Tyler's delighted reactions to everything around him, and a few are selfies of the three of us together. When Sawyer holds up his phone to capture us all with the plaza in the background, I can't help but notice how we look like a family—and the thought sends butterflies careening through my stomach in ways both thrilling and terrifying.

"Let's get you and Tyler some souvenirs before we hit the grocery store," Sawyer says, pocketing his phone and leading us toward a row of shops selling everything from turquoise jewelry to hand-woven rugs. Of course, he finds another pressed penny machine and adds to Tyler's growing collection.

By the time we're ready to head to my new home, I'm practically vibrating with excitement. After six months of living in that cramped apartment next to the constant noise of the car repair shop, the idea of space and silence feels like the greatest luxury imaginable. No more planning our days around library story time and park visits just to escape the din. From what I've seen in Sawyer's photos, the house has enough room for Tyler to really play, and I'll be able to garden again—something I haven't been able to do since we left the house Drew and I shared.

"Want to see the Rio Grande Gorge Bridge before we head out to the community?" Sawyer asks as we leave the town behind, passing the last of the adobe buildings and heading into the high desert landscape. "It's on the way, and you'll get to see the fifth-highest bridge in the United States."

"Absolutely." I love how enthusiastic Sawyer is about playing tour guide. There's a lightness to him here that I never saw in California, like this place has given him permission to be a version of himself that doesn't carry quite so much weight.

The bridge is spectacular—a graceful span of steel and concrete arcing across a chasm so deep it makes my stomach lurch when I peer over the edge. Below us, the Rio Grande cuts its ancient path through layers of volcanic rock, the water just a glittering thread from this height.

"I think I've seen this in movies," I say as Sawyer parks in the designated viewing area.

"It's been in quite a few. Wild Hogs, Natural Born Killers, a bunch of others." He helps me get Tyler situated in his stroller while other tourists mill around with cameras and phones. "It used to be called the bridge to nowhere because when they were building it, funding ran out before they could complete the road on the other side."

We take more photos—selfies with the massive gorge stretching endlessly behind us, artistic shots of Tyler pointing excitedly at the passing cars, panoramic views of the land-scape that stretches to the horizon in every direction. The bridge vibrates slightly under our feet whenever a truck rumbles past, and the wind carries the scent of sage and something wild and clean that I can't identify.

When Tyler starts getting restless, we head back to the SUV and continue our journey. It doesn't take long before Sawyer points out unusual shapes in the distance—curved structures that seem to rise organically from the earth itself, punctuated by the slow rotation of wind turbines.

"Those are some of the rammed earth houses that make up the community," he explains. "Your new neighbors. It's nothing like city living, so it might be a bit of a shock at first."

He turns right off the main road onto what can gener-ously be called a dirt track. Gravel crunches under the tires, and I realize there are no street signs, no painted lines, no infrastructure in the traditional sense. "My place is closest to yours, along with the Pearl—that's Dax and Harlow's house."

"The Pearl?"

"We all name our houses out here. At least, the people I know do. Dax calls his place the Pearl, after his mother, and Todd and I named ours the Daisy."

I look at him curiously. "Daisy?"

Sawyer's smile is soft with memory. "She was our dog

when we were kids. A dachshund with more personality than sense. We loved that little hot dog."

The dirt road winds through an landscape of sagebrush and chamisa, with the Sangre de Cristo mountains rising like ancient guardians to the north. It's so quiet I can hear the wind through the brush, the distant call of a hawk, the gentle whir of the wind turbines. "So this is off-grid living."

"This is it. When you're on the grid, the city or county provides your electricity, gas, water, sewage, roads—all the infrastructure we usually take for granted." Sawyer slows to navigate around a particularly deep rut. "Out here, each house is self-sufficient. Solar panels for electricity, rainwater collection, septic systems, the works. You having second thoughts?"

I give him a pointed look. "I'm tougher than I look, Sawyer."

"I know you are," he says, grinning. "So what are you going to name your place?"

The answer comes without hesitation. "The Willow. After the red willows that gave this place its name."

"The Willow it is." A few moments later, he points to a large structure in the distance, its windows catching the afternoon sun like mirrors. There's a trampoline in the front yard and what looks like a vegetable garden. "That's the Pearl over there. And over to the right is the Daisy. We're all pretty close neighbors out here."

My excitement builds with each passing moment. "Where's mine?"

"Coming up. You ready?" Sawyer turns onto an even smaller track that leads toward a structure that seems to emerge from the hillside itself like something from a fairy tale. The first thing I notice are the south-facing windows that take up almost the entire front wall, followed by the cone-shaped towers on either end that give the whole building an organic, almost alive quality. The teal-colored walls are punctuated by circular shapes in different colors that catch the light and throw it back in rainbow patterns.

"What are those circles?" I ask as Sawyer brings us to a stop.

"Bottle bricks," he says with obvious pride. "You take glass bottles—wine bottles work well—and cut them in half. The bottoms get paired with other bottoms of the same size and color, taped together, and built into the walls. They let in light while maintaining the wall's integrity, and they create these amazing light patterns inside."

He turns off the engine, and sudden silence settles around us like a blanket. No traffic, no machinery, no urban soundtrack at all. Just wind and birds and the distant sound of the wind turbines. "You ready?"

I can't stop smiling. My face actually hurts from grinning so hard. "What do you think?"

Sawyer studies my expression for a moment, and there's something in his eyes that makes my heart skip—warmth and pride and something deeper that I don't dare name. "I think you're as ready as you'll ever be. Let's go see your new home."

I lift Tyler from his car seat and follow Sawyer toward the house, my feet crunching on the gravel path. The scent of sagebrush is stronger here, and I remember reading somewhere that sage is considered a cleansing plant by Native Americans. There's the gentle whir of the wind generator, which sounds almost musical, and I spot a jackrabbit at the edge of what I assume is my yard, calmly munching on something green and apparently unbothered by our presence.

The front entrance is marked by a colorful mosaic made from broken tiles and glass pebbles, creating a mandala-like pattern that catches the light. Sawyer stops at the door and pulls a set of keys from his pocket, holding them out to me with a slight bow.

"All yours."

I don't take them immediately, narrowing my eyes at him. "The lease. I told you I'm not accepting charity, Sawyer."

"It's inside, along with everything else you need to know about living here," he says with a reassuring smile. "Why don't I carry Tyler so you can do the honors?"

I hand over my son, who goes willingly into Sawyer's arms, his attention completely captured by the house in front of us. With trembling fingers, I take the keys and approach the door. The metal is warm from the sun, and when I turn the key, I hear the satisfying click of tumblers falling into place.

I step inside and immediately gasp.

The first thing I notice is the light—golden afternoon sun streaming through those massive south-facing windows, creating patterns on the floor that shift and dance with the movement of clouds outside. The second thing is the plants— an entire indoor garden thriving in planters along the windows and in raised beds integrated into the living space. Tomatoes heavy with fruit, cucumber vines climbing improvised trellises, kale and broccoli and snap peas creating a riot of green against the warm adobe walls.

I stand in the center of the main living area, turning slowly to take it all in. The floors are polished concrete with radiant heating coils underneath, warm under my feet even through my shoes. The walls curve organically, punctuated by those bottle bricks that cast colored light patterns across the surfaces. Some sections are finished smooth as silk, while others show the natural texture of the adobe beneath.

"This is incredible," I breathe, moving toward the kitchen area. "How do you ever want to leave?"

"Work has its demands," Sawyer says, but he's watching my reaction more than looking at the house. "Though I admit, some days it's harder than others."

I'm drawn to run my hands along the adobe walls, surprised by how smooth and warm they feel under my palms. In some places, they seem to sparkle with tiny flecks of light.

"What makes them glitter like that?"

"Mica. It's a mineral we mix into the final plaster coat. When the Spanish conquistadors first came to this area, they thought they'd found one of the legendary Seven Cities of Gold because the buildings seemed to shimmer with precious metal."

"It's beautiful," I whisper, meaning it more than any compliment I've ever given.

As Sawyer guides me through the rest of the house, explaining the systems that make off-grid living possible, I fall more in love with each room. The bedroom is spacious and serene, with built-in adobe benches along the windows that would be perfect for reading. The bathroom features a claw-foot tub positioned to take advantage of mountain views. There's a washer and dryer that run entirely on solar power, a full kitchen with all modern appliances, even Wi-Fi and a large-screen TV.

"Basically, it has everything you'd find in a conventional house," Sawyer explains. "The only difference is where the power comes from. You'll barely notice you're off-grid, except for the silence."

When he finally hands me the lease to review, I'm fighting back tears that seem to come from nowhere and everywhere at once. Maybe it's the relief of finally having a safe, beautiful place to call home. Maybe it's the overwhelming gratitude for Sawyer's kindness in making this possible. Or maybe it's the recognition that for the first time since Drew died, I'm making a choice based on hope instead of fear.

I don't realize I'm crying until Sawyer gently pulls me into his arms, Tyler sandwiched between us like the world's most perfect buffer. I breathe in the scent that's becoming familiar—clean and woodsy and entirely him—while Tyler plants wet baby kisses on my forehead, probably thinking this is all some kind of game.

"It's okay," Sawyer murmurs against my hair, and the simple comfort of being held makes me cry harder.

"I'm sorry for being such a mess," I manage between sobs. "I don't mean to be so emotional. It's just... it's perfect. Better than I ever imagined."

"Maybe it's all the sage in the air," I add with a watery laugh, pulling back to wipe my eyes. "Cleansing the hell out of me."

The sound of an engine approaching breaks the moment, and Sawyer glances out the window. "That should be Todd. He's going to help me unload your trailer."

"He doesn't have to do that," I protest. "I can handle my own stuff."

"We both want to help," Sawyer says firmly. "Seriously, Alma. We're here for whatever you need—moving boxes, figuring out the solar panels, introducing you to the neighbors. The Villier brothers are at your service, no questions asked."

The easy way he says it, like helping me is the most natural thing in the world, makes my heart do something complicated in my chest. "With customer service like that, you'll have women lined up from here to the highway."

He meets my eyes with an intensity that makes my breath catch. "I'm not interested in women plural," he says quietly. "Just one."

CHAPTER NINE

Sawyer

IT'S BEEN three days since I handed Alma the keys to the Willow, and she seems to have settled in quite nicely. At least, that's what I tell myself, considering she hasn't called me once asking for help with anything. Not the solar panel system, not the greywater filters, not even questions about where to shop for groceries.

Part of me is proud of her independence—after all, I gave her a comprehensive tour of every system in the house, showed her the monthly maintenance schedule, and left detailed instructions for everything from resetting the inverter to cleaning the composting toilet. She's also a Marine wife who managed perfectly well during Drew's deployments, which means she knows how to handle herself without a man hovering over her shoulder.

But if I'm being honest, another part of me is disappointed. I'd been hoping for an excuse to see her again, to check on how she and Tyler were adapting to their new environment. Instead, I've been reduced to playing endless rounds of Call of Duty with Todd and pretending I'm not wondering what she's doing every few hours.

When Dax calls this morning asking for help with his greywater botanical system—apparently some of his plants are struggling and he suspects the filters need cleaning—I jump at the chance to get out of the house. Plus, he mentioned having cold beer ready, which doesn't hurt.

Dax meets me outside the Pearl when I arrive, and as always, I'm struck by how much we look alike despite coming from completely different backgrounds. At twenty-nine, he's got the same build as me—broad shoulders, lean hips—along with thick dark hair and blue eyes that women seem to find irresistible. But where my body bears the scars and tension of two combat deployments, Dax moves with the fluid grace of someone who's spent his life working with his hands in pursuit of beauty rather than survival.

After high school, instead of enlisting like I did, he apprenticed under a Japanese master woodworker, eventually establishing Takeshi and Drexel Woodworking & Design after his mentor's death. These days, his custom furniture graces homes from the Hamptons to ski lodges in Gstaad, and he's got a waiting list that stretches two years out. Yet despite all the success and celebrity clients, he's remained grounded —a true Taoseño who's never forgotten his roots.

"Where is everyone?" I ask as we head inside. Usually the twins would be racing to greet me by now, begging me to play superhero or help them build something elaborate out of couch cushions. I've never been much of a kid person, but DJ and Ani-Pea somehow wormed their way under my defenses. Same with Tyler, if I'm being honest.

"Harlow and the kids are at your neighbor's place," Dax

says with a knowing grin as he heads toward the kitchen. "They're having a play date."

"A play date?" The words hit me with unexpected force. I suddenly realize I never got around to introducing Alma to Harlow, too caught up in trying to maintain proper boundaries and give her space. "When did they meet?"

"Yesterday morning. Harlow took the twins over to welcome her to the neighborhood—you know how she is about making sure everyone feels included." He pulls two beers from the refrigerator and tosses one my way. "Turns out your friend is a kindergarten teacher. Now Harlow's talking her ear off about lesson plans and early childhood development."

"Wow." The single word is all I can manage. No wonder Alma hasn't called—she's been busy building the exact kind of connections I should have been facilitating instead of hiding in my house like a coward.

"The kids get along great too," Dax adds, popping open his beer. "Tyler apparently adores the twins, and they're completely smitten with having a baby to fuss over."

I take a long pull of my beer, trying to process this information. "That's good. Really good."

"She's not your girlfriend, is she?" Dax asks suddenly, studying my face with the kind of perceptive intensity that makes him such a good craftsman.

"No," I say quickly. "She's not."

"But you want her to be."

The directness of the statement catches me off guard. "It's complicated."

"How complicated?"

I debate how much to tell him, then decide on a version

of the truth that won't require me to explain the full mess of my feelings. "She's my best friend's widow. The one who died last year."

Dax's expression softens with understanding. "Ah. So you're caught between loyalty to your friend and your feelings for her."

"Something like that." I drain half my beer in one go. "Let's just focus on your plants, okay?"

"Fair enough." But I can see him filing this information away for later analysis. Dax has always been good at reading people—it's part of what makes him such a successful businessman.

We spend the next two hours working on his greywater system, swapping stories about our recent work while carefully avoiding the topic of Alma. I tell him about my latest assignment guarding a tech billionaire during a trip to Saudi Arabia, while he describes the custom staircase he's building for some Hollywood director's Sun Valley retreat. The familiar rhythm of manual labor helps settle my nerves, reminding me why I love this lifestyle—the satisfaction of fixing things with your hands, the peace that comes from being self-sufficient.

We're examining the adobe walls on the eastern side of the Pearl when we hear voices approaching from the main entrance. Dax's entire face lights up with the kind of joy that never fails to make me slightly envious of what he and Harlow have built together.

"There they are," he says as DJ and Ani-Pea burst into the hallway, their bare feet slapping against the polished concrete floors. DJ looks like a miniature version of his father with the same thick dark hair and bright blue eyes, while Ani-

Pea—short for Anita Pearl—is her mother's daughter through and through, all serious hazel eyes and determined chin.

Behind them comes Harlow, looking every inch the successful surgeon even in casual clothes, her dark hair pulled back in a practical ponytail. And beside her...

My breath catches in my throat at the sight of Alma carrying Tyler in her arms. She's wearing a peach sleeveless top that brings out the golden undertones in her skin and white cropped pants that somehow manage to be both practical and elegant. Her auburn hair falls in loose waves over her shoulders, and there's something different about her—a relaxation in her posture, a brightness in her eyes that I haven't seen since before Drew's final deployment.

She looks like she's been kissed by the high desert sun, and the glow suits her perfectly.

"Sawyer!" Harlow greets me with her usual warm hug before chasing after Ani-Pea, who's making a beeline for one of the planters. "Oh no, you don't, little miss. We've talked about this." She scoops up her daughter with practiced ease. "She has an obsession with playing in the soil. Turn your back for two seconds and she's elbow-deep in dirt."

"I should probably build them a proper sandbox," Dax says, moving to kiss Harlow in greeting. "Put it next to the trampoline so they can work off some energy."

"That would be amazing," Harlow says, then turns to include Alma in the conversation. "We had such a wonderful time today. I took Alma on the grand tour—the library, the community center, the farmer's market. Tyler was an absolute angel."

"It sounds like you had a busy day," I manage, my voice

coming out slightly rougher than intended when Alma's eyes meet mine.

"We did," she says softly. "Harlow's been an incredible tour guide. I feel like I'm starting to understand what makes this place so special."

Tyler chooses that moment to reach toward me, his chubby arms extended and a huge grin splitting his face. "Ba-ba!" he babbles excitedly, as if he's been waiting all day to see me.

"Hey there, little man," I say, accepting him into my arms. The weight of him, solid and warm and trusting, does something complicated to my chest. "Did you have fun with the big kids?"

Tyler responds by grabbing a handful of my beard and tugging with the fearless enthusiasm of a child who's never learned that the world can hurt you. Everyone laughs, and for a moment, the tension in my shoulders eases.

"Why don't I take him?" Alma says, stepping closer to retrieve her son. The movement brings her within touching distance, close enough that I catch the scent of her shampoo—something light and floral that makes me think of summer gardens and possibilities I shouldn't be entertaining.

Our fingers brush as Tyler transfers from my arms to hers, and the brief contact sends electricity racing up my arm. From the way her breath catches, I suspect she feels it too.

"I should probably get him home," she says, not quite meeting my eyes. "It's been a long day, and he'll be cranky if he misses his nap."

"But you just got here," Dax protests. "I was about to warm up some of Nana's stuffed sopapillas. You can't leave without trying authentic New Mexican cuisine."

"What are sopapillas?" Alma asks, and Dax actually gasps in horror.

"Sawyer, please tell me you've at least introduced her to the local food scene."

"Was I supposed to?" I ask innocently, though I'm privately kicking myself. I've been so focused on maintaining appropriate boundaries that I've failed at basic hospitality.

"Damn right you were supposed to," Dax says with mock outrage. "Alma, you officially cannot leave until you've experienced Nana's cooking. It's practically a law around here."

Alma looks between Dax and Harlow, then glances at me uncertainly. "Do I have a choice in this matter?"

"Absolutely not," Harlow and I say in unison, which makes everyone laugh.

"Trust me," I add, trying to ignore how natural this all feels—standing here with Alma and Tyler, part of a group of friends sharing an ordinary moment. "Once you try Nana's sopapillas, you'll understand why Dax gets so worked up about them."

"I believe you," Alma says with a smile that makes my heart skip a beat. "But I have to admit, I don't even know what sopapillas are."

"Fate," Dax declares dramatically. "This is clearly destiny intervening to ensure you experience one of life's great pleasures."

While Dax sets about warming the sopapillas—basically a fried dough pastry that's part of New Mexican culinary tradition—the women head to the nursery with all three kids. I carry Tyler's portable playpen in from Alma's SUV without being asked, falling into the kind of easy cooperation that feels dangerously domestic.

Twenty minutes later, all the children are napping, and we're gathered around the Drexels' dining table enjoying carne adovada-stuffed sopapillas smothered in cheese and green chile. For dessert, we have plain sopapillas drizzled with honey, and I watch Alma's face light up with each bite.

"This is incredible," she says, licking honey from her fingers in a gesture so unconsciously sensual it makes my mouth go dry. "I can't believe I've been missing out on this my whole life."

"Welcome to New Mexico," Harlow says with a grin. "Wait until you try green chile cheeseburgers. Or Hatch green chile anything, really."

As Dax and Harlow launch into the story of how they met—a confrontation right here in front of the Pearl that had Dax literally tripping over himself after Harlow called him out for his attitude—I find myself mesmerized by Alma's reactions. She throws her head back when she laughs, completely uninhibited, and her eyes sparkle with genuine delight at their romantic comedy of errors.

I've never seen her this relaxed, this vibrant. Even during the happiest times with Drew, there had always been an underlying tension in her, a watchfulness that came from loving someone who carried darkness inside him. Now, surrounded by new friends in this peaceful place, she looks like she's remembering how to simply exist without constantly scanning for threats.

When she catches me watching her, our eyes lock for a moment that stretches longer than it should. Her cheeks flush pink, and she quickly looks away, but not before I see something in her expression that mirrors the want I'm trying so hard to suppress.

"So do you think you'll stay after your three-month trial period?" Harlow asks, apparently oblivious to the charged moment between Alma and me.

"I honestly don't know yet," Alma says, her voice slightly breathless. "But I have to admit, I'm enjoying myself more than I expected. I was terrified that first night, though."

"Why?" Dax asks with immediate concern. "Did something happen? Is there a safety issue we should know about?"

"No, nothing like that," Alma laughs. "It was just so quiet. Deathly quiet. I could actually hear myself think for the first time in months."

"I know exactly what you mean," Harlow says, nodding sympathetically. "The silence was one of the biggest adjustments when I moved here from Manhattan. You don't realize how much background noise you live with until it's gone."

"Exactly," Alma agrees. "I'd gotten so used to the constant sound of air compressors and machinery from that car repair shop that I'd forgotten what real quiet sounded like."

"What does it sound like now?" I ask before I can stop myself. "The silence, I mean. From inside the Willow."

Everyone turns to look at me, probably surprised by my contribution to the conversation since I've been mostly quiet throughout the meal. But I genuinely want to know—I want to understand how this place is affecting her, whether she's finding the peace I'd hoped she would.

Alma considers the question seriously, tilting her head in that way she does when she's thinking something through. "This might sound corny, but the silence here feels like... coming home to a place you never knew you were looking for.

Like finally being able to breathe after holding your breath for a very long time."

The poetry of her answer hits me square in the chest. This is exactly what I'd hoped for her—this sense of belonging, of peace, of being able to simply exist without constant vigilance.

"That's not corny at all," Harlow says gently. "That's exactly how I felt when I first came here too."

"Would you ever leave?" Alma asks. "Go back to the city?"

Harlow exchanges a look with Dax, their communication wordless and complete. "I don't think so. We travel enough that I don't feel like I'm missing anything from my old life. And this..." She gestures around the table, encompassing all of us, the house, the life they've built. "This is real in a way that nothing in New York ever was."

"I can understand that," Alma says quietly. "I don't think I'd want to travel much while Tyler's still so young anyway. I need to figure out what I'm going to do work-wise first."

"Will you go back to teaching?" Harlow asks.

"I'm not sure. It would depend on the local school district and whether they have openings." Alma pauses, and I can see her working through ideas in real time. "Actually, I've been thinking about starting a blog about homeschooling off-grid. I know enough about early childhood education, and I'd been planning to open my own preschool before..." She doesn't finish the sentence, but we all understand. Before Drew's death changed everything.

"But now that I'm here," she continues, "I could channel that knowledge into creating online content—lesson plans, activities for different age groups, maybe even courses on sustainable education. That way I could work from home and still be present for Tyler."

"That's a brilliant idea," Dax says enthusiastically. "There's definitely a market for that kind of content. Lots of families are choosing alternative education paths these days."

"My mother stayed home with me," he adds, his voice growing softer. "She homeschooled me when I was diagnosed with dyslexia, made sure I didn't fall through the cracks. It made all the difference in my life."

"What about you, Sawyer?" Harlow asks, turning the attention my way. "Did your mother stay home?"

The question hits an old nerve, but I keep my expression neutral. "Yeah, she did."

I don't elaborate, and thankfully, no one pushes. I'm not about to explain that she stayed home because she couldn't hold a job, couldn't be trusted to show up sober or function responsibly for more than a few days at a time. By the time I was ten, Todd was essentially raising me—making sure I had food, helping with homework, making sure I had clean clothes for school. Joining the Marines at eighteen had been as much about giving Todd his freedom back as it was about escaping my mother's chaos.

As the conversation continues—flowing easily between topics like local schools, community events, and which families have children Tyler's age—I find myself watching Alma with increasing fascination. She's engaging with Dax and Harlow like she's known them for years, asking thoughtful questions and sharing insights about child development that reveal the depth of her professional knowledge.

But it's more than that. There's something different about her here, in this place, surrounded by people who accept her without judgment or expectation. The careful guardedness I'd grown used to seeing in her—a protective armor developed during those difficult final months with Drew—has softened into something more open, more genuinely herself.

Every time our eyes meet across the table, I feel that same electric current that's been building between us since the kiss on the highway. She's trying to be subtle about it, but I catch her watching me when she thinks I'm not looking, and there's a heat in her gaze that makes my pulse quicken.

When Dax starts clearing the dishes, I automatically join him in the kitchen while Harlow takes Alma on a tour of their extensive indoor garden. Through the large windows, I can see them moving between the raised beds, Harlow pointing out different plants while Alma asks questions and occasionally reaches out to touch a leaf or examine a fruit.

"So," Dax says casually as he rinses plates, "you dating anyone these days?"

"Why, you interested?" I deflect, loading dishes into the dishwasher with perhaps more force than necessary.

"Sorry, but I'm taken. Long-term arrangement." He holds up his left hand, showing off his wedding ring with a grin. "But seriously, when's the last time you went out with someone?"

"Why are you asking?"

Dax nods toward the women, who are now harvesting kumquats from one of the fruit trees. "Because I think she's incredible, and I think you're an idiot if you don't see it."

"It's not that simple," I mutter.

"Because she was married to your friend."

"Because she's still married to my friend," I correct. "In

here." I tap my chest. "Drew might be dead, but that doesn't mean I get to just move in on his wife like some vulture."

"Is that what you think you'd be doing? Moving in on her?" Dax turns off the water and faces me directly. "Because from where I'm sitting, it looks like two people who care about each other trying very hard not to admit it."

"You don't understand—"

"I understand that you're both alive, both single, and both clearly attracted to each other." His voice is gentle but firm. "I also understand that survivor's guilt can make people do stupid things, like denying themselves happiness because they think they don't deserve it."

The accuracy of his observation hits too close to home. "Drop it, Dax."

"Fine. But answer me this—do you think your friend would want her to be alone for the rest of her life? Would he want his son to grow up without a father figure because you're too noble to acknowledge your feelings?"

I don't answer because I can't. The truth is, I don't know what Drew would want. The Drew I knew before his final deployment might have given us his blessing. But the Drew who died by suicide, consumed by darkness and rage? That's a question I'll never be able to answer.

"Look," Dax says, apparently interpreting my silence correctly. "I'm not saying you should declare your undying love over dessert. But maybe you could start by admitting to yourself that what you're feeling isn't betrayal—it's hope. And hope is a good thing, man. Even when it's scary."

Before I can respond, the women return from their garden tour, arms full of fresh fruit and vegetables. Alma's face is glowing with excitement as she shows off a perfect tomato, and when she looks at me, the smile she gives me is so radiant it takes my breath away.

"Harlow's garden is amazing," she says, moving closer to show me her haul. "She's been teaching me about companion planting and natural pest control. I had no idea there was so much science behind it."

"She's a quick learner," Harlow adds with obvious affection. "I have a feeling the Willow's garden is going to be spectacular under her care."

"I hope so," Alma says, then catches herself looking at me again. This time, she doesn't look away immediately, and for a moment, the rest of the room seems to fade into background noise.

Just then, we hear stirring from the nursery—Tyler's distinctive wake-up babble mixed with the twins' excited chatter. The afternoon nap is officially over, and within minutes, all three children are wide awake and demanding attention.

"Well, so much for quiet adult conversation," Harlow says with a laugh as Ani-Pea races into the main room, her hair sticking up at odd angles.

"Mama! We play outside now?" DJ asks, tugging on Dax's shirt. "Tyler wants to see the trampoline!"

"That sounds like a great idea," Dax says, ruffling his son's hair. "Why don't we all go outside for a bit? Let the kids burn off some energy before dinner."

"Are you sure?" Alma asks, Tyler now fully awake and squirming in her arms. "I don't want to overstay our welcome."

"Are you kidding?" Harlow says. "This is the most relaxed afternoon I've had in weeks. The twins are so entertained by Tyler, they're actually behaving."

As if to prove her point, DJ and Ani-Pea immediately begin organizing an impromptu parade around the living room, with Tyler clapping enthusiastically from Alma's arms.

"Outside it is," I say, surprising myself by speaking up. But seeing Alma here, integrated so naturally into this chosen family, makes something in my chest loosen for the first time in months.

We migrate to the Pearl's backyard, where the late afternoon sun casts everything in golden light. The twins immediately claim the trampoline while Tyler sits contentedly in Alma's lap on one of the outdoor benches, watching their acrobatics with wide-eyed fascination.

"I should check on the evening garden watering," Harlow says after a few minutes. "Dax, want to help me with the greenhouse?"

"Sure thing," he says, but not before catching my eye with a meaningful look. "Sawyer, why don't you show Alma the meditation garden? The light's perfect right now."

The suggestion is so obviously orchestrated that I almost refuse. But Alma's looking at me with curiosity, and Tyler's reaching toward me again, and before I can overthink it, I nod.

"Want to take a walk?" I ask. "There's a nice path that circles around back to the windmill."

"I'd like that," she says softly, and something in her voice makes my pulse quicken.

Maybe Dax is right. Maybe I am in denial.

And maybe it's time I do something about it.

CHAPTER TEN

Alma

"You look beautiful," Sawyer tells me as we step outside the Pearl into the late afternoon light. The golden hour has painted everything in warm honey tones, and I can feel heat creeping up my neck at the simple compliment.

"Thank you." With the kids finally settled and playing quietly under Harlow and Dax's watchful eyes, I have time to breathe for the first time all day. I'm also not eager to return to the empty Willow just yet—the silence that felt so healing this morning now seems to stretch ahead of me like a vast, lonely expanse.

"I'm sorry for not introducing you to Harlow and Dax sooner," Sawyer says, his voice carrying a note of genuine regret. "I should have thought of that the moment you arrived."

"It's okay. You told them I was coming, and that was enough." I follow him as he begins walking up the bermed side of the Pearl, where earth has been mounded against the north wall for insulation. "Sometimes the best connections happen naturally anyway."

He offers his hand to help me navigate the steeper sections, and when I take it, the familiar electricity shoots up my arm. His palm is warm and calloused from years of construction work, completely engulfing my smaller hand in a way that makes me feel simultaneously protected and vulnerable.

From the top of the berm, the view is breathtaking—an endless expanse of high desert stretching toward the mountains, dotted with sagebrush and the occasional rammed earth house rising from the landscape like ancient dwellings. The sky seems impossibly vast here, unmarked by buildings or power lines, just pure blue space punctuated by white clouds that cast moving shadows across the mesa.

"It's beautiful out here," I breathe, meaning it more than any compliment I've ever given. "Like stepping into a completely different world."

"I'm glad you like it. Some people find it too isolated, too quiet."

"The quiet was definitely an adjustment," I admit with a laugh. "The first two nights were rough. I kept waiting for some familiar sound—traffic, sirens, even that damn air compressor from next door. Instead, there was just... silence."

"I'm sorry about that. It's one of the biggest shocks for people coming from the city. The silence and the darkness—no streetlights, no ambient glow from shopping centers. Just stars and space."

"The stars are incredible, though," I say, remembering how I'd stood on my little porch last night, Tyler asleep inside, just staring up at the Milky Way stretched across the sky like a river of light. "I've never seen anything like them."

His eyes find mine, and there's something warm and

inviting in his expression. "We should do some stargazing together one night. I know all the best spots, away from even the small amount of light pollution from town."

The suggestion sends a flutter through my stomach—intimate and romantic in a way that makes my pulse quicken. "I'd like that," I say softly. "But there's something else I want to try first."

He frowns slightly. "What's that?"

I nod toward the large trampoline positioned in front of the Pearl, its black surface gleaming in the afternoon sun. "I haven't been on one of those in years. Do you think Dax and Harlow would mind if I gave it a try? It looks like it's big enough for adults."

Sawyer follows my gaze and grins. "They definitely won't mind. Actually, that's the adult trampoline—Dax's father bought it without realizing he was ordering the full-size version instead of the kids' model. Dax kept it anyway because it's got the basketball hoop attachment, and he likes having something to help him unwind after long days in the workshop."

"There's a kids' version too?"

"In their playroom. You probably saw it during Harlow's tour." He takes my hand again, helping me down the slope toward the trampoline. "Drew mentioned once that you were a gymnast in high school. Is that true?"

The mention of Drew should sting, but somehow it doesn't. Instead, it feels natural—like sharing a memory of an old friend rather than opening a wound. "I was, but I only made it to regionals before I decided to quit."

"Why'd you stop?"

I shrug, trying to articulate something I've never really

examined closely. "It stopped being fun. The pressure, the competition, the constant criticism—it sucked all the joy out of something I used to love. I realized I'm not naturally competitive. I do things because they bring me happiness, and when they stop doing that..." I trail off with another shrug.

"That's probably a healthier approach to life than most people manage," Sawyer says, unzipping the safety netting around the trampoline. "Knowing when to walk away from something that's not serving you anymore."

The words carry more weight than he probably intended, and I wonder if we're still talking about gymnastics or something else entirely.

"You sure this thing can handle me?" I ask, stepping onto the bouncy surface and feeling it give slightly under my weight.

He rolls his eyes with mock exasperation. "If it can handle me and Dax having wrestling matches on it, I think you'll be fine. Or are you trying to chicken out?"

"The hell I am," I say with a laugh, making my way to the center of the trampoline. "But don't watch. I'm seriously out of practice."

"You know I'm going to watch," he says, settling against the netting with his arms crossed. "You know, for safety reasons. In case you need spotting."

"I'm not that out of practice."

"Yeah? Prove it."

The challenge in his voice sends a thrill through me, and I realize how long it's been since someone dared me to be playful, to take a risk just for the joy of it. With Drew, especially toward the end, everything had been about careful navigation, reading his moods, avoiding triggers. This feels like the opposite—pure possibility and freedom.

I start with small bounces, getting a feel for the surface, then gradually build momentum. It doesn't take long for muscle memory to kick in, and soon I'm soaring higher with each jump, laughing with pure delight as the world drops away beneath me. Each ascent feels like shedding another layer of fear and constraint, every landing a small rebellion against the careful, diminished life I'd been living.

The physical exertion is invigorating in a way I'd forgotten was possible. My heart pounds with exertion rather than anxiety, my breathing comes fast from joy rather than panic. For these moments, suspended in air with the vast New Mexican sky above me, I feel more like myself than I have in years.

When I finally stop, breathless and exhilarated, I collapse onto my back in the center of the trampoline. The sky overhead is an endless blue canvas dotted with white clouds that seem close enough to touch. My heart is hammering against my ribs, and every nerve ending feels alive with possibility.

"What are you looking at?" I ask, noticing Sawyer still standing at the edge of the trampoline, that same warm smile playing at his lips.

"You," he says simply. "It didn't take long for the gymnastics training to come back. You looked like you were flying."

"Not everything came back," I admit, though I'm glowing with the compliment. "But it felt amazing. I'd forgotten what it was like to move just for the joy of it." I pat the space beside me on the mat. "Want to join me? Just for lying down—I need to catch my breath before I can even think about more jumping."

He kicks off his sandals and climbs through the netting, the entire surface dipping and swaying as he settles beside me. The movement brings him closer than either of us probably intended, close enough that I can smell his cologne mixed with the clean scent of desert air, close enough to feel the warmth radiating from his skin.

"Thank you for this," I say softly, meaning more than just the trampoline.

"For what?"

"For bringing me here. For showing me that life can still have moments of pure joy in it." I turn my head to look at him, finding him already watching me with an intensity that makes my breath catch. "I'd forgotten that was possible."

We fall into comfortable silence, both of us staring up at the sky while hyperaware of each other's presence. My heart is still racing, though I'm no longer sure if it's from the jumping or from Sawyer's proximity. The space between us seems charged with possibility and danger in equal measure.

"I can't believe Harlow is thirteen years older than Dax," I say finally, needing to break the tension before it becomes overwhelming. "She told me there was a scheduling mix-up when she first came here—they both showed up to use the Pearl at the same time, and instead of one of them leaving, they ended up talking all night."

"That sounds like fate to me," Sawyer says quietly.

"Do you believe in that? Fate, I mean?"

"I think sometimes the universe puts people exactly where they need to be, when they need to be there." His voice carries a weight that makes me think he's not just talking about Dax and Harlow.

"What happens if you fight it?" I ask, my voice barely

above a whisper. "When your mind is screaming that some-thing is wrong, that you shouldn't want what you want, that people will judge you for it?"

"Then you hope your heart's voice is louder and more convincing than your fears."

The words hang in the air between us, heavy with impli-cation. Maybe it's an accident, maybe not, but when Sawyer's hand covers mine on the mat, I don't pull away. His palm is warm and slightly rough, completely enveloping my smaller hand, and the simple contact sends electricity racing through my entire nervous system.

My heart pounds so hard I'm sure he must be able to hear it. The butterflies in my stomach have evolved into something more urgent, more demanding. Everything about this moment—the golden light, the scent of sage on the breeze, the man beside me whose presence has become as essential as breathing—feels like standing on the edge of a cliff, knowing that one more step will change everything.

But before I can find the courage to take that step, Sawyer's phone starts ringing. The sound shatters the moment like glass, and he reluctantly moves his hand away to retrieve the device from his pocket.

"Sorry, I should probably get this," he mutters, climbing toward the edge of the trampoline.

Just then, the front door of the Pearl opens and the sounds of children spill out—Tyler's distinctive babble mixed with the twins' excited chatter. Naptime is officially over, and with it, this stolen moment of intimacy.

After spending another hour at the Pearl—watching the kids play, helping Harlow harvest vegetables for dinner, sharing one more round of Dax's cooking—I'm emotionally and physically exhausted. Tyler is cranky and fighting sleep, and I finally admit defeat.

"I should get him home before he has a complete meltdown," I tell the group, gathering Tyler's scattered toys and my purse.

"Of course," Harlow says warmly. "But you have to come back soon. The kids had such a wonderful time together."

"I'd love that," I say sincerely. "Thank you for making us feel so welcome. This has been exactly what I needed."

Sawyer offers to follow me home, but the Willow is literally visible from the Pearl's front yard—a short drive down a dirt road that's well-marked with solar lights. "It's not necessary," I insist, though part of me wants to say yes, wants to extend this day just a little longer.

The drive home is quiet except for Tyler's intermittent fussing from the backseat. As I pull into my driveway, the Willow looks serene and welcoming in the gathering dusk, its windows glowing warm and golden from the solar-powered interior lights.

But as I carry Tyler inside and begin our bedtime routine, thoughts of Drew creep in uninvited. Not the angry, broken man from those final months, but the Drew I'd fallen in love with—the one who would have loved seeing Tyler learn to walk, who would have been amazed by this place, who might have found his own healing in the silence and space of the high desert.

How I wish things could have been different. How I wish he'd been able to let someone help him before the darkness consumed everything good in him. But as I give Tyler his bath, I realize something has shifted in how I think about the past. The guilt is still there, but it's no longer the crushing weight it once was. Instead, it's becoming something I can carry without being destroyed by it.

Maybe that's what healing looks like—not the absence of pain, but the ability to hold it alongside joy, hope, and the possibility of love.

Tyler's bedtime routine is interrupted by my phone ringing. Frank and Doreen's faces appear on the screen, and I answer on the third ring.

"Hi Doreen, hi Frank," I say as cheerfully as I can manage. "How are you both doing?"

"We wanted to check on our grandson," Doreen says without preamble. "We called earlier, but it just kept ringing."

"Tyler and I were with friends," I explain, switching to video call so they can see him. "We've had a busy day."

The ten-minute call stretches into twenty as they coo over Tyler and pepper me with questions about our new life. I can see the strain in their faces, the way they're holding themselves together while their only connection to Drew babbles happily in my arms, oblivious to the complicated adult emotions swirling around him.

"We miss him so much," Doreen says finally, her voice thick with unshed tears.

"I know you do. And he misses you too. That's why we FaceTime—so you can still be part of his daily life, even from far away."

After we hang up, I feel the familiar tug of guilt. I've taken their grandson across the country, away from the only family he has besides me. But I also know I made the right choice. Tyler needs a mother who's healing, who's learning to embrace joy again, who can model resilience and hope instead of just survival.

I get Tyler settled in his crib and keep him company until he falls asleep, completely exhausted from the day's adventures. Once his breathing evens out, I retreat to the living room with a cup of herbal tea, planning to read for a while before bed.

That's when my phone buzzes with a text from Sawyer.

SAWYER:

You forgot the box Dax made for you.

ALMA:

Sorry, I missed your message earlier. I was getting Tyler ready for bed.

SAWYER:

No worries. I have it with me and can drop it off if you'd like.

My heart does something complicated in my chest. Part of me wants to say yes immediately, wants any excuse to see him again. But another part of me recognizes the danger in how much I'm already depending on him, how easily I could slip into making him the center of my new life here.

ALMA:

That would be great. Thank you.

SAWYER:

OK. Ten minutes.

I stare at the phone after sending my response, wondering if I'm making a mistake. But it's just a box, I tell myself. Just a friend doing a favor. Nothing more complicated than that.

I quickly shower and change into comfortable lounge clothes—an oversized t-shirt and soft pajama pants that make it clear I'm settled in for the evening. No need to dress up or send mixed signals. This is just neighbors helping neighbors, the kind of casual interaction that happens in small communities.

Ten minutes later, I see headlights approaching down my dirt road. Sawyer's truck pulls up beside my SUV, and I notice he's changed clothes too—from his earlier cargo pants into dark jeans and a black t-shirt that emphasizes the breadth of his shoulders. His hair looks damp, like he's recently showered.

"Hey," he says when I open the door, holding out a beautiful wooden box with clean lines and no visible joints or hardware. "Sorry about the confusion back there. It was chaos with all the kids running around."

"Tell me about it," I laugh, accepting the box and running my fingers over its smooth surface. "Dax wasn't kidding when he said the twins were... energetic."

"That's a diplomatic way to put it. Harlow prefers 'spirited' to Dax's less flattering descriptions."

I examine the box more closely, marveling at the craftsmanship. It's clearly made using traditional Japanese joinery —no nails or glue, just perfectly fitted pieces that create something both functional and beautiful. "This is incredible. I was thinking of using it for Tyler's keepsakes—first tooth, locks of hair, that sort of thing."

"Dax would love that. He puts a lot of meaning into his work, especially pieces he gives as gifts."

Sawyer stands in my doorway, hands stuffed in his pockets, and I can sense he wants to say something more. But then his phone starts ringing, and the moment fractures.

"I don't want to keep you," I say, opening the door wider in what I hope looks like a casual dismissal rather than reluctance to see him go. "Thanks for bringing this by."

He glances at his phone but doesn't answer the call. "Actually, Dax mentioned you had some questions about the water system? Something about pressure settings?"

"Oh, that." I wave my hand dismissively. "It's nothing urgent. I may have forgotten a few details about the filtration sequence and pressure monitoring, but I can figure it out."

"I could come by tomorrow afternoon and walk through it with you again, if you'd like. Make sure everything's running optimally."

The offer sends a warm flutter through my chest. "That would be really helpful. Thank you."

He pauses at the threshold, and for a moment, I think he might say something about what happened on the trampoline, about the way our hands found each other, about the electricity that seems to arc between us whenever we're in the same space.

Instead, he says, "I'm glad you decided to move here, Al. You looked really happy today. More like yourself than I've seen you in a long time."

I'd be happier if you stayed, I think but don't say. "Dax and Harlow are wonderful people. You're lucky to have friends like that."

"They're your friends now too."

"Thanks to you." We linger in the doorway for another heartbeat, the space between us humming with unspoken possibilities. Then his phone buzzes again—a text this time—and reality intrudes.

"That must be important," I say, trying to keep my voice light. "You should probably get going."

"It's just—" he starts, then stops himself. "You're right. I should head out. I'll see you tomorrow?"

"Tomorrow," I confirm, stepping back so he can leave.

As his truck disappears down the dirt road, I lean against my closed front door and let out a shaky breath. The wooden box is still warm from his hands, and I clutch it against my chest like a talisman.

This is dangerous territory we're navigating, and I know it. The growing attraction, the easy intimacy, the way he's becoming essential to my sense of home here—it's all happening too fast, built on a foundation of shared grief and complicated loyalty.

But as I lock up the house and prepare for bed, I can't bring myself to regret any of it. For the first time since Drew's death, I feel alive in my own skin. I feel like a woman who deserves love and joy and the possibility of a future that isn't defined by loss and fear.

Not anymore.

CHAPTER ELEVEN

Sawyer

I hate having to brush Alma off, but I need a clean slate if I'm going to pursue what's been building between us. There's a part of my past in town that requires closure—a chapter that needs to be definitively ended before I can even think about starting something new.

I spot Sage at a corner table in the Love Apple, a farm-to-table restaurant housed in what used to be the Placitas Chapel, an old Catholic church with thick adobe walls and exposed vigas. She's exactly as I remember her—ethereal in that way that made me think she might disappear if I looked away too long. Tonight she's wearing a flowing skirt with tiny bells sewn into the hem and a sleeveless top that shows off the intricate henna designs on her forearms. Bangles catch the lamplight on her wrists, and her dark hair falls in a simple braid down her back.

Sage isn't her real name, but it fits her perfectly. Her actual name is sealed away in an expunged juvenile record somewhere—something she told me once during pillow talk that I've pretended to forget, more for her sake than mine.

She smiles when she sees me approaching, rising to wrap me in one of those lingering hugs that used to make my pulse race. Now I feel only a fond warmth, like embracing a sister or a dear friend from childhood.

"Sawyer," she says, pulling back to study my face with those grey-green eyes that always seemed to see too much. "You look different. Settled."

Sage DeSantos is the only person who ever saw me at my absolute worst and helped me find my way back. When I left Walter Reed—body patched together but mind still fractured—I was drowning in a cocktail of pain medications and rage that made Drew's struggles look manageable by comparison. The night I pressed the barrel of my service weapon against the roof of my mouth, tasting metal and desperation, I knew I needed help that went beyond what the VA could provide.

I found Sage through a mutual friend who'd heard about her work with trauma survivors—women who'd survived abuse and had problems with touch, with trust, with existing in their own bodies. At first, I didn't think she was the right fit for me. But when I threw out my back one day, she fixed it with a touch that seemed to reach directly into the knot of pain and untangle it.

When she moved her practice to Sedona, I followed her there for ten sessions of something she called Structural Bodywork. It was brutal—like having my entire nervous system rewired while conscious. I'd leave her table feeling like I'd been put through an emotional meat grinder, sometimes crying or raging for hours afterward without understanding why.

But it worked. Whatever she did managed to unlock trauma that had burrowed so deep into my muscles I hadn't even known it was there—not just from the IED blast and the surgeries, but from years of hypervigilance, from my mother's chaos, from carrying Drew's weight along with my own. She taught me that the body remembers everything, stores every moment of terror and loss in places the mind can't reach.

Eventually, inevitably, we became lovers.

"You do look different," she says now as we settle into our seats. "Lighter, somehow. You've met someone."

It's not a question. With Sage, it never is.

"How can you tell?"

She reaches across the table and takes my hand, turning it palm up in that gesture I remember so well. "Your hands are steadier. Less tension in your shoulders. And there's something in your eyes that wasn't there before." She traces a line on my palm with her finger—a touch that once would have sent electricity through my entire body. Now it feels clinical, detached. "Hope, maybe."

"You're not reading my palm."

"No," she laughs, a sound like wind chimes. "I'm reading your face. You're practically glowing, Sawyer. She must be special."

The mention of Alma sends warmth spreading through my chest, and I realize Sage is right—I am different now. The hypervigilance that once kept me scanning every room for threats has softened into something more manageable. The rage that used to simmer just beneath my surface has cooled to occasional flashes of irritation.

"She is," I say simply.

"Tell me about her."

I hesitate, then decide honesty is the least I owe her. "You know who she is. I talked about her during our sessions."

Sage's expression grows thoughtful. "Drew's wife. The one you were in love with but never acted on."

"Drew's widow now."

"Ah." She nods slowly, understanding flickering in her eyes. "And you're here because you need to close our chapter before you can open a new one with her."

This is why I fell for Sage in the first place—her ability to cut straight through pretense to the truth underneath. "Something like that."

"Are you worried about betraying his memory? Or are you worried about whether your feelings are real, or just proximity and shared grief?"

The questions hit closer to home than I want to admit. "Both, maybe."

Sage leans back in her chair, studying me with the same intense focus she used to bring to our sessions. "Do you remember what I told you about guilt during our work together? How it can become an addiction, a way to avoid moving forward because staying stuck feels safer than risking something new?"

I remember. I also remember how angry those words made me at the time, how I'd accused her of not understanding the weight of what I'd carried home from Afghanistan.

"You were right," I admit now. "About the guilt being a prison I was building for myself."

"I usually am," she says with a small smile. "The question is: what are you going to do with that knowledge?"

Before I can answer, the server arrives to take our orders. We both choose the ruby trout—a local specialty that Sage insists is life-changing. As the server walks away, an comfortable silence settles between us.

"I've been thinking about what you said," I tell her finally. "About how the people we love don't die so we can spend the rest of our lives punishing ourselves for surviving them."

"And?"

"I think Drew would want Alma to be happy. He loved her enough to want that for her, even if it means letting her go."

"Do you think he'd want her to be happy with you specifically?"

The question I've been avoiding. "I don't know. But I think I have to trust that if she chooses me, it's because she sees something worth choosing. Not because she's settling or because I'm convenient."

Sage nods approvingly. "That's very mature of you. Much more mature than the man who used to rage at me for suggesting his guilt might not be as noble as he thought."

"I was pretty awful during some of those sessions."

"You were in pain. People in pain lash out—it's what they do." She pauses as our food arrives, then continues, "The work you did, Sawyer, the healing—that was real. Don't let anyone, including yourself, diminish that."

We eat in comfortable silence for a while, and I'm struck by how different this feels from our past dinners together. There's no undercurrent of desire, no tension crackling between us. Just two people who were important to each other once, sharing a meal and finding closure.

"I should probably tell you," Sage says eventually, "I'm going back to school. Physical therapy. Working with people like you made me realize I want to do more, but in a more conventional medical setting."

"That's incredible, Sage. You'll be amazing at it."

"I hope so." She takes a sip of wine, her bangles chiming softly. "But what about you? Are you ready for this new chapter you're writing?"

The question hangs in the air between us, heavy with implication. Am I ready? Ready to risk loving someone who might reject me? Ready to build something new on the foundation of something lost? Ready to stop defining myself by what I've survived and start defining myself by what I might become?

"I think so," I say finally. "For the first time in years, I actually think I might be."

Sage reaches across the table and squeezes my hand—a gesture of friendship, nothing more. "Then I'm happy for you. Both of you."

The next afternoon, I knock on Alma's door and see her through the glass, moving across the living room in a pink sleeveless dress that flows around her calves like water. She's wearing one of those baby carriers across her chest, but Tyler has escaped and is zooming around the open space pushing a colorful wagon that plays music with each step.

"Hey Sawyer," she says, opening the door with a smile that makes my heart skip. "Sorry I had to reschedule earlier. Grocery shopping with a toddler takes about three times longer than it should."

"No problem. Gave me time to take care of some things

around the house." I'd texted her this morning about coming over to walk through the water system again, but she'd been dealing with Tyler's meltdown in the produce section of the market.

"How do you like my sign?" She points proudly to a hand-painted plaque above the door featuring the word "Willow" in colorful letters, each one decorated with a different pattern—polka dots, stripes, flowers, butterflies.

"It's perfect. Very you." I hold out a small terracotta pot containing a plant with glossy dark green leaves, along with a small bag from a local chocolatier. "I realized I never gave you a proper housewarming gift."

"You didn't have to do that," she says, accepting both items with obvious pleasure. "But thank you. What kind of plant is this?"

"Dwarf macadamia tree. Macadamia integrifolia, if you want to get technical. I thought it would be a nice addition to your indoor garden. And since I remembered you have a weakness for chocolate..." I trail off, suddenly feeling foolish. It's such a small gesture compared to everything she's given up to be here.

"I love chocolate, and I have a feeling I'm going to love fresh macadamia nuts even more." Her smile is radiant, transforming her entire face. "Come in."

As I step inside, Tyler abandons his wagon and makes a beeline for my legs, chattering excitedly in that mixture of babble and real words that passes for toddler conversation.

"Let me wrangle him first," Alma says, chasing after her son with exaggerated cowboy movements that make him shriek with laughter. "Ever since we moved here, he's discovered he has room to really run. Unfortunately, that means a lot more space for me to chase him through."

She scoops Tyler up and settles him into the baby carrier, where he continues to babble happily while reaching for everything within grabbing distance. As I follow her through the house, I notice how she's made the space her own—family photos on the shelves, a few decorative pieces I recognize from her old house with Drew, Tyler's toys scattered in colorful abundance across the living area.

We head to the utility closet that houses the solar power system—the nerve center of off-grid living with its banks of batteries, inverters, and monitoring equipment. Even though I've already walked her through this once, there are nuances to the system that take time to internalize, especially when you're used to just flipping switches and having everything work.

I explain the daily monitoring routine, how to read the battery levels, what to do if the inverter starts beeping. The twenty minutes pass too quickly, and I find myself lingering over details just to stay close to her a little longer.

"Any plans for the rest of the day?" Alma asks as we return to the living room. She sets Tyler on the floor where he immediately crawls toward his wagon, pulling himself up with the determined focus of someone on an important mission.

"Nothing urgent."

"Would you like to stay for dinner?" She opens the oven door, and the scent of roasting beef fills the air. "I may have gotten a little ambitious at the grocery store."

"I'd love to," I say, stepping aside as Tyler zooms past pushing his musical wagon. The sound of his laughter echoing through the spacious room makes something warm unfurl in my chest. "Place agrees with him."

"He loves having room to explore. And the quiet means he sleeps through the night now, which is a miracle I didn't dare hope for." She moves to the kitchen counter where a large salad bowl sits next to a draining rack full of fresh greens. "These are from the indoor garden, and the cucumbers are from Dax and Harlow's place. I've heard of farm-to-table, but this is even better."

"Garden-to-table," I suggest, and she laughs.

"Exactly. Want to help? You can handle the salad while I deal with the green beans."

Working beside her in the kitchen feels natural in a way that should probably alarm me. The easy rhythm of domestic cooperation, the way she hums softly while she works, the occasional brush of her arm against mine as we move around each other—it all feels like something we've been doing for years rather than days.

We're discussing the care and feeding of macadamia trees when I spot headlights approaching through the large front windows.

What's Todd doing here?

"Oh good, he made it," Alma says, grabbing an extra plate and silverware from the cabinet. "I ran into Todd in town while I was shopping and invited him to join us. I hope you don't mind."

"Of course not," I lie, watching my brother park his Jeep next to my truck.

But I do mind. I mind more than I should, more than is reasonable or fair. This was supposed to be our evening—

mine and Alma's. A chance to build on whatever's been growing between us without interference or complications.

Todd emerges from his vehicle wearing his usual casual uniform of jeans and a faded t-shirt, looking every inch the laid-back creative type he is. Before I moved to Taos, he'd been living in LA, waiting tables and writing screenplays in a tiny apartment that somehow cost more per month than my entire house here. When I got injured, he'd just sold his first script—a real breakthrough moment in his career—but he dropped everything to be with me through the worst of it.

He'd spent months at Walter Reed, typing on his laptop while I lay drugged and furious in that hospital bed, never leaving my side no matter how awful I became. Later, he told me he'd been terrified that if the doctors had to amputate my leg, I'd find a way to kill myself. He wasn't wrong—I was absolutely that fucked up.

After my discharge, I moved in with him in LA and got a taste of his life—the parties, the industry connections, the casual hedonism that seemed to define everyone in his circle. For a while, it was the perfect distraction from the demons I'd brought home. But I couldn't handle the noise, the crowds, the way my hypervigilance made every social gathering feel like a potential combat zone. The Fourth of July nearly broke me—all those fireworks exploding over the Hollywood Hills sounded exactly like mortar rounds, and I'd spent the night crouched in Todd's bathroom, shaking and sweating and hating myself for being so weak.

When I finally escaped to Taos, Todd followed—ostensibly to check on me, but he never left. This place suited him too, gave him the quiet he needed to write without the constant pressure and artifice of LA.

"Hey Alma, thanks for the invitation," Todd says as she opens the door. He hands her a gorgeous bouquet of mixed wildflowers that makes my practical macadamia plant look pathetic by comparison.

Of course he brings flowers. Of course they're perfect.

"These are beautiful," Alma says, accepting the bouquet with obvious delight. "Let me get them in water."

"Hey man," Todd claps me on the shoulder with that easy familiarity that's always defined our relationship. "Good to see you."

"You too," I manage, though the words taste like sawdust.

Todd immediately gravitates toward Tyler, who's managed to get mashed potatoes in his hair during the few minutes we were distracted. "Hey there, little man. Looks like you're winning the battle against dinner."

Within minutes, we're all seated around Alma's dining table, and Todd is holding court with the kind of effortless charm that's always come naturally to him. He asks thoughtful questions about how she's adjusting to off-grid living, compliments her hand-painted sign with genuine enthusiasm, shares funny stories from his Hollywood days that have her laughing until tears form in the corners of her eyes.

I watch her face light up as she listens to him, the way her eyes sparkle when she laughs, the graceful gestures of her hands as she talks. She's relaxed in a way I rarely see—no undercurrent of tension, no careful monitoring of mood or tone. With Todd, she can just be herself without worrying about complicated history or unspoken expectations.

The realization sits like lead in my stomach. Todd doesn't remind her of Drew—he never served with us, never shared that particular bond of brotherhood and trauma. He's not carrying the weight of survivor's guilt or complicated loyalty. He's just a charming, talented man who can make her laugh without any baggage attached.

Maybe that's what she needs. Maybe what I interpreted as growing attraction was just gratitude, or loneliness, or the simple human need for connection after months of isolation.

Halfway through dinner, I've completely lost my appetite. I push back from the table with more force than necessary, the chair legs scraping loudly against the floor.

"Sorry, I need some air," I mutter, not waiting for a response.

Outside, the night air is crisp and clean, the full moon casting everything in silver light. The silence that usually soothes me feels oppressive tonight, filled with the sound of Alma's laughter drifting through the windows behind me.

I should go back in. I should stop acting like a jealous teenager and remember that Alma is free to have dinner with whoever she wants. She's free to laugh at Todd's jokes, to appreciate his flowers, to choose him over me if that's what makes her happy.

But knowing what I should do and being able to do it are two different things.

"What's eating you?" Todd's voice cuts through my brooding as he steps outside, closing the door softly behind him.

"Nothing. Just needed some fresh air."

"Bullshit." He joins me at the edge of the porch, leaning against the railing. "You've been shooting daggers at me all evening. What's the problem?"

"There's no problem."

"Right. That's why you stormed out of there like your ass was on fire." Todd studies my face in the moonlight. "Oh. Oh, I see what this is about."

"You don't see anything."

"I see my little brother being an idiot about a woman he's clearly crazy about." Todd's voice is gentle but firm. "Sawyer, I'm not here to steal your girl."

"She's not my—"

"Spare me. I've got eyes, and I'm not blind." He chuckles softly. "The chemistry between you two is so thick you could cut it with a knife. You can't stop looking at each other while pretending you're not looking at each other."

"That's not true."

"Come on, man. She wouldn't have uprooted her entire life to move out here with you if she didn't feel something. And you wouldn't have offered her your best property if you weren't hoping it might lead somewhere." He gestures toward the house behind us, where warm light spills from the windows like something from a fairy tale. "This place is perfect for her and Tyler. You built it for her, didn't you? Even if you didn't realize it at the time."

The accusation hits too close to home. Had I been thinking of Alma when Todd and I designed the Willow? Had some part of me been imagining her in that kitchen, Tyler playing in those wide-open spaces?

"She's Drew's wife," I say finally.

"She's Drew's widow," Todd corrects. "There's a difference. And if you think staying away from her honors his memory, you're kidding yourself. You're just cheating both of you out of a chance at happiness."

"It's not that simple."

"Isn't it?" Todd pulls his keys from his pocket, signaling his intention to leave. "Look, I know how close you and Drew were. I know he saved your life, and I'm grateful to him for that. But surviving doesn't mean you owe him your entire future. It means you get to live—really live, not just exist."

He heads toward his Jeep, then pauses and turns back to me. "You know what I think Drew would want? I think he'd want his son to have a good man in his life. I think he'd want Alma to be loved by someone who sees how incredible she is. And I think he'd be pissed as hell if he knew you were throwing away a chance at happiness because you think suffering is somehow more noble than joy."

The engine starts with a soft rumble, and Todd's headlights sweep across the desert as he turns around. I watch his taillights disappear into the darkness, his words echoing in the sudden silence.

Through the window, I can see Alma cleaning up the kitchen while Tyler plays at her feet. She looks content, settled, like she belongs here in a way that has nothing to do with me.

Maybe Todd's right.

Maybe I've been so focused on what I think I owe the dead that I've forgotten what I owe the living.

CHAPTER TWELVE

Alma

I WATCH the headlights of Todd's Jeep slice through the darkness as he drives away, his words still echoing in my mind. *You're just cheating both of you out of a chance at happiness.* The silence that follows his departure feels heavy with possibility and fear in equal measure.

Seconds later, the front door opens and Sawyer steps back inside, looking uncertain and slightly embarrassed. I can see the internal war playing out across his features—the want battling against whatever sense of loyalty or guilt he's been carrying.

"Hey stranger, everything okay?" I ask playfully, hoping to ease some of the tension that's been building all evening.

He flashes me a sheepish smile that makes my heart skip. "Yeah, just needed to clear my head."

"Did you really think Todd was flirting with me?" The question slips out before I can stop it, and I see his cheeks flush slightly.

"Maybe a little," he admits, moving to help me clear the remaining dishes from the table.

"You don't have to help with this," I start to say, but our fingers brush as we reach for the same plate and I freeze. The contact sends electricity shooting through my entire nervous system—definitely not static, definitely not accidental.

"Thank you for dinner, Al. It was incredible." He glances toward Tyler, who's managed to get more mashed peas in his hair than in his mouth. "And I think he agrees with my assessment."

I lift Tyler from his high chair, noting how Sawyer's eyes follow the movement with surprising tenderness. "I need to get this little mess cleaned up and ready for bed."

"Let me handle the dishes," Sawyer says. "I can check the water pressure while I'm at it—make sure everything's running smoothly."

I arch an eyebrow at him. "Did you just make that up? Because the water pressure is fine."

"I prefer to call it quality control," he says with a grin that's both boyish and devastating.

"Okay," I concede, secretly relieved he's staying. "But don't feel obligated to find problems that don't exist."

As I carry a protesting Tyler to the bathroom, I tell myself not to rush through bedtime routine, but it's useless. My heart is racing like I'm sixteen again, preparing for my first real date. The awareness that Sawyer is just rooms away, that we're finally alone together without interruption or obligation, makes every nerve ending sing with anticipation.

He's just washing dishes, Alma. Get a grip.

But even as I try to rationalize away my body's response, I can't ignore the way my hands shake slightly as I bathe Tyler, the way my pulse quickens every time I hear Sawyer moving around in the kitchen.

Half an hour later, I emerge from Tyler's nursery to find Sawyer putting away the last of the clean dishes. He moves through my kitchen with easy familiarity, and something about the domestic scene makes my chest tight with longing. He's tall and broad-shouldered, moving with that careful precision that speaks to his military training, but there's gentleness in how he handles my things, respect for the space I've made my own.

"How was the water pressure?" I ask as he turns to face me, drying his hands on the dish towel.

"Like everything else about this place—perfect," he replies, but his voice has gone slightly rough, and the way he's looking at me makes heat pool low in my belly.

I know I'm about to step into dangerous territory, but I can't keep dancing around this anymore. "Sawyer, about the other day—"

"I'm not sorry for kissing you," he interrupts, his honesty catching me off guard.

"I'm not either." The admission hangs between us like a bridge I'm finally brave enough to cross. "But why does it feel like you're pulling away from me?"

Something vulnerable flickers across his features. "Because I promised Drew I'd take care of you, not take advantage of you."

"Who says you're taking advantage of me?" The question comes out more heated than I intended. "You've helped me more than anyone has in months. You offered me this place when you didn't have to. You drove across the country with Tyler and me when you could have just put us on a plane. That's not taking advantage—that's being..." I search for the right word, "...that's being everything I needed when I didn't even know what I needed."

"That's the problem, Al," he murmurs, closing the distance between us with deliberate steps. "I don't want to be just what you need. I don't want to be just a friend to you. Not anymore."

The silence that follows is pregnant with possibility. Ever since that moment in my hallway over a year ago—when he cupped my face and asked if I was okay, when I saw something in his eyes that went far beyond friendly concern—I've wondered if I was imagining the connection between us. But standing here now, seeing the heat in his gaze, feeling the electric tension crackling in the space between our bodies, I know I wasn't imagining anything.

When he reaches up to cup my face in his hands, it's the same gesture from that day, but this time there's no fear of Drew walking in, no guilt strong enough to stop what's been building between us for longer than either of us wants to admit.

"I don't want you to be just a friend either," I whisper, my voice barely audible over the thundering of my heart. "That day you came to the house and asked if I was okay—"

"I was worried about you," he says softly, his thumbs tracing gentle circles on my cheekbones. "I let my emotions get the best of me. I went too far and it almost cost me my friendship with Drew. I had to step away."

My heart sinks at the memory of how abruptly he'd disappeared from our lives after that confrontation. "Is that what you're planning to do now? Step away again?"

Still cradling my face, Sawyer shakes his head slowly. "No. I'm done running from this."

"What are you going to do then?"

"This," he murmurs, lowering his head until our lips are barely a breath apart.

The kiss starts gentle, almost reverent, as if we're both afraid this moment might shatter if we move too quickly. But when I don't pull away—when I instead step closer and slide my hands around his neck—something breaks open between us.

His arms come around my waist, pulling me against the solid warmth of his chest, and the kiss deepens into something hungrier, more desperate. It tastes like coming home and starting over all at once, like every moment of longing and denial has been building to this.

When we finally break apart, both breathing hard, I rest my forehead against his and try to find words for the magnitude of what I'm feeling.

"Alma," he says quietly, "I need you to be sure about this. Because if we cross this line, there's no going back. I won't be able to pretend anymore that what I feel for you is just friendship or loyalty to Drew's memory."

I pull back to look into his eyes—those hazel-green depths that have haunted my dreams and my waking moments alike. "I'm sure," I whisper. "I've been sure for longer than I've been brave enough to admit."

Something shifts in his expression then, the last of his resistance crumbling. When he kisses me again, it's with a certainty that takes my breath away, his hands moving to explore the curve of my waist, the line of my spine, as if he's been waiting forever for permission to touch me this way.

"I want you," I whisper against his ear, and feel him shudder in response.

"Are you absolutely certain?" he asks, pulling back to search my face. "Because I've wanted this—wanted you—for so long that I'm not sure I'll be able to stop once we start."

I pull away, looking into his hazel-green eyes, hoping he can see all the heat, all the desire, all the built-up tension that's bursting in the seams since that first kiss. No, long before that, when we stood in that hallway more than a year ago, and he asked me if everything was okay. I nod, biting my lip as his gaze moves down my face to my mouth.

As one corner of his mouth lifts in a knowing smile, Sawyer scoops my legs out from under me and carries me toward the bedroom. I wrap my arms around his neck, inhaling his scent and sucking on his neck hungrily. When he reaches the bed, I lower my feet to the floor, unwrapping my arms from around his neck. Sawyer pulls my dress over my head and tosses it to the bed.

I gather his shirt in my hands and whisk them off his shoulders, gasping at the sight of his chiseled chest and the tattoos that each tell a story, from the Asian tiger on his left bicep to the phoenix on his right. And then there are the scars that mark his skin where there are no tattoos to obscure them. When I trail my fingers along a scar that reminds me of a bullet entry wound, he grasps my fingers as if telling me it's not time for that.

We kiss again, almost desperate longing for a connection firmly in place, his hands fisting my hair as his tongue slips between my teeth. I tug at his belt, our lips still connected, but he grips my wrist again.

"I want to see you first," he murmurs, his mouth warm against my lips. "I want to remember the moment I see your body for the first time."

Sawyer continues to kiss me, the metal buckle of his belt pressing against my belly as he squeezes my ass with his big hands before he moves them lower. I gasp as he trails a finger between my legs, briefly dipping into my wetness. Sawyer growls in delight, pulling away from our kiss to gaze at me as I step back and bring hands up my back to unhook my bra.

I slip my bra off my shoulders, knowing this is the first time I've had anyone see me naked in a long time. But I push the thought away, watching Sawyer's eyes grow dark and heavy as he runs his hands over my sensitive nipples.

"You're so beautiful, Alma," he whispers, sitting on the edge of the bed and pulling me closer so I'm standing in front of him. He hooks his thumbs into the sides of my thong and slowly pulls it down, taking his time. With anyone else, I'd probably have died of embarrassment at being exposed to a man's gaze so up close but right now, all I want is to show myself to him. I want Sawyer to look at me, touch me, taste me, and most of all, fuck me in way that would make up for all the time we've spent denying ourselves of this moment.

As I stand before him, Sawyer doesn't speak. There's something so intimate about being exposed and open to his admiration especially after so much waiting. I'm so wet, impatiently waiting for him as he takes his time running his hands over my belly and back up to cup my breasts.

"You're such a tease," I moan as Sawyer rolls my nipples between his fingers.

He bites his lower lip before gripping me by my ass cheeks and pulling me toward him. I gasp as he lowers his knees to the floor, his tongue snaking between my pussy lips. I hold onto his shoulders for support as he licks my slit with his tongue, running it back and forth, pausing each time to suck on the sensitive nub.

"Sawyer," I gasp as he pauses and looks up at me.

"You taste so fucking good, Al," he murmurs, letting his hot breath tickle my clit. He licks me again and I grip his shoulders, my fingers digging into his skin as he brings me to a quick and hard orgasm, my knees threatening to buckle beneath me. As Sawyer lets go of my waist and stands up, I crumble to my knees in front of him, starving for his cock.

He unbuttons his pants, his cock springing before me. I wrap my hand around his thick shaft, stroking him. Sawyer's eyes narrow as he watches me part my lips and slide his smooth, glistening head into my mouth. I let out a moan as I slide him deeper into my mouth, tasting him. He groans, his hands gathering my hair in a pony tail and gently guiding my head as I suck him, loving the taste and feel of him in my mouth.

"Fuck, Al," he groans, guiding my head off of him and pulling me to my feet and pushing me down on the bed. "I want to be inside you."

"Do you have protection?" I whisper, the mere thought of needing one after so long sounding strange coming from my mouth. But as I watch him retrieve his wallet from his pants and pull out a shiny silver square wrapper, I sigh. At least, one of us is prepared.

Sawyer tears the wrapper with his teeth and rolls it on his dick. I scoot over to the middle of the bed as he follows, using his knees to push my knees apart. With one hand on the bed to support himself, he lowers his body to mine, his mouth finding my lips again as he guides his cock against my open-ing. Sawyer doesn't press forward at first, instead letting his smooth head rest against my folds. I whimper in anticipation, trying to push myself against him. He slips his arms under my back and holding me close to him, I wrap my hands tightly around his neck and lift my hips as he slides his cock into me for the first time.

We both moan in unison, our eyes locked onto each other. It feels surreal at first, the feeling of being filled for the first time after so long, my pussy stretching to accommodate him. Kissing me again, his breath hot against my mouth, Sawyer moves slowly in and out, rocking back and forth. There is no need for words this time, only us, our bodies meeting and parting, the heat between us building as I feel myself inch closer and closer to shattering in his arms. My hands explore the muscular terrain of his back, over his shoulders and down over his ribs until they rest on his hips and pull him into me as deep as he can go until he fully seats himself into me and I cry out, my orgasm claiming me. Sawyer follows shortly after and I cling to him, feeling his body shudders with his release.

Moments later, I feel his hand on my forehead, pushing my hair from my face. "I'll always take care of you, Alma," he murmurs before kissing me, his kiss gentle this time. "Both of you. I promise."

I don't answer, not wanting my vulnerability to show even when I can no longer hide it. For isn't this what it's all about, finding someone you can be vulnerable with, no longer afraid of showing who we really are?

CHAPTER THIRTEEN

Sawyer

A WEEK LATER, I take Alma and Tyler around Taos like the tourists they are, though I have to admit this is new territory for me too. Armed with a colorful brochure and with Tyler secured in a backpack carrier that makes me look like the world's most domestic tour guide, I'm winging it completely.

We start our walking tour at Taos Plaza, beginning at the Hotel La Fonda where Alma and Tyler spent their first night in New Mexico—a detail that feels significant now, like the opening chapter of a story we're still writing. From there, we explore the Old County Courthouse and Our Lady of Guadalupe Church, me reading from the brochure like I actually know what I'm talking about.

In all my years living here, I've never bothered with the official tourist attractions. I can explain the intricacies of solar panel efficiency and greywater systems until someone's eyes glaze over, but Taos history? I leave that to the locals like Dax, who actually grew up with these stories.

Around noon, Dax, Harlow, and the twins meet us at the Blumenschein House on Ledoux Street. From there, we make our way to the Harwood Museum of Art as one enthusiastic group. Dax immediately takes over as the real tour guide, and everywhere we go, locals greet him as "that Anaya boy"—his mother's family name carrying the weight of generations. The Anayas have been part of this landscape since the 1800s, Spanish colonists who put down roots in this high desert and never left.

As if one native Taoseño isn't enough, Dax's older sister Sarah meets us at the Fechin Home, accompanied by her longtime boyfriend Benny and their stories of raising ten-year-old Dyami. Their son is off with cousins today, probably riding bikes around the acequia roads when he's not glued to video games—the perfect age for adventure and independence.

Together, we make quite the tour group, and we're definitely not quiet about it. The conversation flows between art history and family gossip, with frequent detours into discussions of food—where to find the best green chile rellenos, what makes authentic posole, though everyone agrees that nothing beats Dax's grandmother Nana's cooking. Benny argues good-naturedly that his Navajo hominy stew gives her a run for her money, which always leads to plans for another family dinner where we can settle the debate.

As I watch Alma seamlessly integrate into this conversation—asking thoughtful questions about adobe restoration, swapping parenting tips with Harlow and Sarah, laughing at Dax's stories about growing up between two cultures—I'm struck by how naturally she fits here. There's a lightness to her that wasn't there in California, a sense of belonging that goes beyond just finding a nice place to live.

She's beautiful, of course—I've always known that, was

genuinely happy for Drew when he found such a keeper. But it's more than that now. It's watching her discover joy again, seeing her face light up when Tyler claps at street musicians, the way she unconsciously leans into me when we're walking close together.

"How are you liking that backpack model, the one that comes with the baby?" Alma asks teasingly when the others drift over to join Harlow near the playground. I've taken the carrier off and Tyler is now crawling around with the twins under various watchful eyes.

"Best investment I ever made," I reply, grinning as color rises in her cheeks. "Sturdy, comfortable, and surprisingly stylish. Though I have to admit, the mom and baby who come with it are definitely the premium features."

"Would you like to post a testimonial on the official website?"

"Absolutely." I notice a bit of cinnamon sugar on her lower lip from the pastry we'd shared earlier. "You've got something right here," I say, pulling her closer and kissing her thoroughly, tasting sweetness and possibility. "Thank you for letting me play tourist guide today. I should confess—I've never actually done this before."

She laughs, the sound making something warm unfurl in my chest. "I wondered about that. Here I was thinking you were this expert on local history."

"That's what brochures are for. But with Dax here now, we get the real stories—the ones they don't print for tourists."

"I can tell. He knows so much more than any guidebook could capture."

"You should hear his Nana tell stories about this place. She's lived through eight decades of changes, and her late husband was one of the most respected potters in the region. Their daughter—Dax and Sarah's mother—inherited the artistic gene." I pause, watching her take in the plaza around us, the way the afternoon light catches the adobe buildings. "You love it here, don't you?"

Alma adjusts her wide-brimmed hat, and I catch something wistful crossing her features. "I do. More than I expected to." She's quiet for a moment, then adds softly, "I wish Drew had been able to visit you here at least once. I wish he could have seen all this—the houses, the community, the peace you've found. Maybe it would have made a difference for him."

The words hit me like a physical blow, and I have to clear my throat before I can respond. The guilt I thought I'd started to process comes rushing back—all the ways I failed my best friend, all the opportunities I missed to help him.

"Yeah," I manage, the word coming out rougher than intended.

"Oh God, I'm sorry," Alma stammers, realizing the weight of what she's just said. "I didn't mean to bring that up, especially not today—"

"No, Al." I lean my forehead against hers, looking into those dark eyes that have seen so much loss and are finally learning to see possibility again. "I never want you to think you can't mention Drew around me. He was part of both our lives, part of how we got here. I miss him too."

The admission feels like releasing a breath I'd been holding. Drew will always be between us in some way, but maybe that doesn't have to be a wall. Maybe it can be a bridge—a reminder of love and loss that makes us appreciate what we have now.

Two weeks later, with Tyler enjoying a playdate with the twins at the Pearl, I take Alma west of Taos to the small community of Pilar for a day of river rafting on the Rio Grande. Our guide, a weathered local named Miguel, fills us in on the area's history as we navigate the water—stories of the Genízaro people, the mixed-race communities who made their lives along these riverbanks long before statehood was even a dream.

The water levels are lower than usual, Miguel explains—drought has been a concern throughout the region for the past couple of years. But there's still enough flow for excitement, enough white water to make Alma shriek with laughter as we hit the rapids.

Watching her face as we navigate the churning water, seeing her throw back her head and laugh with pure joy as spray soaks her hair, I feel something shift inside my chest. It's more than attraction, more than the comfortable affection I've felt growing between us. This is something deeper, something that makes my breath catch and my pulse quicken in ways that have nothing to do with the adrenaline of the rapids.

I'm in love with her. Really, truly falling in love in a way that's both exhilarating and terrifying.

The realization hits me like the cold river water—sudden and complete and impossible to ignore. This isn't just physical desire or the bond of shared trauma or even the satisfaction of seeing her heal. This is the real thing, the kind of love that changes the entire landscape of your life.

When she turns to look at me, river water sparkling in her

hair and that expression of pure joy lighting up her face, I feel it like a punch straight through my ribcage. I want to tell her, want to shout it over the sound of rushing water, but something holds me back. It's too soon, too intense, too much to lay on someone who's still figuring out how to rebuild her life.

But God, I'm in love with her.

The knowledge sits in my chest like a secret I'm not quite ready to share but can no longer deny.

By the time we pick up Tyler at three that afternoon, Alma is sun-tired and happy, the adrenaline from our river adventure having mellowed into contentment. When I park my truck in front of the Willow, there's an unfamiliar car with rental plates sitting next to her SUV.

"You expecting someone?" I ask as Alma lifts Tyler from his car seat.

"No, not that I know of."

I approach the rental car cautiously, noting that the windows are cracked and the hood is still warm—whoever's here arrived recently and is probably somewhere nearby. My question gets answered when Kevin emerges from around the back of the house, looking like he's been exploring the property.

He's cleaned up since I last saw him—hair trimmed short, wearing a crisp white t-shirt and new jeans that suggest this visit required some planning.

"Kevin, what are you doing here?" Alma asks, surprise and wariness warring in her voice. "Are Frank and Doreen with you?"

"Nah, just me this time," he replies, positioning himself by the front door like he belongs here. "I had some airline miles to burn, figured why not come see my nephew in person? Unless I'm supposed to call ahead and schedule visits now?"

"Of course not," Alma says, though I can hear the tension underneath her politeness. "Come in."

For the next hour, I watch Alma carefully navigate conversation with Kevin, steering away from certain topics while he peppers her with questions about off-grid living. He's playing interested tourist, asking about solar panels and water systems, but I'm not buying the act. I see how he looks at her when he thinks no one's watching—there's judgment there, resentment, a fundamental lack of respect that sets my teeth on edge.

When Alma puts Tyler down for his nap, Kevin asks for a tour of the property. I immediately volunteer to handle it, not wanting Alma alone with him for any extended period. After all, Todd and I designed and built this place—I know every system, every detail, every feature better than anyone.

Kevin doesn't look pleased by my intervention, but I pretend not to notice. For the next twenty minutes, I walk him through the technical aspects of sustainable living, though it's clear he couldn't care less about water recirculation or DC-powered appliances. What he does care about is taking photographs—lots of them, claiming his parents are curious about Alma's new living situation.

"Why didn't Frank and Doreen come with you?" I ask as we head back toward the house. Kevin's already turning red from the brief exposure to high altitude sun.

"Dad's tied up with a big project, and Mom hates flying. She's terrified of planes, won't get near an airport." He wipes sweat from his forehead. "So I figured I'd use my miles and check things out for them."

"How long are you planning to stay in the area?"

"Just a few hours. I'm driving down to Santa Fe where there's actually stuff to do." His tone carries clear disdain. "It's pretty dead out here. Nothing happening."

"There's plenty to do if you know where to look." And the last thing I want is Kevin looking. I want him to find Taos boring, want him to leave and never come back.

"Maybe for you, but what about Alma? She's a city girl," he says with that same dismissive tone. "What does she know about living in the middle of nowhere?"

"More than you might think. She's adapting remarkably well."

"That's because you're fucking her, man."

The words hit like a slap, and I don't give him a chance to elaborate. I grab the front of his shirt and push him against the side of the house, my face inches from his.

"What she does in her private life is none of your business," I say through clenched teeth. "You need to show some respect for your sister-in-law. Drew would never have tolerated you speaking about her this way."

"Yeah, would he have approved of you fucking his wife?" Kevin counters, his eyes bright with malicious satisfaction. "Or is he rolling in his grave knowing his best friend had the hots for his wife the whole time?"

I release him and step back, watching him straighten his rumpled shirt. "That's not what happened."

"Keep telling yourself that, man. Maybe someday you'll believe it." He adjusts his collar with exaggerated dignity. "Drew told me about the last time you came to their house. Said you made a move on Alma, and seeing what I see now, he called it right. Is that why you stayed away for a whole year? Figured people would forget?"

The accusation lands too close to a truth I'm still learning to live with. "I'm done talking to you."

I hold the door open as Alma emerges from the nursery, concern written across her features at the tension she can obviously feel.

"Make sure you say goodbye to your sister-in-law before you leave," I tell Kevin, keeping my voice carefully neutral. "And remember your manners."

I wait until Kevin makes his stiff farewell and drives away, my jaw clenched until the dust from his rental car settles. Only when Alma wraps her arms around my waist do I allow myself to relax.

"Thank you for staying," she says quietly. "That means a lot to me. He does love Tyler, I know that."

"I can see that. But I don't like the way he treats you." The understatement of the year. "Was he always like this? Angry and disrespectful?"

Alma doesn't answer immediately. When she does, her voice is soft with sadness. "No, he changed after Drew died. Kevin idolized his big brother, was so proud of his military service. When Drew died by suicide..." She shakes her head. "I guess I was the easiest person to blame. After all, I left him when he needed me most. I let him down, let all of them down."

"You didn't let anyone down, Al," I say fiercely, pulling her closer. "You had your reasons for leaving, and no one should fault you for protecting yourself and Tyler."

I press a kiss to the top of her head, grateful I was here

when Kevin showed up unannounced. What would he have said to her if she'd been alone? How would he have treated her without a witness?

Learning that Drew told his family I'd made a move on Alma explains so much about their hostility toward her. They probably think she was having an affair, that she left Drew for me. The timeline would work, from their perspective—I disappear from their lives, she leaves Drew, he dies, and then she moves across the country to be near me.

The worst part is that Kevin isn't entirely wrong. I did always care for Alma in ways that went beyond friendship. I never acted on those feelings because she was Drew's wife, but they were there. I respected her, was amazed by how she could make any space feel like home, how she could make Drew laugh even during his darkest moments.

"Looks like Tyler's waking up," Alma says, glancing at the baby monitor in her hand. "Want to stay for dinner? I harvested bok choy this morning and was planning to make Asian stir-fry with tofu."

I shake my head reluctantly. "I can't tonight. Dax, Todd, and Gabe are having guys' night at my place."

Alma laughs, the tension from Kevin's visit finally starting to ease. "Is that where you all drink beer and pretend you're still twenty-five?"

"We grill steaks too. And then we sit around like the boring adults we've become and argue about video game strategies." I follow her into the house, closing the door firmly behind us. "What about you? Any exciting plans for the evening?"

"I'm working on lesson plans—or play plans, really.

Educational activities for toddlers. Learning through play concepts."

"That sounds riveting."

She rolls her eyes playfully. "Not as riveting as your virtual warfare, but I'll manage. Though I'd probably get bored shooting everything that moves."

"We don't shoot everything, Al. Just the bad guys. There's strategy involved."

From the nursery comes the sound of Tyler laughing at some toy, and the normalcy of it helps wash away the last residue of Kevin's visit.

"I'd still be bored out of my mind," she says as my phone buzzes with an incoming text.

I pull it out to see a message from my supervisor at Blackwater Ridge Security. As Alma disappears into the nursery, I read the message and type a quick response.

"Everything okay?" she asks, emerging with Tyler, who's contentedly chewing on his favorite purple octopus.

"One of the guys injured his back and I'm needed next week." I hit send and pocket the phone. "Looks like I'm flying to Hong Kong."

"Where to this time?"

"Hong Kong. But I don't want to go."

She tilts her head curiously. "Why not? I thought you liked the travel."

I pull both her and Tyler into a gentle embrace. "Because I don't want to leave you two."

"Sawyer, we'll be fine."

What if Kevin comes back? The thought flashes through my mind, but I don't voice it. The last thing I want is for her to spend the week worrying about Drew's hostile little brother and whatever agenda he might have.

"Really," she continues, as if reading my concerned thoughts. "Tyler and I will be fine. You can call when you get there, and we'll figure out video chats despite the time difference."

"Eighteen hours ahead, I think."

"So? I've got a packed schedule anyway. Doctor visits for both Tyler and me, playdates with Harlow and the twins, library activities. Plus I need to work on my social media content and plan out my blog posts." She adjusts Tyler on her hip as he tries to grab a handful of her hair. "I'll be too busy to miss you properly."

The casual way she says it makes my chest tight. Will she miss me? The way I know I'll miss her?

"You sure you'll be okay?"

"Sawyer, don't use me as an excuse to avoid work," she says with gentle firmness. "Work is work. You have responsibilities."

"Would you want me to stay tonight?" The question slips out before I can stop it, revealing more need than I intended.

She shakes her head with a soft smile. "Enjoy your guys' night. Have fun and stop worrying about me. I'm not as fragile as you think."

But as the words leave her lips, I know I won't stop worrying. Not with Kevin still in the area, not with the memory of his hostile words still echoing in my head. I also can't smother her with my protective instincts—she's been taking care of herself for months before I came back into her life.

"Just promise me you'll lock your doors and don't let

anyone in while I'm gone," I say, trying to keep the request casual.

She gives me a quick kiss that tastes like promise and possibility. "I lived in Los Angeles for years, Sawyer. Of course I'm going to lock everything. Old habits die hard."

CHAPTER FOURTEEN

Alma

It's 0600 Hong Kong time when my phone rings, but I've been waiting for this call like an addict waiting for his next fix. That makes it 4 PM in Taos—the perfect time to catch Alma and Tyler before dinner.

"Oh my, you look absolutely delicious!" Alma's voice fills my sterile hotel room with warmth and excitement. "I love seeing a man in a suit. It does something to me."

"Really? In that case, take your fill, Al." I step back from the phone propped on the coffee table, letting her appreciate the full view. I'm probably blushing, but I don't care. I finish adjusting my tie until it's perfect—the tailored suit fits like armor, designed to allow full range of motion if things go sideways. Only my shoes betray my real job; they're too practical for a businessman, too ready for action.

"How are things over there?" she asks, settling Tyler on her lap.

"Boring, which in my line of work is infinitely better than not boring. How about you?"

"It rained earlier today—these clouds appeared out of

nowhere and just opened up. Then as quickly as they came, they disappeared, and now there's this incredible smell in the air..."

"Petrichor," I say with a grin. "The scent that comes after rain hits dry earth."

"Yes, that's it! It means more water for the cisterns, right?"

"Exactly." The Willow's rainwater collection system is one of the features I'm most proud of—reservoirs hidden in the bermed soil that insulates the house, filtering roof runoff for use throughout the home.

For the next ten minutes, we chat about her week—playdates with Harlow and the twins, her growing social media following as she documents off-grid living with a toddler, the small victories and daily rhythms of her new life. Her enthusiasm is infectious, and Tyler's even more so as he climbs down from her lap to stand at the coffee table where the iPad is propped.

He reaches his chubby arms toward me, babbling excitedly. "Da-da! Da-da!"

It's become his favorite thing, calling me by a name he can't quite pronounce yet—the "S" sound still beyond his eighteen-month-old vocabulary. I laugh as he tries to grab the tablet, but Alma quickly moves it out of reach. Last time he managed to end our call with one enthusiastic swipe.

"He just woke up from his nap and he's getting hungry, so we can't talk much longer," Alma says, pulling him back onto her lap. "But seriously, you should wear suits more often, Mr. Villier. They do things to me you can only imagine."

She blows me a kiss, then guides Tyler's hand to his

mouth so he can blow one too. The simple gesture makes my chest tight with longing.

"Bye bye, little man. See you both soon," I say before the screen goes dark.

Suddenly I find myself wishing Tyler would one day call me something different—not just Da-da, but Daddy. The thought should probably alarm me more than it does.

I pull Drew's compass from my trouser pocket, running my thumb over the cracked glass face. His name is scratched into the back in childlike script, probably carved during one of our countless hours on watch.

"I know we didn't part on good terms," I murmur to the empty room. "But I never gave up on you. You know that, right?" I turn the compass over, studying the face that guided us through so many missions. "I'm keeping that promise I made you, though. I'm here for her now... for both of them."

As I slip the compass back into my pocket, I know we're moving fast—maybe too fast by conventional standards. But I've known Alma for years. She was more than just Drew's wife; she was my friend too, someone I trusted and respected long before these complicated feelings developed.

My phone buzzes with an email notification—one I've been expecting. I could have rushed the results, but since I was traveling anyway, I let them follow the normal timeline. Still, it's important enough that I requested both email and hard copy delivery.

I'd gotten tested two days after Alma and I first slept together. I wanted her to know I was taking this seriously, that what we have isn't some casual rebound or convenience. The results confirm what I already knew, but seeing it in writing feels official, responsible. Clean across the board.

Just because I wasn't into commitment before doesn't mean I was reckless about health.

My phone buzzes again—a reminder that I have five minutes to relieve my colleague at Heath's suite next door. I check my reflection one final time, adjusting my tie and trying to shake the restless energy that comes from being so far from home.

Three more days. Then I can get back to Taos, back to Alma and Tyler. Back to hearing that little voice call me Da-da, even though the guilt of it sometimes threatens to swallow me whole.

It's a name I don't deserve—it belongs to a man Tyler will never meet. But I'm not planning to change the narrative either. Tyler is Drew's son and always will be. I just hope I knew Drew well enough to believe that despite how we parted, he'd want his wife and child protected, loved, cared for with everything I have to give.

Because I want more than just that. I want so much more.

***

I wake with a start, my hand automatically reaching for my left leg as the remnants of the nightmare fade back into whatever dark corner of my mind houses them. It's been a while since the last episode—maybe a month, maybe more. Even though my rational mind knows my leg is intact, my body performs its own check anyway. Muscle memory, the therapists called it. My nervous system's way of verifying I'm still whole.

"Bad dream?"

The question comes from Heath, who's sitting across

from me in the cabin of his private jet. At thirty-two, he's already one of the richest men in the world, but right now he looks like the kid I used to fish with during summer vacations. He sets a steaming cup of coffee next to a magnetic chess board where, judging by the absence of his queen, I apparently won our last game.

"Maybe," I say, pressing the button to bring my seat upright. "How long was I out?"

"Not long. We should be landing soon." Heath glances at his platinum watch, a piece that probably costs more than most people's cars.

"That should be me telling you that."

"True, but you're my friend first, bodyguard second. I can tell you whatever I damn well please."

"Ha ha," I reply dryly as Lorelei, the flight attendant, appears with fresh coffee. Black, the way I've been drinking it since the Marines taught me that cream and sugar were luxuries you couldn't count on.

Heath and I are an unlikely pair—the young billionaire and the broken-down Marine. But we've known each other since we were kids spending summers at Lake Winnipesaukee. Heath lived in the massive estate on the water, the one my grandmother always called "the house where the servants outnumber the family." Todd and I would see the bodyguards but never the actual residents, until one summer when Heath, his mother Rosalie, and their security detail actually moved in for the season.

We first spotted one of the bodyguards teaching him to fish on their private dock. Todd and I swam over and asked if he wanted to hang out with us instead. Heath said yes; his bodyguard said absolutely not and immediately escorted him back to the house.

Eventually, that bodyguard—Clyde Fredricks, though everyone called him Fred—relented and allowed his charge to play with the two feral kids next door who wore thrift-store clothes and had no curfew. It was an unlikely friendship, but it worked. Even as Heath went on to Ivy League schools while I enlisted, we stayed in touch.

When I came back from Afghanistan, he offered me work as security when he traveled abroad. Maybe it was pity, maybe genuine need—with my leg, I wasn't exactly prime bodyguard material. But the pay was good, the suits were tailored, and the work kept me busy when the silence of Taos became too much.

I can hear the other two bodyguards moving around in the back of the cabin—both veterans like me, one former Army Ranger, the other ex-Recon Marine. Good men who understand that protecting someone isn't just about taking bullets; it's about reading situations, preventing problems before they start.

"Why didn't Fred hire Drew when he applied to Black-water Ridge?" I ask suddenly. The question has been bothering me for months, but I've never found the right time to bring it up.

Heath's expression grows careful. "You know I don't handle hiring decisions. Fred runs that side of the operation."

"But you must know why he was rejected. I gave Drew a strong recommendation—exemplary service record, proven under fire. Yet Fred passed on him."

"Does it really matter now?" Heath's voice is gentle but firm. "He's gone, Sawyer."

"It matters to me."

Heath sighs, setting down his coffee. "Look, you know the standards Fred maintains. No matter how good a recommendation is, it comes down to one question: can this person do the job under extreme pressure? Maybe Fred had concerns."

"About what? Drew's record was spotless."

"Not about his military service," Heath says carefully. "But Fred does comprehensive background checks, psychological evaluations. Sometimes good soldiers struggle with civilian transitions. PTSD, substance issues, family problems —any of those can be disqualifying factors."

The implication hits me like a cold wind. Fred must have seen something in Drew's evaluation, some red flag that I missed or chose to ignore. Maybe his drinking was already showing up in official records. Maybe his mental health struggles were more apparent to an outside observer than to someone who loved him.

"Fred keeps everyone safe by hiring people who can stay stable under pressure," Heath continues. "I trust his judgment. And he trusts you, or you wouldn't be here."

"I'll ask him about it when we get back," I say finally.

"I'm sorry about your friend," Heath adds quietly. "I know you two were close."

"Were," I emphasize. "We had a falling out before he died. Two months of not speaking before he..." I can't finish the sentence. Even now, the words stick in my throat.

"I'm sorry to hear that too."

I feel Heath studying me for a moment before he asks, "What happened to his widow? Are you still in contact?"

"She's renting one of my properties in Taos," I reply carefully. "The house Todd and I just finished."

Heath's eyebrows shoot up with obvious interest, and I immediately regret saying anything.

"What does that look mean?" I ask suspiciously.

"You're awfully defensive for someone who's just playing landlord," he says with a knowing grin.

"You're talking in riddles, man."

"Sometimes life isn't as complicated as we make it, Sawyer," Heath says. "Sometimes everything you need is right in front of you, and the only thing stopping you from reaching for it is your own fear."

The Willow is mostly dark when I arrive, just a few lights glowing warm in the living room windows. Heath's jet had landed in LA just in time for me to catch the last commercial flight to Santa Fe, and now here I am, home again after what felt like the longest week of my life.

Alma is waiting by the front door as I park next to her SUV, and just the sight of her silhouetted against the doorframe makes my chest tight with something I'm finally ready to call love. As I make my way up the path, a shooting star streaks across the brilliant canopy of desert stars overhead, and I can't help but take it as a good sign.

The moment I step through the door and drop my carry-on, I sweep Alma into my arms, lifting her and spinning her around as she squeals with laughter. She feels perfect against me, all warm curves and soft skin that smells like roses and lavender and home.

"Where's Tyler?" I ask as I set her down, noting how quiet the house is, most lights dimmed low.

"Asleep," she says softly, biting her lower lip in that way that makes my pulse quicken. "I thought we might appreciate some privacy."

I could have changed on the plane, swapped this tailored suit for my usual cargo pants and t-shirt. But I remembered what she'd said during our video calls about how good I looked in formal wear, and judging by the way she's looking at me now—like I'm her next meal—the effort was worth it.

I pull Alma to me and kiss her. The feel of her breasts pressing against my chest has my cock instantly hard, like a steel rod in my trousers. I press my hips against her and her eyes widen. Fuck, I'm so hard.

"I've missed you. Can't you tell?" I growl into her neck, scooping her up and feeling her legs wrap around me as I make my way to the bedroom and hoping I don't walk right into a damn wall. The moment we get to the bedroom, I set Alma down, still kissing her. I can't get enough of her. She's wearing a cute dress, but she's not too worried about me getting it off her. She's intent on getting me out of my suit first.

"There's nothing I love more than seeing you in a suit," she murmurs in my ear as she loosens my tie. "That way I can take it off you, piece by piece."

"Not yet." I slide the straps of her dress, pulling them down her shoulders and off her body until it's a puddle at her feet. She's naked underneath and I take a deep intake of breath. Holy fuck. "You're so beautiful, baby."

I take a step back and let her undress me slowly, watching her concentrate as she starts with my coat, sliding them off my shoulders first and draping it over the edge of the bed. We continue to kiss as she works on the tie and then my shirt, marveling at my own patience. But by the time we get to my belt, my cock feels like a lead pipe in my pants and I'm done waiting.

"Get on the bed."

Alma slides her body to the middle of the bed, watching me as I undress. When I reach for my wallet to retrieve a condom, she shakes her head. "Is it okay if we... if we don't use that?" When I frown, she continues, "While you were away, I went to see a doctor. I mean, I had to find one anyway, now that I live here, but I'm now on the... on the Pill."

I crawl over her on the bed. "You sure this is what you want?"

"Yes. I want to feel you inside me. You. All of you." Alma grips my shoulders, pulling me down for a kiss. I slid my hand under her neck as my tongue slipped between her lips, relishing her taste, her warmth, knowing that soon, there'd be nothing between us. It'll be just us. Connected. Whole.

I pull away, blazing a trail of kisses along her neck downward before stopping over a perky nipple, my hands now cupping each breast. She moans as I suck each one, making sure to give them equal attention. When my hand drifts lower between her legs, I find her so wet and ready for me.

As I press against her and slowly slide the head of my cock past her folds, Alma rocks her hips slightly. I pause, feeling myself inside her tight pussy. I should be enjoying this, savoring it all.

All the years since I've known her as my best friend's wife, keeping my distance, doing everything that would make her life easier while he was away—changing light bulbs in the garage because it turned out she was afraid of heights, cleaning out the rain gutters so she didn't have to pay someone else to do it, or carrying the Christmas tree inside her house so she'd have something to hang her cute handmade ornaments and not be lonely on the day when most families would be together—all that was going straight to hell. She's never been just my best friend's wife, she was the woman I'd secretly adored, the woman I admired, and now her son—no, their son—is calling me a name that's not mine.

She looks up at me, her brow furrowing at my hesitation. "What's wrong?"

I lean my forehead against hers, her voice, her words, her gaze becoming the keys that I wish could unlock the gates of time and return us back to that night at the bar. This time I'd have been the one to walk over to her and make her smile, not Drew.

"I want you, Sawyer," she whispers, rocking her hips against me, pushing up to grind her clit against my pelvic bone as I thrust inside her, feeling her pussy clamp around my cock. With each pump of my cock inside her, I watch Alma come apart, kissing her closed lids and her half-open mouth. She wraps her legs around me, holding onto me as we both come together, her pussy squeezing and pulsing around me as the sound of her voice calling out my name fill the room. As my own release comes, I can't see or feel anything but her. It's as if she's become my world.

No, she is my world.

Afterward, as we lie tangled in the moonlight streaming through the bedroom windows, Alma traces lazy patterns on my chest while I play with her hair.

"I love you," I say suddenly, the words spilling out before I can second-guess them. "I'm completely, utterly in love with you, Alma Thomas."

She goes very still for a moment, and I hold my breath, wondering if I've moved too fast, revealed too much. Then she lifts her head to look at me, her eyes bright with unshed tears.

"I'm madly in love with you too, Sawyer," she whispers. "You've made me happier than I probably deserve to be."

"You deserve all of it," I tell her, cupping her face in my hands. "Every bit of happiness this world has to offer."

As I kiss her again, soft and slow and full of promise, I realize that Heath was right. Sometimes everything you need really is right in front of you, and the only thing standing in your way is the courage to reach for it.

Tonight, finally, I did.

CHAPTER FIFTEEN

Alma

It's been two months since the night Sawyer returned from Hong Kong declaring his love, and we've fallen into a rhythm that feels surprisingly natural. I spend my days with Tyler, building my social media presence and developing lesson plans for homeschooling families, while Sawyer splits his time between teaching sustainable building workshops with Todd and his colleagues, and his security work that takes him to places I can only imagine.

It's fascinating to watch him navigate these two completely different worlds—one where he gets his hands dirty building homes from the earth itself, and another where he wears tailored suits and protects billionaires in five-star hotels. Sawyer thrives in both environments, adapting with an ease that speaks to his fundamental resilience.

Some days I find myself wondering if Drew could have managed the same kind of adaptation, then remind myself that comparisons aren't fair to either of them. Despite their deep friendship, Drew and Sawyer were fundamentally different men. Drew needed structure, certainty, clear hierarchies. Sawyer flows like water, finding his shape in whatever container holds him.

Life in the high desert continues to feel like a miracle I'm afraid to examine too closely. Some mornings I still have to pinch myself when I wake to dancing sunlight streaming through the glass bottle bricks, casting rainbow patterns on the adobe walls. When I step outside, I breathe in the scent of green earth and growing things, of hollyhocks blooming against the backdrop of endless sky.

What if I'd said no to Sawyer's offer? I'd still be living next to that car repair shop, probably going deaf from the constant noise. But that's not my reality anymore. Tyler and I are here, we're happy, and I'm building something that feels like it might actually last.

I love that Sawyer doesn't let me live rent-free—though I'm sure he would if Todd didn't intervene with practical concerns about business partnerships and property values. I want to pay my own way, to prove that I'm not here as charity case or damsel in distress. Yes, I spent almost a year in that terrible apartment, but that was about needing time to process shock and new motherhood, not about needing rescue.

Things are different now. Better. I've even set up a Christmas tree this year—the first one since Drew's death. Last year, I couldn't bear the thought of celebrating anything.

My blog has taken off beyond my wildest expectations. Apparently, there's genuine interest in how city dwellers can adapt to off-grid living, and my perspective as a single mother navigating solar power and homegrown vegetables resonates with people. The photos I post daily—of my indoor garden thriving, of Tyler playing against the backdrop of sage and mountains—draw hundreds of comments from curious followers.

Before his last trip, Sawyer bought me a professional camera and taught me about composition and lighting. Todd chimed in with technical advice about capturing the unique quality of high desert light through the Willow's tilted windows. It turns out I'm more comfortable in front of the camera than I expected, maybe because I'm finally comfortable in my own skin.

The only people who aren't celebrating my transformation are Drew's parents. They hate seeing Tyler's photos on social media, can't understand how I could make money from sharing pieces of our life online. No matter how many times I explain that Tyler and I are thriving here, they insist I've lost my mind and need professional help. How could a rational widow abandon city life to become, in their words, "a hippie in the desert, endangering her child by living off the grid"?

Sawyer has witnessed enough of their phone calls to be genuinely baffled by my patience with their criticism. He can't understand how I tolerated that kind of treatment for so long. But grief and guilt were my constant companions for a year, and I'd bought into their narrative that because I'd failed Drew, a guilt-ridden half-life was what I deserved.

My phone buzzes on the kitchen counter, pulling me from my thoughts. It's a text from Sawyer, who's been working on a new rammed earth house with students learning foundation techniques—stacking tires and filling them with tamped soil, back-breaking work that he approaches with the enthusiasm of someone who genuinely loves teaching.

SAWYER:

Just finished with the crew and heading to
shower. Are we still on for dinner?

I glance at the slow cooker where beef bourguignon has
been simmering all afternoon, filling the Willow with rich,
comforting aromas.

ALMA:

Definitely still on. I miss you.

SAWYER:

Miss you too. Be there in 30.

ALMA:

Take your time. I'll be right here.

SAWYER:

Want to do some stargazing tonight?

ALMA:

Of course. I have the app ready.

Lately, Sawyer has been teaching me about constellations, knowledge he picked up from his boss Heath, who
apparently knows enough celestial navigation to guide a ship
across an ocean using only stars. Sawyer told me the skies in
Afghanistan and Iraq were often just as brilliant as they are
here in Taos—a stark contrast to the reality that no matter
how beautiful the night sky, the following morning could
bring death.

But here, those same stars represent peace, mastery over
his own fate, better control over the flashbacks that occasionally surface. I still remember the episode triggered by our

blown tire on the interstate—the way his face went pale and cold sweat beaded his forehead, how he seemed to disappear entirely into some internal battlefield. It scared me because it was so reminiscent of Drew's episodes, but Sawyer pulled himself back. He kissed me, and everything changed between us.

These days, the three of us often lie on blankets and pillows spread in front of the large windows, Tyler nestled between us as we trace constellations overhead. It feels like family. It feels like home.

I'm so lost in these thoughts that the sharp knock on the front door makes me jump. With Tyler balanced on my hip, I walk to the entrance and see an older man in a blue work shirt with "Service Pros" embroidered on the pocket, beige slacks, official clipboard in hand.

"Can I help you?" I ask, opening the door but not inviting him in.

"Are you Miss Alma Thomas?"

"Yes."

He extends a manila envelope with the gravity of someone who knows he's delivering bad news. "I have legal documents for you, ma'am."

I frown, accepting the envelope with my free hand. "What kind of legal documents?"

"I can't provide details, ma'am. Everything you need to know is in there."

After he leaves, I set Tyler on the floor and stare at the envelope like it might spontaneously combust. Who would be serving me papers? What could I possibly have done?

The moment I tear open the envelope and scan the first page, the floor seems to drop away beneath my feet. I lean against the wall, trying to focus on the words, but tears blur my vision. Still, I understand the intent, the devastating implications.

The sound of Sawyer's truck pulling up snaps me back to the present. Tyler, who's been playing at my feet, immediately perks up and calls out the name he's been using since Sawyer's Hong Kong trip.

"Da-da!"

Sawyer's face darkens the moment he sees my expression. Usually I'd be running to greet him, but I can't move. My feet feel like they've turned to lead, and any movement might shatter what's left of my composure.

"Who was that who just left? What did he want?"

When I can't find my voice, Sawyer gently takes the envelope and papers from my trembling hands. He flips through the pages, his jaw tightening with each one.

"Can they actually do this?" he asks finally.

I nod, the simple movement feeling monumental. "Apparently they can. I have to be in LA in three weeks."

"I can't believe they're questioning your mental stability," he says, anger creeping into his voice as he continues reading. "They're claiming you're unfit to raise Tyler on your own."

"I should have seen this coming." The words come out as barely a whisper.

"How the hell can Frank and Doreen sue for custody?" Sawyer mutters as I lift Tyler into my arms, needing the comfort of his warm weight against me.

Because they think I've lost my mind, I think but can't say aloud. I'm afraid if I start talking, I'll break down completely. I can't imagine Tyler and me back in LA, not after discovering all the possibilities that have opened up here in Taos.

"Alma, look at me," Sawyer says, his fingers gently tilting my chin upward. "We're going to fight this."

"Do I have a choice? If I don't fight, they get exactly what they want."

"And they won't get what they want," he says fiercely. "You're an amazing mother. You and Tyler are thriving here. You've built a support system, started a career, created stability for both of you. Any court can see that."

"I don't mind them wanting visitation rights," I say, the words tumbling out in a rush. "I've never tried to keep Tyler from them. But I'm terrified they'll take him and disappear. They've already overridden my decisions in the past, kept him longer than agreed, ignored my parenting choices. That's why I started staying the entire time when they had visits."

The tears come then, hot and unstoppable. Sawyer pulls Tyler and me against his chest, and I let myself sob into his shirt.

"That's not going to happen," he says firmly. "We're going to fight this together." He pauses, pulling back to study my face with sudden intensity. "Why don't we get married? They can't pull this kind of maneuver if we're married."

I stare into his eyes, seeing nothing but sincerity and determination. This is Sawyer—when has he ever been anything but completely honest? He's delivered on every promise he's made since I've known him. A chance to start over, a home of my own, new friends and opportunities— check, check, and check.

But marriage as a legal strategy?

"We can't get married for this," I blurt out, the words coming faster than my thoughts. "Sawyer, I'm grateful for everything you've done, but I can't marry you just to win a custody battle. If we're going to get married, I want it to be because we're both ready, because we choose each other freely, not because Drew's parents are forcing our hand."

When he doesn't immediately protest, I continue, "I hope you understand where I'm coming from."

He swallows hard, and I watch something flicker across his features—hurt, maybe, or disappointment. "You're right."

"Sawyer, I'm sorry—"

"It's okay, Al. I understand." His smile doesn't quite reach his eyes. He turns his attention to Tyler, taking him from my arms with gentle hands. "Hey, little man, how was your day?"

As I follow him into the living room, I find myself wishing desperately that I could take back my refusal and say yes. Marriage would solve everything, would end this custody nightmare before it really begins. But I can't build a marriage on fear and legal strategy.

I want to do things the right way, even if it's harder. I need to face this head-on, because if I don't, Frank and Doreen will never stop trying to control my life and Tyler's future.

But as I watch Sawyer with Tyler, seeing the love and tenderness in every interaction, part of me wonders if I've just made the biggest mistake of my life.

CHAPTER SIXTEEN

Sawyer

Three weeks since Alma got served those papers. Three weeks watching the light fade from her face as each phone call with her lawyer came and went. The fact that they had to serve her right before Christmas is more than cruel—it's despicable, and I hate seeing the woman I love slowly disappearing under the weight of their legal assault.

It's like watching a desert rose start to wither, and it kills me knowing there's so little I can do to help. I want to punch someone and make them pay for trying to beat her into submission. For a year after Drew killed himself, the demons won whenever I stayed away from her. But I'm not letting them win again.

Unfortunately, right now, waiting in this stuffy LA County courthouse is about to do me in as we wait for Frank, Doreen and their lawyer to arrive before the mediation meeting can start. At least it doesn't go straight into the court hearing, which is tomorrow. But no matter how much I hate it, I have to remain positive for Alma.

The courthouse smells like fear and broken promises, old coffee and desperation. I squeeze Alma's hand as we sit on the hard wooden bench, watching her nibble what's left of her cuticles—a nervous habit that's gotten worse since this nightmare began. She's probably already destroyed half her fingernails by now.

"You okay?" she asks, flashing me an apologetic smile, her slender hand dwarfed in mine.

"Yeah, I'm good. I work security, remember? We usually do a lot more waiting than actual chasing after bad guys, although I prefer the waiting, to be honest."

"Just not this type of waiting."

"I didn't say that." I squeeze her hand, hating how terrible this is for her. "I only want things to work out for you and Tyler."

While I'm keeping Alma company in LA, Harlow and Dax are taking care of Tyler for us in Taos. It was Alma's first time to be away from her son overnight, and it showed. She's been miserable, barely sleeping, checking her phone constantly for updates. Last night at the hotel, she kept a brave front, but after Harlow directed the camera at Tyler's sleeping face during their video call, Alma almost broke down completely.

I want to punch someone so bad for putting her through all this hell, but I have to play the game too—whatever twisted game Drew's parents think they're playing.

I get it. They want full custody of their grandson, and they don't care who they hurt in the process. They're not even playing fair.

They're not only using Alma's decision to move to Taos

and live off-grid—which they consider unsafe and populated with unsavory characters—they're also using hearsay from Kevin about her emotional and mental state as part of their evidence. Flimsy at best, and I know it won't stand up in court. But the damage is done. Even if Alma proves them wrong, the emotional toll it's taking on her leaves me feeling as useless as I felt when I suggested we get married.

I'm sure it was a surprise for her just as much as it was for me. I'd never asked anyone to marry me before. Hell, I'd never even thought about getting married before. It was never in the cards, not even a consideration. I like my independence. I didn't mind seeing friends settling down, always getting asked to be best man but never becoming the groom. But people change, and judging from my recent failed proposal, I certainly have.

Suggesting marriage had come out of desperation, but I meant every word. I want to marry Alma, and it's not only to get rid of this custody case, but because I'm in love with her. I love her. Being married would mean that Frank and Doreen could no longer sue her for custody of Tyler, and that's a good thing, right?

Unfortunately, I never factored in hearing Alma say no.

And so for the past three weeks, I've had to swallow my pride and keep myself busy. I've had to tell myself that her refusal wasn't personal. Alma simply didn't have any other choice, definitely not one she could feel good about.

Still, I wish I could make all this legal bullshit go away. But even if I could—hell, I could pull enough strings with Heath to get her the best lawyer money can buy and blow this custody case out of the water—Alma refuses any help beyond what she's already getting. She tells me she's got her lawyer handled. I understand her need for independence, but it's frustrating as hell.

The moment we see Alma's lawyer step out of the elevator, we get up and she introduces me to him. Gordon Cromwell is probably in his late fifties, with broad shoulders encased in an ill-fitting brown suit and a shaved head that gleams under the fluorescent lights. When he sees the tattoo on my right arm, he tells me he did two tours in Vietnam. It's one way to break the ice, but we're not here to trade war stories, although I do appreciate him trying to establish common ground.

He turns to Alma with obvious concern. "Can we speak privately before the meeting starts?"

As I pull out my phone, distracting myself by checking emails that don't matter, I can hear bits and pieces of their hushed conversation from across the hallway.

"You'll need to bring it up, Alma," I hear Gordon say, his voice carrying the weight of experience. "They have to know about Drew and what happened between you two."

"No, I'm not going to bring it up. I can't." Alma's voice drops to barely a whisper. "We'll have to go ahead without saying anything about it."

I hear Gordon exhale heavily, the sound of a lawyer who knows his client is about to handicap their own case. "If that's how you want to proceed, then we'll do our best with what we've got, but I got to warn you—even though the court usually sides with the mother in these situations, without the full picture..."

Gordon's voice lowers and I can't hear anything anymore. Whatever Alma is hiding about her marriage to Drew, it's eating at her. I can see it in the rigid set of her shoulders, the way she keeps glancing toward the conference room like she's walking toward her execution.

Before long, Frank and Doreen arrive with their lawyer—a sharp-dressed woman in her forties who looks like she eats opposing counsel for breakfast and asks for seconds. Behind them, Kevin follows, that familiar smirk already plastered across his face.

"I knew it," I mutter under my breath. All those pictures he was taking of the Willow during his "innocent" visit had been for this case.

"What's he doing here?" Kevin demands, his hands thrust in his trouser pockets as he glares at me.

Doreen turns to their lawyer with obvious irritation. "He's not joining us inside, is he? This mediation meeting is only for family members, and he's not family."

"No, he's not joining us, Doreen," Alma says, her voice soft but firm. There's steel underneath the quiet tone that makes me proud of her.

"I didn't ask you," Doreen snaps, and I force myself not to say anything. Have they always treated Alma with such open contempt? I glance at Alma, but she avoids my gaze, her jaw clenched tight. This is where I get to wish all over again that she'd said yes to my proposal. Marrying me would have made me family. It would have made all this nonsense of mediation and custody hearings go away.

"Good, because this is not his business," Doreen adds with satisfaction. "All we want is the best for our grandson."

"So you're going to take him away from his mother?" I ask, unable to keep quiet any longer. "That's not what's best for Tyler at all. That's what's best for you."

Alma squeezes my hand in warning. "Sawyer…"

"You caused all this," Frank tells me, his face reddening with anger. "If it weren't for you, Alma would still be living in LA and we'd have no problems seeing our only grandson every week. He's our only link to Drew."

Their lawyer clears her throat and pushes the door to the conference room open with professional efficiency. "Mr. Thomas, Mrs. Thomas, why don't we step inside and begin the meeting? The mediator is ready." She turns to Kevin with barely concealed annoyance. "Are you joining us as well?"

As Kevin disappears inside the conference room with obvious self-importance, Alma turns to face me. The fluorescent lights make her look pale, fragile in a way that makes my chest tighten with protective fury.

"If you need to go somewhere..."

"I'll be fine, Al. Don't worry about me." I watch her step inside the room followed by Gordon, the door closing behind them with a soft click that sounds like a jail cell locking. Then I'm alone on that bench, pretending to read through emails while the words blend together meaninglessly.

All I want right now is to be inside that room with Alma. I want to tell Frank and Doreen that what they're doing is causing more harm than good, that Alma and Tyler are happy living in Taos. Who knew Alma's enthusiasm over living off the grid would translate so well to social media? Each day, I check her Instagram and blog posts, beaming with pride at the rapidly growing numbers of followers she gets and the comments and questions about her life raising Tyler in sustainable housing. It's only been a few months, but watching her bloom has been like witnessing a miracle.

Why the hell would Frank and Doreen want to smother that? Have they forgotten how much Drew loved his wife, how much he gushed about her every chance he got even before he married her? The guy was completely smitten with her. He was so proud of her it was almost embarrassing to watch sometimes.

Drew probably set the bar for the woman I'd want to marry one day, even though at that time, I had no idea marriage was something I'd ever want. All I knew was that I was comfortable with Alma. I trusted her in a way I trusted very few people.

Propping my forearms on my knees, I pull up my Photos app and scroll through my albums. Some contain photos I've uploaded from my previous deployments—first Saudi Arabia where my unit didn't see much action, then Iraq where we did, and finally Afghanistan where we saw too much and I almost lost my leg.

As I swipe through pictures of friends, some who didn't return alive and some who did but were broken inside, I feel my chest grow heavy with familiar weight. I shouldn't be looking at these pictures, not even to kill time. Have I forgotten how easily they can bring back the darkness, how the threat of flashbacks lurks just a swipe away? I'd worked too fucking hard to get better, so why risk it now?

Just as I'm about to close the app, a picture flashes on my screen that makes me pause. It's Drew and me in Afghanistan, taken a few weeks before that IED blast killed Smith and Jonas. I study the image, recognizing the scratches on Drew's face caused by tree bark exploding next to him from an Afghan sniper's bullet. If that round had shifted a few millimeters to the right, it would have found Drew. To the left? It would have found me.

Maybe it was windage. Maybe spin drift. Who knew?

What we did know that day was that one of us had been close to getting our heads blown off. That evening, as we sat around the fire with the rest of the guys in our unit, Drew took me aside and asked me to take care of Alma if anything happened to him.

This was more than just visiting his family to express condolences and share a few stories about his service. No, this was a promise to take care of a woman he hadn't even married yet. But what good is that promise if I can't do anything to stop the people wanting to take Tyler away from her?

The conference room door opens after what feels like hours, and a frustrated Alma steps out with Gordon. Frank, Doreen, and their lawyer follow right behind them, looking just as unhappy. They don't even say goodbye to her—they keep walking toward the elevator like she doesn't exist.

"What happened? Did you reach a decision?"

"No," Alma replies, her voice hollow with exhaustion. "It didn't get anywhere."

"Custody hearing goes on as scheduled tomorrow. One o'clock," Gordon says before turning to look at Alma with obvious frustration. "I seriously urge you to think about what I said, Miss Thomas. It's something they should know."

"Something who should know?" I ask, though I'm starting to piece together what Gordon is driving at. "What are you talking about?"

"Nothing," Alma replies quickly, avoiding my gaze like she's done since this whole nightmare started.

"Nothing?" I frown, my voice sharpening. "If Gordon thinks whatever it is could keep Tyler safe from this mess, it can't be nothing, Al."

"I told you, Sawyer. It's nothing," she snaps, then immediately looks ashamed of her tone. Gordon presses his lips together, clearly not happy with how things are going, but he knows better than to push a client who's already at her breaking point.

"Can we go now?" she asks quietly.

As we make our way toward the parking garage, Alma doesn't say anything, but she doesn't have to. I can tell that whatever Gordon meant is weighing heavily on her, but I'm not going to push it. She'll tell me when she's ready—if she'll ever tell me at all.

With Alma needing to meet her lawyer again that afternoon, I change into something more comfortable and take an Uber to the cemetery. I tell the driver to wait until I'm done and get out of the car. This time I don't bring any beer. It's just Drew and me.

I sit cross-legged on the grass in front of his grave, studying the words etched into the black granite. Two bouquets of flowers are arranged on both sides of his headstone, and a small American flag stands at attention right in front of it. I'm guessing they're from his parents, but I don't look at the cards to confirm. I'd planned on making this visit during my next layover in LA, wanting to assure Drew that I'm taking care of Alma just like I promised. I just never counted on having to do it under these circumstances, with his parents suing her for custody of Tyler.

For the next few minutes, I sit staring at the words on his gravestone, letting random thoughts pop into my head. Funny moments during our deployment when Drew would tell his crazy and morbid sniper stories. The time I woke up in the hospital in Maryland to find him and Alma sitting by my bed after another surgery to repair my leg, the threat of amputation leaving me an emotional fucking mess who was convinced life would be over if it happened.

Somehow, out of all the visits from members of my unit, I remember Drew and Alma's visit the most. They sat with me for three days and cheered me up with silly card games and stories, giving Todd a break from keeping an eye on me.

"So I hear you could lose your leg, Villier," he'd said one day, his voice carrying that particular brand of dark humor that got us through the worst moments overseas. "It's still better than losing your life, because what about me, man? You can't leave me here by my lonesome! I'd go straight to hell and drag you back because it ain't your time, devil dog."

I smile as the memories come, one after another, of the man who helped get me back on track. So why the fuck couldn't I do it right when it was my turn?

Another memory surfaces—seeing Alma sitting on the chair next to my hospital bed, her brow furrowed in concentration as she read a book in her lap. I figured she was probably studying one of her education textbooks, but for some reason, I needed to hear her voice.

"What are you reading?" My voice emerged as a croak, my mouth dry from the medication.

She looked up, surprised, before smiling. Her cheeks reddened as if embarrassed. "Poetry."

"You love poetry?"

She shook her head. "I wouldn't say love. But I like it. And not just any poetry—larger than life type of poetry. The type that I read when I want to feel brave."

"You're brave, Alma. You married a Marine."

"Not brave enough, but I try." She poured water from the pink pitcher into a plastic cup. "Would you like some water?"

I nodded as she put a straw in the cup and brought it toward me. I took a few sips, licking my dry lips as she returned the cup to the table. "Thanks."

"Any time, Sawyer."

"So what poem is it? The one you were reading?" I asked as I settled back down on the pillows. "Do you mind reading it to me?"

She frowned, hesitating at first. Then she pulled her chair closer and cleared her throat, beginning:

"Out of the night that covers me, black as the pit from pole to pole—"

"I thank whatever gods may be," I continued as she glanced up, surprised. "For my unconquerable soul."

"You're good," she said, impressed.

"I don't remember much, but you should go on. Maybe it will come back to me."

Alma smiled, and this time she didn't look at the book as she continued. This time I didn't want to interrupt or impress her either. After listening to everyone else around me talk medical shit about my leg and the possibility of losing it, I wanted to hear something else. I wanted to hear Alma's voice.

"In the fell clutch of circumstance, I have not winced nor cried out aloud. Under the bludgeoning of chance, my head is bloody, but unbowed."

Alma stopped to look at me, as if waiting for permission to continue, and I nodded.

"Beyond this place of wrath and tears looms but the horror of the shade, and yet the menace of the years finds, and shall find me, unafraid."

"It matters not how strait the gate, how charged with punishments the scroll," I continued, my voice cracking as she lifted her gaze to meet mine. "I am the master of my fate, I am the captain of my soul."

We didn't talk for a few minutes afterward, both of us locked in some kind of meditation until a nurse popped her head in to check on my leg and then left.

Alma smiled. "I'd never have pegged you as a poetry man."

"I'm not, but we had to memorize a poem in eighth grade. My girlfriend chose 'Annabel Lee' by Edgar Allan Poe, and I picked 'Invictus' by William Ernest Henley."

"Did it work? To impress her, I mean?"

I shook my head. It was a lie—I didn't pick that poem to impress anyone. I chose it because I needed something to help me handle my mother's drinking and the parade of men she brought home. "Nah, she said it was too macho for her. Too angry."

"I don't think it's a poem one would pick to impress someone," Alma said thoughtfully. "It's more to spur you to do something noble, something that scares the crap out of you."

That conversation had stayed with me through all the dark months that followed. Now, sitting at Drew's grave, I realize Alma was right. Sometimes you need words that make you brave enough to do what scares you most.

I don't know how long I sit staring at Drew's headstone, but by the time my leg starts feeling numb, I get up and dust the grass from the seat of my jeans.

"I'm going to take care of her, man. I promise I'll take care of her and Tyler," I mutter under my breath. "I wish you could have gotten to know your son, Drew, because he's such a beautiful boy. I wish you'd stayed alive long enough to see him, because maybe you would have found a reason to fight harder."

My throat tightens, my mouth turning dry as the next thought comes unbidden. "But then if you had, I wouldn't be here, would I? I wouldn't be with her."

CHAPTER SEVENTEEN

Alma

THE HOTEL ROOM is dark when I wake with a start, the remnants of another dream with Drew's face hovering over me fading into the shadows. For a moment, I forget where I am—the unfamiliar weight of expensive linens, the hum of LA traffic filtering through reinforced windows. Then my hand touches Sawyer's back, his skin warm and solid beneath my palm, and I remember. The courthouse. The mediation. Tomorrow's hearing that could change everything.

I touch the base of the bedside lamp and soft light fills the space. The hotel clock blinks 4:17 AM in accusatory red digits.

Beside me, Sawyer rolls onto his back, covering his eyes with his forearm. "Everything okay?" His voice is thick with sleep, but I can hear the underlying concern that's been present since yesterday's disaster.

I want to say yes, to spare him more worry. But I spent an entire year after Drew died pretending everything was fine when it wasn't, building walls around my pain until no one could reach me anymore. I won't make that mistake again.

"Actually, I'm not sure," I admit, shifting onto my side to face him. I trace lazy patterns across his naked chest, feeling his muscles ripple beneath my touch. "I'm sorry about what happened today. I didn't mean to snap at you in the hallway."

Sawyer captures my hand and brings it to his lips, his beard tickling my skin in a way that sends warmth spreading through my chest. "You don't have to apologize for being under pressure. I can only imagine how brutal that mediation was." He chuckles dryly. "I'd have punched something if it were me."

Despite everything, I smile. "Then I'm glad you weren't in there."

"I wish you didn't have to carry this burden alone, Alma. Whatever you need to face tomorrow, I'm here for it. For you."

"I know, and I'm grateful you flew all the way here," I whisper, guilt threading through my voice. "You didn't have to leave work behind for this mess."

"For you and Tyler? I'd do anything."

Something in his tone makes me study his profile in the lamplight—the strong line of his jaw, the way his dark hair falls across his forehead. "Anything?"

"Yes. Anything."

I scoot closer, feeling his arms wrap around me automatically, pulling me against his broad chest. I inhale his scent—something woodsy and clean that's become synonymous with safety, with home. But underneath my relief at his presence lurks a darker knowledge, a secret that's been eating at me since Gordon first mentioned it.

"I miss you holding me like this," I murmur as he tucks a strand of hair behind my ear.

"Promise me there won't be any secrets between us, Al." His voice is gentle but firm, and I feel something twist in my stomach at the words.

I bite my lip, knowing I'm about to lie to the man I love. "I promise."

The words taste like ash in my mouth, but what choice do I have? Tomorrow I may have to break the promise I made to Drew, the one thing I swore I'd never reveal. But I can't tell Sawyer about that decision—not yet, not when he's already carrying so much guilt about failing Drew. How can I explain that the man he idolizes, the friend whose memory he's spent two years protecting, became someone neither of us would recognize?

As Sawyer pulls me closer, I feel his warm breath against the top of my head, the soft brush of his lips against my hair. His fingers stroke through the auburn strands, and when I tilt my face up to look at him, his mouth descends on mine. He tastes of peppermint and something uniquely him—strength and promises and the possibility of a future I'm terrified I might lose.

Suddenly I don't want to think anymore. I don't want to rehearse tomorrow's revelations or imagine the look in Sawyer's eyes when he learns the truth about Drew. I want him to hold me, kiss me, make love to me like we have all the time in the world instead of these few stolen hours before everything changes.

"I love you, Sawyer," I whisper against his lips, and I hear his breath hitch in response.

"I love you too, Al," he murmurs, his kiss deepening as he guides me back against the pillows. His hands find the hem of my nightshirt, sliding it up and over my head with practiced ease. When his mouth follows the path his hands have traced —jaw, neck, the sensitive hollow of my throat—I arch beneath him, desperate for his touch to erase everything else.

His fingers hook into my panties, sliding them down my legs with deliberate slowness that makes me gasp. When he settles between my thighs, his mouth finding me with an intimacy that makes my vision blur, I lose myself completely in the sensation. This is what I need—to feel alive, cherished, desired. To remember that whatever tomorrow brings, this moment is real.

Later, as we move together in the lamplight, I watch his face above me and memorize every detail—the way his eyes darken with passion, the slight furrow of concentration between his brows, the reverent way he whispers my name like a prayer. I want to hold onto this version of us, before the truth fractures everything we've built.

"I need you," I breathe against his ear as he moves within me, and I mean it in every possible way. I need his strength, his protection, his love. I need him to still look at me this way tomorrow, even after he knows what kind of woman I really am—the kind who abandoned her husband when he needed her most, who kept silent about his demons until it was too late.

When release finally claims us both, I cling to him like he's the only solid thing in a world that's about to shift on its axis. And maybe he is.

Hours later, we arrive at the county courthouse two hours before the scheduled hearing. I requested this last-minute meeting with Frank and Doreen, and surprisingly, they agreed. Gordon warned me they're probably expecting me to cave to their demands, but that's not why I called this meeting.

I can't stop thinking about what Gordon said yesterday—about telling the court why I really left Drew. The truth I've buried for over a year, the promise I made to a dying man that I'm about to break. How will Frank and Doreen accept the reality that their perfect son gave me no choice but to leave?

There's only one problem. They didn't make a promise to Drew. They didn't swear to keep the darkest parts of him hidden behind closed doors, to preserve his reputation as the war hero who saved his brothers-in-arms.

I did.

I take a deep breath and straighten my shoulders, forcing myself to find the strength I've been rebuilding brick by brick since moving to Taos. I've allowed myself to be beaten down for a year since Drew died, accepting blame and guilt and shame like they were my due. But I can't do that anymore. What message am I sending Tyler if he grows up watching his mother refuse to stand up for herself? If I can't fight for us, how can I expect anyone else to?

"You look beautiful," Sawyer says, squeezing my hand as we enter the courthouse lobby. "You're going to do great in there."

I'd searched desperately for something appropriate to wear, finally finding a complete ensemble at a thrift store in Torrance yesterday—a navy blue skirt suit with matching closed-toe pumps. I need to make a good impression, to show the court that living off-grid doesn't make me irresponsible or unfit. The clothes feel like armor, professional and serious in a way my usual flowing dresses aren't.

Sawyer looks equally polished in a light blue dress shirt under a tailored charcoal jacket, black trousers, and leather shoes. It's such a departure from his usual cargo pants and work boots that I barely recognize him. But the way he carries himself—confident, protective, ready for battle—that's purely Sawyer.

"I need to speak with Gordon first," I tell him as we spot my lawyer waiting by the elevators.

Sawyer gives my hand a gentle tug. "No secrets, remember?"

The words hit me like a physical blow, but I force my expression to remain neutral. "You may not like what you're about to hear."

"Doesn't mean I'm going to let you face this alone," he says firmly, just as the elevator doors open to reveal Frank and Doreen with their lawyer.

"You ready for this?" Gordon murmurs to me as we all file into the conference room.

I nod, though my mouth feels like cotton. "As ready as I'll ever be."

"Are you here to negotiate?" Doreen asks the moment the door closes, her voice sharp with anticipation. "Because all we want is reasonable access to our grandson, which means you and Tyler need to move back to California where you belong."

"None of this off-the-grid nonsense," Frank adds with

obvious disdain. "What happens when you decide to give up on Tyler the way you gave up on our son? Who's going to be there to protect him when you abandon him too?"

The accusation hits exactly where they intended, but instead of crumbling, I feel something steel-hard form in my chest. "I never gave up on your son, Frank. But I had to make an impossible choice—one that probably saved both Tyler's life and mine."

"What's that supposed to mean?" their lawyer interjects, clearly irritated by the dramatic turn.

I clear my throat, drawing on every ounce of courage I've rebuilt over the past months. "I left Drew because he was physically abusing me."

The silence that follows is deafening. Even the courthouse sounds from the hallway seem to fade away.

"Excuse me?" Frank stammers, his face draining of color.

"What are you talking about?" Doreen's voice rises to nearly a shout.

"After his final deployment and discharge from the Marines, Drew struggled severely with PTSD," I begin, forcing my voice to remain steady even as my heart hammers against my ribs. "He was having violent flashbacks, most of them related to losing members of his unit in Afghanistan." I can feel Sawyer's shocked stare burning into the side of my face, but I don't dare look at him. Not yet. "Despite getting treatment at the VA—therapy, medications—his condition kept deteriorating."

"That's impossible," Doreen says flatly. "Drew was fine. He never mentioned any problems."

"He didn't want anyone to know," I continue, my voice growing stronger with each word. "Especially not you. Drew was too proud to admit he was struggling, too afraid of seeming weak. But he wasn't fine, Doreen. He was so far from fine that I started sleeping in the guest room because I was afraid of what might happen during his nightmares."

"Drew would never hurt you," Frank says, but there's uncertainty creeping into his voice now.

"The morning I finally left him, Drew woke up from a flashback and didn't recognize me. He thought I was the enemy." I can feel tears threatening, but I blink them back. This is too important for tears. "He wrapped his hands around my throat and squeezed until I couldn't breathe. If he hadn't snapped out of it when he did…"

"No," Doreen whispers, shaking her head violently. "No, you're lying. You're making this up to win custody."

Gordon slides a thick manila folder across the table to their lawyer. "Hospital report from the day after the incident. ER photos, documentation of injuries, police report—everything you need to verify Mrs. Thomas's account."

I watch Frank's hands shake as he opens the folder, his face going ashen as he stares at the first photograph. It shows me standing against a hospital backdrop, purple and black bruises circling my throat like a necklace of violence. The image is even more shocking than I remembered—the bruising so severe it took weeks to fade completely.

"Oh my God," Frank breathes.

"Did you know about this?" Doreen demands, turning to Sawyer with wild eyes.

"No, ma'am," Sawyer replies, his voice carefully controlled. But I can see the tension in his jaw, the way his hands have clenched into fists on the table. "I knew Drew was struggling with PTSD, but I had no idea it had escalated to this."

"Why didn't you tell anyone?" Frank asks, still staring at the photos with horrified fascination.

"Because Drew begged me not to," I say simply. "He was horrified by what he'd done, terrified that people would see him as a monster instead of a hero. He made me promise that if anything happened to him, I wouldn't tell anyone about his darker moments."

"But you just did," their lawyer points out.

"Because I won't let you take Tyler away from me based on lies," I say fiercely. "Yes, I left Drew when he needed me most. But I was eight months pregnant, and I was terrified that the next time he had an episode, he might not wake up in time to stop himself. I couldn't risk Tyler's life—or mine."

Doreen is crying now, tears streaming down her carefully made-up face. "You could have lost the baby. Oh God, Frank, how could we not have known?"

"Drew was always distant toward the end," Frank admits, his voice cracking. "Angry, impatient, especially with Kevin. I told myself it was just the adjustment to civilian life. He'd served six years, four combat deployments—of course leaving the Corps would be difficult."

"The holes in the walls at your house," Doreen says suddenly, looking at me with dawning horror. "The broken furniture, the way you always seemed nervous when we visited—that was all because of this?"

I nod, unable to trust my voice.

"Why didn't you call the police after it happened?" their lawyer asks.

"The doctor did—he was a mandatory reporter. But I asked him to send everything to the VA first, hoping they could use it to get Drew into an inpatient program." I take a shaky breath. "Drew was supposed to start intensive therapy the week after he died. He was finally ready to get serious help."

"Mr. Davis," Frank says to his lawyer, his voice hollow with shock. "My wife and I no longer wish to proceed with the custody hearing. We need time to process this information."

"Are you certain?" Davis asks, clearly frustrated by this turn of events.

"Completely certain," Doreen says, standing on unsteady legs. She walks around the table and pulls me into a fierce embrace that smells of expensive perfume and regret. "I'm so sorry, honey. We had no idea what you went through. You should have told us."

But even as she holds me, even as Frank mutters apologies and their lawyer shuffles papers with barely concealed annoyance, all I can focus on is Sawyer's silence. He hasn't said a word since learning the truth about Drew, hasn't met my eyes, hasn't reached for my hand.

When Doreen finally releases me, I turn to face the man I love, the man whose respect and trust I may have just lost forever. His jaw is clenched tight, his hazel eyes filled with something I can't quite read—anger, disappointment, betrayal.

"Sawyer," I begin, but he's already standing, already moving toward the door.

"I need some air," he says without looking back.

As the conference room empties around me, as Gordon packs away the evidence of my broken promise to Drew, I sit alone at the polished table and wonder if saving Tyler's future was worth destroying my own.

Because the look in Sawyer's eyes as he walked away told me everything I needed to know about the price of truth.

Some secrets, once revealed, can never be taken back. And some trust, once broken, might be impossible to rebuild.

CHAPTER EIGHTEEN

Sawyer

It takes all my self-control not to return to the cemetery, dig Drew up, and beat the shit out of him for what he did to Alma. The rage burns so hot in my chest I can barely breathe, a living thing with claws that tears at my ribs with each heartbeat.

I'd tried calling him after that day in the hallway—after he accused me of making a move on his wife, after our friendship shattered over a moment of concern that maybe carried more weight than it should have. But he never picked up, never responded to my texts. Instead, he poisoned his family against me, told Kevin I'd tried to seduce Alma.

Maybe I had crossed a line that day. Maybe my worry for her safety had been colored by feelings I'd buried so deep I'd almost convinced myself they didn't exist. The memory plays on repeat—the way she looked at me when I cupped her face, asking if she was okay. The moment that stretched too long between us, electric with possibility and danger.

But acknowledging my guilt doesn't change the timeline that's now burned into my brain like evidence at a crime scene.

The last time I visited their house and saw Drew's erratic behavior. The way Alma had seemed smaller somehow, more careful with her words, walking on eggshells in her own home. The phone call I ignored when she desperately needed help.

He choked her a month after I stopped visiting. She called me and I hung up on her. She left him three weeks later, and three weeks after that, he was dead.

Where the fuck was I when it mattered?

I close my eyes, but there's no escaping the hospital photos burned into my retinas—the purple and yellow bruises circling Alma's throat like a necklace of violence, the clear imprints of Drew's fingers marking exactly how close she'd come to dying. My best friend's hands around the neck of the woman carrying his child.

What if he hadn't woken up from that flashback? What if I'd lost them both—him to his demons, her to his violence, Tyler never born at all?

The thought makes my stomach lurch, and I press my palms against my eyes until stars burst behind my lids.

For Alma's sake, I keep it together for the rest of the day. I smile when I have to, talk when expected, pretend everything is fine as we navigate airports and flights and the long drive home to Taos. The custody battle is over—Frank and Doreen will visit Tyler as grandparents should, and everyone keeps saying everything will be alright.

But I know nothing will ever be normal again. There's before I knew what Drew did to Alma, and there's after. The after feels like standing on the edge of a cliff, looking down at the wreckage of everything I thought I understood about my best friend, about myself, about the life we've built.

"Are you disgusted with me for leaving Drew when he needed me most?" Alma asks as we drive the familiar route from Santa Fe to Taos, Tyler sleeping peacefully in his car seat.

The question hits like a physical blow. I grip the steering wheel tighter, anger flaring—not at her, never at her, but at the fact that she's been carrying this misplaced guilt alongside everything else.

"Of course not, Al. Why would you even think that?"

"You've barely said two words to me since we left LA."

The accusation lands with pinpoint accuracy because it's true. I've been locked in my own head, replaying every conversation with Drew, every missed sign, every moment I could have done something different. "I'm tired, that's all. It's been a hell of a couple days."

I reach for her hand, finding her fingers cold as ice. Has she been sitting there this entire time thinking I blame her for any of this? The thought makes my chest tight with protective fury.

"Thanks for coming with me, Sawyer," she says quietly. "I couldn't have done this without you."

"No problem." I squeeze her hand, keeping my eyes on the road ahead where the familiar landscape of high desert unfolds under the vast New Mexico sky. "Al, can I ask you something? I need to understand the timeline."

"Sure."

"The day you called me and I hung up on you—that's when it happened? When Drew..." The word sticks in my throat like broken glass. Even knowing the truth, it feels impossible to say. "When he hurt you?"

Alma turns toward the passenger window, her reflection ghostlike in the glass. "Yes."

That single word detonates in my chest like an IED. Yes. Such a small sound for such a massive failure on my part.

"I'm sorry, Al." My voice comes out rougher than intended. "I should have picked up. I should have listened. I should have—"

"You didn't know," she interrupts, her forgiveness somehow making it worse. "What's done is done."

But it's not done. It will never be done. I abandoned her when she needed help most, all because I was too much of a coward to face the truth of Drew's accusation—that I'd always wanted his wife for myself.

When we reach the Pearl to collect Tyler, I stay outside by the truck while Alma and Harlow disappear into the nursery. The night air is crisp and clean, stars scattered across the darkness like broken glass, but my mind won't quiet.

"What are you doing out here all by yourself?" Dax asks, closing the door behind him with obvious concern. "Everything alright?"

"Just giving the women time to catch up." The lie tastes bitter on my tongue.

Dax leans against the truck and crosses his arms, studying my face with that perceptive intensity that makes him such a good craftsman. "I thought everything went well in LA. The custody lawsuit got dropped, right?"

"Yeah, it did."

"Then how come you look like someone kicked your dog?"

I focus on the mountains silhouetted against the star-filled sky, their ancient presence both comforting and accusatory. "It's complicated."

"Most things worth having are." Dax taps his fingers against the truck's side panel, a nervous habit I've noticed when he's thinking through a problem. "Do you want to talk about it?"

Before I can answer, the front door bursts open and chaos erupts—Harlow and Alma emerging with Tyler and Alma's overnight bag, the twins shrieking in their pajamas like they've made the great escape from bedtime. DJ's wearing dinosaur pajamas, and Ani-Pea has lopsided pigtails that stick out at odd angles.

I move to help Alma secure Tyler in his car seat, and his little face lights up when he sees me. He reaches for me with those chubby toddler hands, babbling excitedly.

"Da-da!" he says clearly, and my heart clenches painfully.

For a moment—watching the easy goodbye between friends, listening to children's laughter, feeling Tyler's small hand grip my finger—I'm lost in a scene that feels like it belongs to someone else. This warmth, this sense of family, this contentment that I've never known before.

But the guilt crashes over me like a wave. This moment should never have been mine. Drew should be the one kissing Tyler goodnight, the one making easy conversation with neighbors, the one holding his wife close and whispering that everything will be okay.

It should never have been me.

The drive home passes in heavy silence except for Tyler's soft breathing and the hum of tires on asphalt. When we pull into our driveway, the rammed earth house looks like something from a dream with its curved walls and solar panels gleaming under starlight. But even this place we've built together feels tainted now, like I'm squatting in someone else's life.

The next morning, I throw myself into the physical labor of tire-packing at a new eco-home construction site. The repetitive motion of ramming soil into tires that will form the foundation walls should be meditative, therapeutic even. Instead, it feels like punishment.

BAM!

The mallet connects with packed earth, sending vibrations up my arms. Fuck PTSD and the flashbacks that drag you back to hell with no return ticket.

BAM!

Another strike, harder this time. Sweat beads on my forehead despite the cool morning air. I knew Drew's condition had deteriorated—I could see it in his hypervigilance, the way he jumped at sudden sounds, the hollow look in his eyes. But I never imagined it had escalated to attempted murder.

BAM!

The tire wall takes shape with each impact, creating the solid foundation that will keep this family safe and warm. The irony isn't lost on me—I'm helping build something that will protect strangers while I failed to protect my own found family when they needed me most.

Sweat drips from my face as I continue the punishing rhythm. When someone offers me a water break, I wave them off. I'm used to working myself ragged, pushing until exhaustion forces the demons back into their cages. It's what helped me heal years ago, this marriage of physical exertion and purposeful creation.

But today the work feels hollow. Every strike of the mallet brings another wave of questions that circle like vultures. Why didn't Drew call me when the flashbacks got bad? Why didn't I recognize the signs when they were right in front of me? Why did I let him brush me off every time I tried to check on him?

The hospital photos replay in my mind—those purple bruises mapping exactly where Drew's fingers had pressed, how close Alma had come to dying. He could have killed her. He could have killed them both.

I get that he had PTSD. Hell, I've been there—the night terrors, the hypervigilance, the way trauma can twist your mind until you can't tell friend from enemy. What I don't understand is why he never reached out, even after I'd offered to help. Why didn't I push harder when he gave me those hollow reassurances?

I've never felt more helpless than listening to Alma recount that hospital report like she was the one who'd done something wrong. Maybe that's what happens when you keep a secret too long—you start believing you're at fault for someone else's violence.

And for what? So his parents could preserve their image of the war hero son? So I could maintain my worship of the man who saved my life?

With the tire finally packed solid, I stop and catch my breath. My shirt is soaked with sweat, hands raw despite work gloves. A young volunteer from New Jersey—here to learn sustainable building—hands me water, and I drain it gratefully. She's told me other things about herself, but I can't focus beyond the noise in my head.

I'm too busy seeing alternative scenarios play out like films I can't turn off. If I'd taken Alma's call that day instead of hanging up. If I'd dropped everything to help. I would have driven straight to LA, insisted Drew get inpatient treatment, stayed until he got proper help. He and Alma would have worked through it together. He would have been there for Tyler's birth, first steps, first words.

But I did none of that. I hung up and went back to my own problems, my own guilt, my own selfish desire to avoid confronting my feelings for my best friend's wife.

Instead of Drew experiencing those milestones as Tyler's father, I'm the one witnessing them now. I'm the one sleeping next to his wife, the one she turns to when nightmares come calling.

"Hey, Sawyer!" A volunteer with sun-bleached surfer hair calls out. "Your girlfriend brought lunch for the crew."

The word 'girlfriend' hits like a slap. Girlfriend?

She's Drew's widow. She used to be his wife. The distinction matters, even if no one else sees it.

I drop the mallet and step down from the tire wall, my legs unsteady. Past volunteers and friends, past people who've taught me everything about building something that lasts—I don't care that they're staring as I walk away, filthy and covered in dust and sweat.

"Sawyer!" Alma's voice carries across the construction site, but I keep walking. I get into my truck and gun the engine, backing up fast enough to kick up gravel and dust clouds. Let them wonder what's wrong with Sawyer Villier now.

I need to get away from that version of myself who could have saved his best friend but chose not to. Because if he had, he never would have inherited the life he has now.

The truth burns like acid in my throat.

I drive to one of my favorite spots overlooking the Rio Grande Gorge, where the earth opens into eight hundred feet of empty air and the New Mexican sky stretches endlessly overhead. The sunset paints everything in reds and golds and purples against the backdrop of sagebrush and distant mountains. In my current state, I can barely appreciate any of it.

I sit on the edge of the canyon, wind whipping up from the depths, feeling like I might blow away with the next gust. My phone buzzes with texts—Todd checking on me, probably already verifying that all weapons are secure at the house. He knows the signs when I disappear like this.

But this isn't about old trauma or PTSD triggers. This is about realizing that the man I considered a hero had almost murdered the woman I love. This is about understanding that I abandoned her to fend for herself because I was too much of a coward to face what Drew had accused me of—that I'd always wanted Alma for myself.

My phone buzzes again, Alma's name on the screen. I reach to answer, then stop. I can't keep pretending I deserve her. She deserves someone who would have been there when she needed help, someone whose judgment wouldn't have been clouded by guilt and desire.

She always deserved better than me.

The sun sinks toward the horizon, painting the gorge in deeper shades. Somewhere behind me, traffic hums on the distant highway—people heading home to their families, their uncomplicated loves, their clear consciences.

I close my eyes and let the wind wash over me, carrying scents of sage and dust and coming rain. Tomorrow I'll have to face them all again—Alma, Tyler, the community that's become my family. Tomorrow I'll have to figure out how to live with what I failed to do, what it cost, and what it's given me in return.

But tonight I sit with my ghosts and my guilt, watching light fade over the Rio Grande Gorge, wondering how you forgive yourself for surviving when your best friend didn't—and for inheriting the life he should have had.

CHAPTER NINETEEN

Alma

I watch Sawyer walk away from the construction site, his shoulders rigid with something that looks like rage and grief all tangled together. As Tyler squirms in my arms, the dust cloud from Sawyer's truck hangs in the air long after he's disappeared down the unpaved road.

"Everything okay?" asks the volunteer from New Jersey, the one with kind eyes who'd been working the tire wall with Sawyer. She's young, maybe mid-twenties, here to learn about sustainable building but clearly picking up on the tension that just exploded across the job site.

"I'm sure it's fine," I lie, forcing a smile that feels like broken glass. "He probably just remembered something he needed to take care of."

But it's not fine. Nothing about this is fine. The way Sawyer looked at me before he drove off—like I was a stranger, like everything we've built together was suddenly contaminated by the truth I finally told.

I distribute the sandwiches among the volunteers with mechanical efficiency, making small talk about the progress on the foundation, the unseasonably warm weather, anything but the real reason my boyfriend just stormed off like the earth was on fire. When I run out of distractions, I pack up the empty cooler, secure Tyler in his car seat, and drive home to the Willow, my hands shaking on the steering wheel.

The house feels too quiet when I step inside and release Tyler from his carrier. He looks up at me with those bright blue eyes—Drew's eyes—and reaches his chubby arms toward me.

"Ma-ma!" he calls, and the pure joy in his voice nearly undoes me.

I lift him into my arms, burying my face in his soft hair that smells like baby shampoo and innocence. He doesn't know that his world just shifted on its axis. He doesn't understand that the man he calls Da-da might not come home tonight, might not be able to look at us the same way after learning what kind of monster his real father became.

"It's okay, baby," I whisper, though I'm not sure who I'm trying to convince. "Everything's going to be okay."

But even as I say the words, I know they might be lies. The look in Sawyer's eyes when he learned the truth about Drew—the shock, the horror, the way he pulled away from me like I was something poisonous—that look is burned into my memory like a brand.

He could only bottle his emotions up for so long—until today.

I should have told him sooner. Should have found a way to explain what really happened in those final months before I left Drew. But how do you tell the man you love that his hero, his best friend, the person who saved his life, had become someone capable of attempted murder? How do you destroy someone's faith in the person they've spent two years grieving?

The answer is: you don't. You keep that secret locked away where it can't hurt anyone else, even if it eats you alive from the inside.

But Frank and Doreen forced my hand. Their custody lawsuit would have brought everything into the light anyway, and at least this way I controlled the narrative. I told the truth on my terms, in my words, instead of having it dragged out of me in a courtroom where Tyler's future hung in the balance.

Still, the cost might be everything I've built with Sawyer.

Tyler squirms in my arms, reaching for his favorite toy— the purple octopus that's been his constant companion since we moved to Taos. I set him down in his playpen and watch him immediately become absorbed in making the toy's tentacles dance. Such simple joy, such uncomplicated happiness. I envy him that innocence.

My phone buzzes with a text from Harlow: *How did things go at the site? Dax said Sawyer left early?*

I stare at the message for a long moment, then type back: *Everything's fine. Just some work stuff he needed to handle.*

Another lie. I'm getting good at those.

The afternoon stretches endlessly ahead of me. I try to distract myself with household tasks—laundry, cleaning the kitchen, tending to the indoor garden that's become my pride and joy. The tomatoes are coming in beautifully, heavy and red on their vines, and the kale is so vibrant it almost seems to glow in the afternoon light streaming through the south-facing windows.

This house, this life we've built together—it all feels so fragile now. Like a soap bubble that could burst with the wrong word, the wrong look, the wrong truth finally spoken aloud.

When Tyler goes down for his nap, I find myself pacing the living room like a caged animal. The silence that used to feel healing now feels oppressive, filled with all the things Sawyer and I aren't saying to each other. I keep checking my phone, hoping for a text, a call, anything that might give me a clue about where his head is.

Nothing.

By the time the sun starts its descent toward the mountains, painting the sky in those brilliant oranges and purples that never fail to take my breath away, I can't stand the waiting anymore. I strap Tyler into his car seat and drive the short distance to Todd and Sawyer's place, hoping to find answers or at least someone who might know where Sawyer goes when the world becomes too much to handle.

The Daisy sits quiet and dark, no vehicles in the driveway. But as I'm turning around to leave, Todd's truck appears on the dirt road, dust billowing behind it like a brown cloud.

He pulls up beside me and rolls down his window, taking in my expression with the same perceptive intensity I've noticed runs in the Villier family.

"Let me guess," he says. "You're looking for my idiot brother."

The casual way he says it, like this is a routine occurrence, makes something in my chest both tighten and relax simultaneously. "He left the job site this afternoon. Hasn't answered his phone."

Todd nods, unsurprised. "Gorge?"

"The what?"

"Rio Grande Gorge. It's where he goes to think. To

punish himself, mostly." Todd's expression gentles. "Want me to go get him?"

Relief floods through me so suddenly I have to grip the steering wheel to keep my hands from shaking. "Would you? I mean, if you don't mind. I don't want to impose, but—"

"Alma." Todd's voice is kind but firm. "You're family. You don't impose, you just ask for help when you need it. That's what family does."

Family. The word hits me like a blessing and a curse all at once. Is that what we are? Even after today, even after everything Sawyer learned about Drew and the way it clearly shattered something inside him?

"I should have told him sooner," I say, the confession spilling out before I can stop it. "About Drew, about what really happened. But I was so afraid—"

"Of what?"

"Of losing him. Of seeing that look in his eyes, like I'm something broken that can't be fixed." The words come out in a rush, all the fears I've been carrying since we left LA. "Drew was his hero, Todd. His best friend. The man who saved his life. How do you tell someone that their hero became a monster?"

Todd is quiet for a long moment, his fingers drumming against his steering wheel. "You know what I think?"

I shake my head.

"I think my brother has been carrying around guilt over Drew's death for two years. Guilt that he couldn't save him, couldn't be there when it mattered. And now he's probably blaming himself for not seeing the signs, for not protecting you." Todd's voice is gentle but direct. "That's not about you being broken, Alma. That's about him feeling like he failed the two people who mattered most to him."

The insight hits like a revelation. Of course. Of course Sawyer would take this on himself, would find a way to make Drew's violence his own responsibility. It's so perfectly, heartbreakingly him—the man who carries the weight of the world on his shoulders and never thinks to ask if some of that weight belongs to someone else.

"Can you bring him home?" I ask quietly.

"I can try. But Alma?" Todd waits until I meet his eyes. "When he comes back—and he will come back—you two are going to have to talk. Really talk. No more secrets, no more protecting each other from hard truths. If you want this to work, you have to trust each other with the messy stuff too."

I nod, my throat too tight for words.

As Todd drives away toward the gorge, I head home with Tyler, who's been remarkably patient through our impromptu adventure. The Willow welcomes us back with its warm adobe walls and the scent of lavender drifting in through the open windows. This place that Sawyer built with his own hands, that we've made into a home together.

I feed Tyler dinner and give him his bath, going through the familiar motions of our evening routine while my mind races with everything I want to say to Sawyer when he comes back. If he comes back.

But he has to come back. We have to find a way through this, because the alternative—losing each other over truths that should have been shared long ago—is unthinkable.

When Tyler is finally asleep, I curl up on the couch with my phone in my lap, waiting. The house settles around me with its familiar creaks and sighs, solar panels adjusting to the cooling air, water pumps cycling through their automatic routines. All the sustainable systems that Sawyer taught me to understand and maintain, the technology that makes our off-grid life possible.

But none of that matters if the heart of our home—the love we've built together—can't survive the weight of the past.

CHAPTER TWENTY

THE SUN BLEEDS red across the gorge when I hear the crunch of tires on gravel. I don't need to turn around to know it's Todd's truck—he's the only one who knows to find me here. This ledge has been my thinking spot since I first came to Taos, back when the demons rode shotgun everywhere I went. Some days, the emptiness of the gorge was the only thing that made sense.

"Thought I'd find your sorry ass out here," Todd says, boots scuffing against rock as he approaches. He settles beside me on the tailgate, two bottles of beer appearing from nowhere. The glass is already sweating in the evening heat. "Alma called."

Of course she did. My chest tightens at the thought of her worrying, probably pacing the eco-home with Tyler on her hip. It's what she does when she's anxious—I've seen it enough times to know.

"How'd you know to find me here?" I ask, though we both know the answer.

"Same way I always know." He takes a pull from his beer,

eyes on the horizon. "You get that look—like you're carrying the weight of every ghost from over there." He doesn't need to specify where there is. We both know. "Plus, this is where you come to punish yourself. Has been since you got back."

The gorge stretches before us, eight hundred feet of empty air and redemption. I've spent more hours than I care to count staring into its depths, wondering if answers hide at the bottom.

The wind whips up from the canyon, carrying the scent of sage and desert rain and for a moment it hits me, how for some, this is the last thing they'll take in before they take that final step, hoping for some kind of peace.

But not for me even though I'm sure Todd must be scared out of his head wondering if I'd do just that.

"Did you know?" The words scrape out of my throat. "About Drew and Alma? About what he did to her?"

Todd's silence is answer enough. The bottle in my hand might as well be full of sand for all I want to drink it.

"Jesus Christ." I drag a hand down my face, feeling the grit of construction dust under my fingers. "Was I the only one who didn't see it? His best friend, and I couldn't even—" The beer bottle creaks in my grip, and I set it down before I shatter it. "I should've known something was wrong. The signs were all there."

"You saw what he wanted you to see," Todd says quietly. "What you needed to see, maybe. Sometimes the people closest to us are the hardest to really look at. Hell, remember how long it took me to notice what was happening with you after you got back?"

"I should've been there. When she called–"

"But you weren't." Todd's voice is gentle but firm. "And

beating yourself up about it now won't change that. Won't help her either. You think Alma wants to see you tearing yourself apart over this?"

"You don't understand." The words taste like ash in my mouth. "I stayed away because I was afraid he was right about me. About how I felt about her. What kind of friend does that make me? I let my own guilt, my own feelings, keep me from helping them both."

"A human one." Todd shifts, and I can feel his eyes on me. "Remember that night you brought me out here, right after you got settled? When you couldn't sleep more than an hour without seeing Smith step on that IED?"

I nod tightly. That night, I'd been the one showing Todd the gorge, trying to share what this place meant to me, how the vast emptiness somehow made the noise in my head bearable. But I'd been drinking too much, thinking too much about all the ways I'd failed my brothers-in-arms.

"You told me something I never forgot. You said the hardest part wasn't the trauma—it was forgiving yourself for surviving it." He pauses, letting the words sink in. "Maybe this isn't so different."

The laugh that escapes me is hollow. "So what, I'm supposed to forgive myself for falling in love with my best friend's wife? For wanting her even when he was alive? For not being there when they both needed me?"

"No." Todd's voice is steady. "You're supposed to forgive yourself for being human. For having feelings you couldn't control. And maybe for not being perfect when your friend needed you." He pauses. "You're not God, Sawyer. You can't save everyone, even the people you love most."

I close my eyes against the burning in my throat. "She deserves better."

"Better than what? Better than someone who drops everything to fly across the country to help her keep her son? Better than someone who builds her a home with his own hands? Someone who loves her enough to torture himself with guilt over feelings he never acted on?" Todd shakes his head. "You know what I see when I look at you two? I see a woman who's finally living again, and a man who's so afraid of happiness he might just talk himself out of it."

"You don't get it—"

"No, you don't get it." Todd's voice sharpens. "That woman moved her entire life to Taos. Not for the weather, not for the sustainable homes and harvested water. For you. She moved herself and her kid out here for you. And you're out here wallowing in guilt over things you can't change instead of being there for her now." He shakes his head. "You want to honor Drew's memory? Then be the man he couldn't be for her, Sawyer. Be present. Be whole."

The truth of his words hits me hard. I think of Alma at the job site today, probably worried sick. Of Tyler, who lights up every time I walk through the door. Of the day he called me Da-da. Of the life we've started building, brick by brick, day by day.

"Drew's gone, Sawyer," Todd says softly. "And yeah, maybe you could've done things differently. We all could've. But Alma's here. She's alive. She chose to build a new life—with you. Question is, are you gonna let guilt over the past rob you both of a future?"

The sun dips behind the mountains, painting the sky in colors that remind me of Alma's garden—purples and oranges, life springing from harsh soil. Maybe Todd's right. Maybe it's time to stop looking for answers at the bottom of the gorge.

"Come on," Todd says, sliding off the tailgate. "Let's get you home."

Home. The word catches in my throat. The thought of facing Alma after walking away from the job site, after everything I've learned about Drew, about my own failures—my fingers tighten on the truck door.

"I don't know if I can face her," I admit, the words barely audible over the wind. "After everything I've learned, after failing her so completely—"

"So you're going to fail her again by disappearing?" Todd's words hit their mark. "That what you want her to teach Tyler? That when things get hard, the people you love just... vanish?"

The parallel to Drew's final choice isn't lost on me. I close my eyes, feeling the weight of it all pressing down on my chest.

"I'll drop you at home and then I've got to leave to meet some of the guys," Todd says, softer now. "What you do after that is up to you. But Sawyer?" He waits until I look at him. "Sometimes the bravest thing isn't charging into battle. Sometimes it's just showing up, even when you think you don't deserve to."

As we drive back toward the lights of Taos, I think about what Todd said. About forgiveness and futures, about the weight of ghosts and the warmth of the living. The truck's headlights cut through the gathering darkness, illuminating the familiar stretch of road that leads from the gorge back to civilization. Back to her.

The radio crackles with some old country song about second chances and lost time, and Todd reaches over to turn it down. The silence between us isn't uncomfortable—it's the kind of quiet that comes from understanding, from years of brotherhood forged in shared concern and mutual protection. He doesn't need to fill the space with more words. He's said what needed saying.

Through the passenger window, I watch the landscape shift from wild desert to the outskirts of town. Adobe houses dot the hillsides, their flat roofs and rounded corners softened by porch lights and the warm glow of windows. This place has become home in ways I never expected when I first rolled into town three years ago, looking for somewhere to build something meaningful.

"You remember when I first brought you out here?" I ask suddenly. "When you were still living in LA, thinking I'd lost my mind moving to the desert?"

Todd glances over, a small smile playing at the corners of his mouth. "Course I do. You were so convinced this place would fix everything that was broken in you. All that talk about sustainable living and getting back to basics."

"I thought you were going to stage an intervention." I lean my head against the window, watching the lights of Taos grow brighter. "Drag me back to civilization whether I wanted to go or not."

"And now?"

"Now I think maybe I was right about this place. It did fix something." The admission comes easier than I expected. "Not just the building and the clean living, but having you here. Having family."

We pass the turnoff to the main plaza, where tourists are

probably wandering between galleries and restaurants, blissfully unaware of the weight some of us carry. The truck rumbles past the familiar landmarks—the hardware store where I buy supplies, the diner where Alma and I sometimes grab breakfast on Saturday mornings, the park where Tyler chases pigeons with pure, unbridled joy.

"She's good for you," Todd says quietly. "Alma. Even before everything went to shit with Drew, I could see it. The way you looked at her, the way she looked at you when she thought no one was watching."

My throat tightens. "That's what makes it so fucked up."

"No, that's what makes it human." He turns onto the dirt road that leads to our place—to the eco-home that Alma and I have been building together, one sustainable dream at a time. "Love doesn't follow rules, Sawyer. It doesn't wait for permission or check with your moral compass before it shows up. It just is."

The headlights sweep across the familiar curve of the Willow's walls, and I can see the warm light spilling from the windows. Home. The word doesn't catch in my throat this time—it settles there, warm and solid.

Todd pulls to a stop beside my truck, the engine ticking as it cools. "You want some advice from your older, wiser brother?"

"Do I have a choice?"

"Not really." He grins, but it fades quickly. "Stop trying to earn forgiveness you don't need. Drew made his choices, you made yours, and Alma made hers. She chose you, Sawyer. Not because she had to, not because you're some consolation prize, but because she wants to. Because she loves you."

The words hit something deep in my chest, a knot of fear and shame I've been carrying for months. Maybe years.

"What if I can't be what she needs? What if I'm just as broken as Drew was, just in different ways?"

"Then you figure it out together." Todd reaches over and grips my shoulder. "That's what love is, little brother. Not being perfect, but being present. Not having all the answers, but being willing to keep showing up anyway."

I watch Todd's taillights disappear down the unpaved road, leaving me alone outside our eco-home. The desert night wraps around me like a familiar blanket, stars wheeling overhead in their ancient patterns. The air smells of cooling earth and the lavender Alma planted by the front door, a scent that has become synonymous with peace in my mind.

Inside the Willow, I can see movement through the windows—Alma's silhouette as she moves through the kitchen, probably cleaning up after dinner. Tyler's toys are scattered across the front porch, a reminder of the life we've built here, imperfect and complicated but real.

My phone sits heavy in my pocket, Alma's missed calls like small weights on my conscience. Seven calls. Two voicemails. A handful of texts that I haven't had the courage to read. I should call her. I need to call her. But the words tangle in my throat before I can even reach for the phone. What could I possibly say to make this right?

The front door opens, and Alma steps onto the porch. She's changed out of her work clothes into one of my old flannels, the sleeves rolled up to her elbows. Her hair falls loose around her shoulders, catching the porch light like spun gold. She looks tired, worried, beautiful.

"I saw the headlights," she says quietly. "Figured it was either you or Todd come to drag you home."

"Both, actually." I take a step closer, my boots crunching on the gravel. "Todd found me at the gorge."

She nods, understanding flooding her features. She knows about my thinking spot, about the nights I disappear there when the weight gets too heavy. "Tyler's asleep. Finally. He kept asking where you were, why you left so suddenly."

The guilt hits fresh and sharp. "I'm sorry. I didn't know what else to do. After everything you told me, everything about Drew—"

"So you ran." There's no accusation in her voice, just sad understanding. "Just like he used to."

The parallel stops me cold. Drew, disappearing for days when things got hard. Drew, leaving her to wonder and worry and pick up the pieces. And here I am, doing the same damn thing.

"I'm not him," I say, more to myself than to her.

"No," she agrees softly. "You're not. But you're here now, and that's what matters."

She steps down from the porch, closing the distance between us. Up close, I can see the worry lines around her eyes, the tension in her shoulders. This woman who has already lost so much, and I made her wonder if she was losing me too.

"I'm sorry," I say again, the words feeling inadequate. "I should have stayed. Should have talked to you instead of running off like some scared kid."

"You're talking to me now." She reaches out, her fingers brushing mine. "That's a start."

The touch grounds me, reminds me of all the ways we fit together—working side by side on the house, lazy Sunday mornings with Tyler between us, quiet evenings on the porch watching the sunset paint the mountains gold. This is real. This is worth fighting for.

"I don't know how to do this," I admit, my voice rough. "How to love you without feeling like I'm betraying him. How to be what you need when I'm still figuring out how to live with myself."

"We figure it out together," she says, echoing Todd's words. "One day at a time. That's all any of us can do."

Maybe that's what living really means—not having all the answers, but being here anyway. Ready or not, willing to try. The stars wheel overhead, ancient and patient, witnesses to all the small human dramas playing out below. And for the first time in hours, I think maybe that's enough.

"Come inside," Alma says, her hand slipping into mine. "Come home."

CHAPTER TWENTY-ONE

Alma

THE DOOR CLOSES behind us with a soft click, shutting out the desert night and all its ghosts. For a moment, we stand in the entryway of our home, the weight of everything that's happened settling between us like dust after a storm.

The Willow wraps around us with its familiar warmth—solar-heated floors beneath my feet, the faint scent of herbs from my kitchen garden, the lived-in comfort of the life we've built together. It should feel like sanctuary, but right now it feels charged with electricity, as if the air itself is holding its breath.

I release Sawyer's hand and move toward the kitchen, my movements careful and deliberate. I need to give him space to process, even though every instinct screams at me to hold onto him, to make sure he doesn't disappear again. The tension in my shoulders has been building since this morning when he walked away from the construction site, leaving me standing there with a cooler full of sandwiches and the sinking realization that learning the truth about Drew might have broken something between us.

"Are you hungry?" I ask, busying myself with unnecessary tasks—straightening dish towels, adjusting the herbs on the windowsill. "I saved you a plate from dinner. Tyler kept asking where you went."

I hear Sawyer's sharp intake of breath behind me, and I know the mention of Tyler hits him hard. This morning, after I finally told him the truth about Drew's violence—about the choking, the hospital report, the real reason I left—Sawyer had walked out without a word. I can picture what he's thinking now: Tyler watching another father figure disappear when things got difficult.

"I'm sorry," Sawyer says, his voice rough with exhaustion. "I should have called. Should have explained—"

"Should have, could have." I turn to face him, and I can see the toll this day has taken written in every line of his face. "We could spend all night talking about what we should have done differently, Sawyer. But I'm tired of should-haves. I'm tired of walking on eggshells around the past."

He's standing in the middle of our living room looking lost, and it breaks my heart. This man who builds homes with his bare hands, who can coax life from desert soil, who makes Tyler laugh until his cheeks hurt—he looks like he doesn't know where he belongs in his own space.

"Sit down," I say gently, gesturing toward the couch. "Please."

He moves like he's walking through water, every step heavy with the weight of what he's learned. When he finally settles onto the cushions, I can see how much this revelation has cost him—the knowledge that his best friend, his hero, had become someone capable of attempted murder.

I want to go to him, to curl up beside him like I have so

many evenings before, but something holds me back. Maybe it's self-preservation. Maybe it's the fear that if I get too close, he'll pull away again. Instead, I lean against the kitchen counter, maintaining the distance while I try to find the right words.

"Tyler asked where you went," I say quietly. "When he kept looking for you around the house this afternoon."

Sawyer's head drops into his hands. "What did you tell him?"

"The truth. That you needed some time to think." The words come out sharper than I intended, and I see Sawyer flinch. "Because that's what I hoped was happening, Sawyer. That you were processing what you learned about Drew, not running away from it. From us."

"That's not—" He starts to protest, but I hold up a hand.

"Let me finish." I take a deep breath, trying to steady myself. "I know what you learned today shook you. I know discovering the truth about Drew's violence, about what he did to me during those episodes, brought up every guilt and regret you've been carrying about not seeing the signs. But what I can't understand is how you could learn something that devastating and think the answer was to shut me out completely."

"I wasn't running away," Sawyer says, but his voice lacks conviction.

"Then what would you call it?"

The silence stretches between us, filled only by the soft hum of the refrigerator and the distant sound of wind through the desert outside. Sawyer lifts his head, and when he looks at me, I can see all the pain he's been carrying reflected in his eyes.

"I was drowning," he says finally. "When I learned what Drew had done to you, when I realized I was his battle buddy and I missed every single sign that he was that far gone—I felt like I was drowning. And the worst part was knowing that part of me, some sick part of me, felt almost relieved."

"Relieved?"

"Because it meant I didn't have to feel guilty anymore about wanting you. About loving you when you belonged to him. About being so wrapped up in my own feelings that I completely missed how far gone my best friend was." His voice breaks on the words. "What kind of battle buddy does that make me? What kind of friend misses that his brother in arms was having violent episodes?"

I push away from the counter, unable to maintain the distance anymore. I cross to the couch and sit beside him, close enough that our knees almost touch. "It makes you human, Sawyer. Flawed and complicated and human."

"You don't understand—"

"I understand more than you think." I reach for his hands, and after a moment's hesitation, he lets me take them. His skin is rough from construction work, warm and familiar. "I understand guilt, Sawyer. I understand shame and regret and the weight of what-ifs. I've been carrying them for over a year."

"That's different. You were a victim—"

"Was I?" The question stops him short. "Or was I a woman who stayed in a situation I knew was getting worse because I was too proud to admit I couldn't fix it? Too scared to face the judgment that would come with leaving?"

Sawyer's grip on my hands tightens. "Alma—"

"I loved Drew," I continue, needing him to understand.

"But I also resented him. For making me afraid in my own home, for turning our marriage into something I didn't recognize. And yes, there were moments—especially near the end—when I wondered what my life would be like without him. What does that make me?"

"Someone who was trying to survive."

"Exactly." I lean closer, willing him to really hear me. "Just like you were trying to survive having feelings you couldn't control. Just like Drew was trying to survive demons that were bigger than all of us combined."

I can see the war happening behind Sawyer's eyes, the battle between his guilt and his desire to believe what I'm telling him. It's the same battle I've been fighting since Drew died, the same one that brought me to Taos in the first place.

"I won't lie to you," I say softly. "There were times during our marriage when I thought about you. When Drew would be having one of his bad days, and I'd remember how easy things felt with you, how safe. I'd remember that day at Walter Reed when I read you poetry, and how you looked at me like I was something precious. And I felt guilty about it then, too."

Sawyer's eyes widen slightly. "You never said—"

"Because it felt like a betrayal. But feelings aren't betrayals, Sawyer. Actions are. And neither of us acted on anything while Drew was alive."

"But I wanted to." His voice is barely a whisper. "That last day, at your house, when I asked if you were okay—I came so close to telling you how I felt."

"But you didn't. And I didn't either, even though part of me wanted you to." I take a shaky breath. "We're not perfect,

Sawyer. We're just human beings trying to do the right thing in impossible circumstances."

I watch something shift in his expression, a crack appearing in the wall of guilt he's built around himself. "I loved him," he says, and it sounds like a confession. "But I loved you too, and I hated myself for it."

"I know." I brush a tear from his cheek that I hadn't realized had fallen. "But Drew is gone, and we're still here. We have a choice to make—we can let guilt and shame poison whatever chance we have at happiness, or we can choose to live. Really live."

"What if I can't? What if I'm too broken, like he was?"

"Then we'll figure it out together." The words come out with such certainty that they surprise even me. "Sawyer, I didn't move to Taos just for a fresh start. I moved here for you. For us. For the possibility of building something real and honest and good."

I stand up from the couch and extend my hand to him. "Come with me."

He looks confused but takes my hand, letting me pull him to his feet. I lead him down the hallway to Tyler's room, where my son sleeps peacefully in his toddler bed, surrounded by stuffed animals and picture books. The night light casts gentle shadows on the walls, and Tyler's breathing is soft and even.

"Look at him," I whisper. "Do you see someone who's been damaged by loving you? By having you in his life?"

Sawyer's breath catches. "He kept calling for 'Da-da' this afternoon," he says quietly. "Todd said he seemed confused when I didn't come home."

"Because you're his father in every way that matters.

Because you've shown him what love looks like when it's patient and kind and consistent." I turn to face Sawyer in the dim light. "That little boy doesn't care about our complicated history or our guilt or our fears. He just knows that you make him feel safe and loved."

We stand there for a moment, watching Tyler sleep, and I can feel some of the tension leaving Sawyer's body. This is what we're fighting for—not just our own happiness, but Tyler's future, his understanding of what love and commitment really mean.

"I don't want to hurt him," Sawyer says finally. "Or you. I don't want to be like Drew, letting my demons win."

"Then don't let them." I take his hand again, leading him back toward our bedroom. "But also don't think you have to be perfect. Don't think you have to carry everything alone."

In our room, I turn to face him fully. The moonlight streams through the windows, casting everything in silver, and I can see the man I fell in love with underneath all the pain and doubt. He's still there, still fighting to be better, still choosing to show up even when it's hard.

"I love you," I say simply. "Not despite your flaws or your guilt or your complicated feelings about Drew. I love you because of who you are when you think no one's watching— the man who builds Tyler a fort out of couch cushions, who tends my garden when I'm too busy to water it, who holds me when I have nightmares about the past."

"Alma—"

"I love you because you came to LA when I needed you, because you fought for Tyler when his grandparents tried to take him away, because you saw something worth saving in both of us when we couldn't see it ourselves." I step closer, until there's barely any space between us. "And I love you because even when you're scared, even when your demons are screaming at you to run, you came home. You're here."

For a long moment, we just look at each other. I can see the moment his resolve finally breaks, when the walls he's built around his heart start to crumble. His hands come up to cup my face, thumbs brushing across my cheekbones.

"I love you too," he whispers. "So much it terrifies me."

"Good," I say, smiling through the tears I didn't realize were falling. "Love should be a little terrifying. It means it matters."

When he kisses me, it tastes like coming home and starting over all at once. It tastes like forgiveness—for Drew, for ourselves, for all the complicated ways we've arrived at this moment. And when we finally pull apart, I know we're going to be okay. Not perfect, not without struggles, but okay.

"No more running," I say against his lips.

"No more running," he agrees. "We face it together."

"Together," I repeat, and for the first time in days, the word feels like a promise we can actually keep.

Alma

IT's chaos everywhere I look, but it's the best kind of chaos—the kind that comes with extended family like the Drexels. Harlow once told me she'd found the true meaning of family when she met Dax, because you don't just get the man in the deal, you get his entire world of people who love him.

I finally get to meet Nana, Dax's grandmother, around whom Sawyer is always on his best behavior according to the stories I've heard. Legend has it she caught him rummaging through her recyclables looking for bottles to use in his first eco-home and mistook him for a homeless soul. Thinking he must be starving, she invited him to dinner, and he never really left. She calls him mijo—my son—the same way she calls Dax and Gabe.

"Are you enjoying yourself in Taos, mija?" Nana and I sit side by side at the head of the long table that dominates the Pearl's dining area. Around us, conversation flows in both English and Spanish, punctuated by laughter and the occasional shriek of delight from the nursery where Tyler, DJ, and

Ani-Pea are playing under the watchful eye of one of Dax's cousins.

Nana made half the dishes gracing our table, vegetables harvested from her own garden with help from the twins. Once a month, she opens her home to teach authentic New Mexican cuisine, which is how I learned to make my first batch of sopapillas. I'm addicted to them drizzled with honey and have to restrain myself from making them weekly.

"Very much, Nana. I'm happier here than I've been in years."

"I've never seen Sawyer so happy either. He's found his soul, su alma," she says, tapping her finger over her heart. "That's what your name means in Spanish. Heart. Soul. Did you know that?"

Heat rises in my cheeks as I nod. "Sí, Nana."

I'm learning Spanish because I want Tyler to grow up bilingual like DJ and Ani-Pea. It's hard to believe how Taos gives me everything I could ever need—community, purpose, love. The only thing missing are my regular visits to Drew's grave, where I used to tell him everything.

But missing him doesn't mean I'm not happy. I am. Like any place, Taos isn't perfect. It's a small town—sometimes too small—but I understand why everyone loves it here, whether they're Taoseños like Nana or transplants like Sawyer and Harlow. It's not just the clean air and endless sky. The people make it special. And the food—Nana makes the best New Mexican cuisine, green chile on everything except sopapillas, which demand honey and powdered sugar when I'm feeling sinful.

Even Frank and Doreen seem enchanted, and I love watching them smile and laugh when they're not overwhelmed by the boisterous company. They've always been reserved, and Drew was the same way around them.

Since that awful day in the courthouse, this is Frank and Doreen's second visit to Taos. Things aren't perfect between us, but they're better, and we're taking it one day at a time. They're happy to spend time with Tyler, and I'd never keep him from them. We'll visit LA in a few months. Kevin is a different story—he hasn't forgiven me and probably never will. Drew was his hero, and learning the truth shattered that image.

"Have you seen the macadamia tree growing in the garden?" Sarah asks as Frank and Doreen follow her toward the indoor growing space. Behind them, Dyami races past, chased by three cousins his age.

Even though the twins' birthday isn't until next week— when there'll be another party at a venue in town—today is the family celebration that only the Drexels can pull off. The Pearl overflows with guests who spill onto the front lawn with its patch of artificial grass where Dyami and friends currently occupy the trampoline. Dax and Todd man the grill while Gabe handles music selection, occasionally pulling someone onto the makeshift dance floor.

I stand as Frank and Doreen return, their hands full of macadamia nuts ready to be cracked open.

"Have a seat," I say, pulling out my chair for Doreen.

"Oh, you don't need to—"

"I have to find Sawyer anyway." I smile as she settles into the chair, Frank taking the empty seat beside Nana and Daniel, Dax's father who flew in from New York. Next to him sit Addison, one of Harlow's surgical colleagues, and her husband Jordan. Their daughter Piper, about Tyler's age, is playing in the nursery under Sarah and Benny's supervision.

I've yet to keep track of everyone—if not for Sawyer's whispered reminders, I'd be completely lost. I only wish Drew could have experienced this warmth, this sense of belonging. It's the only bittersweet note in an otherwise perfect evening, but I've learned that even though he's gone, he'll always be part of me.

"Hey, beautiful, want to take a walk and watch the sunset?" Sawyer appears beside me, his voice low and intimate. "We haven't been alone since we got here."

"I'd love that." He takes my hand, guiding me outside where solar lights line the path like breadcrumbs leading us home.

We climb the bermed hill behind the Pearl, part of the home's innovative design that provides natural insulation. From here, we can see for miles across the high desert, the sky painted in brilliant yellows, oranges, and purples as the sun sinks toward the horizon.

Sawyer stands behind me, arms circling my waist, his bearded chin resting on my shoulder. Who would have thought I'd find myself in the middle of the high desert, living off-grid in a community of strange-looking houses with the most wonderful, quirky people? Certainly not me. But my three-month trial period came and went, and Tyler and I are still here, loving every day we wake up in our earthen home with vegetables and flowers growing under the same roof.

"Can I ask you a question?"

I turn to face him, and our lips meet in a soft kiss that makes me forget everything else. The sunset, the party, the question—it all fades except for this man who holds me like I'm precious.

"You were saying?" I ask when we finally part.

Sawyer's face has gone pale, and I frown. "Are you alright?"

But then I notice something else—the Pearl has gone quiet. How can a place filled with so many people suddenly fall silent?

"What's going on?" I step back, confused.

"Hang on." Sawyer pushes aside pebbles with his foot, then reaches into his pocket. Before I can process what's happening, he drops to one knee, and my hand flies to my mouth.

"Sawyer..."

"Great. My mind went completely blank. I rehearsed this all week." He clears his throat, looking up at me with eyes that shine with love and vulnerability. "Alma Thomas, I know you said no the first time I asked you to marry me—and I understood. The timing was terrible."

I stifle a giggle. "Yes, it was. But your intentions were admirable."

"Well, my intentions right now are crystal clear," he says, his voice gaining strength. "I love you so much, Al. More than I ever thought possible."

"You don't need words, Sawyer. I see it every day in how you love Tyler, how you've built this life for us."

"Alma," he whispers, his voice suddenly thick with emotion. "Will you marry me?"

I drop to my knees in front of him, cupping his face in my hands, my heart threatening to burst from my chest. "Yes,

Sawyer Villier," I whisper, pressing my forehead to his. "Yes, yes, and yes."

The ring he slides onto my finger is unlike anything I've ever seen—mahogany wood with a birch liner, inlaid with crushed green malachite that catches the dying light. It's earthy and unique and absolutely perfect.

When he stands and kisses me, his mouth warm against my lips, I hear a rustling sound. From the corner of my eye, I catch Dyami's head popping up near the trampoline area before disappearing again. Then he reappears, grinning from ear to ear.

"She said yes!"

Cheers erupt from below, and I don't need to look to know everyone has been waiting for this moment.

"You're all sneaky," I say against Sawyer's lips, laughing as heat floods my cheeks. "Who else knew?"

"Everyone."

I pull back, ready to protest, then catch sight of the sunset —a masterpiece of yellows, oranges, and reds stretching across the endless New Mexican sky. Instead of complaining, I chuckle and turn to watch the light fade over our chosen home.

Of course everyone knew. This community that's become our family, these people who've embraced Tyler and me with open hearts—they've been rooting for us all along.

As the last light fades and the first stars appear overhead, I think about how far we've come. From that terrible day in the courthouse to this perfect moment on a rooftop in the high desert, surrounded by love and laughter and the promise of forever.

Sometimes the best things in life come when you're brave

enough to say yes to the unexpected. And sometimes, if you're very lucky, you find exactly what you never knew you were looking for.

Five Months After That...

By LA standards, the Santa Fe Municipal Airport is refreshingly quiet and orderly. It's also surprisingly small—many people don't even know it exists. But as long as it offers direct flights to Los Angeles, it tops our list of preferred airports.

On the bench beside me, Doreen and Tyler are deep in their farewell ritual while Sawyer accompanies Frank to check their luggage at the far end of the terminal. Tyler's lower lip trembles with the threat of tears—he can't understand why Grandma and Grandpa are leaving after only five days when there's still so much to explore from a toddler's perspective.

"We'll be back in a few months, sweetheart," Doreen says, glancing at me for confirmation.

"That's right, Ty. Before you know it, they'll be here again," I add as Tyler looks up at me with those sky-blue eyes that are pure Drew. He's his father's carbon copy in every way—the wheat-blond hair, the stubborn set of his jaw, even the way his whole face lights up when he laughs.

"And we'll FaceTime every week," Doreen promises. "Right?"

Tyler nods solemnly before throwing his arms around her neck. "Miss you, Gamma."

"I'm going to miss you too, dear. So very much."

I can see Doreen fighting back tears, and my heart goes out to her. She and Frank genuinely adore their grandson and have made every effort to visit regularly. With Frank in the process of selling his contracting business to a longtime colleague, they're looking forward to having more time for Tyler—though I'm not sure if that means relocating to New Mexico or just more frequent visits.

While we've managed to rebuild our relationship since the custody nightmare, Kevin remains a different story. I'm grateful he hasn't shown up unannounced or tagged along with his parents. One day I might forgive his cruelty, but I won't be forced to entertain him until I'm ready.

Baby steps, as Sawyer reminds me. It's been baby steps for all of us—from the day he proposed five months ago to our intimate wedding ceremony two months later at the Pearl, surrounded by the chosen family who've made Taos home.

One day at a time.

When Frank rejoins us, he sweeps Tyler into his arms with practiced ease. "Who's my favorite little man?"

"Me!" Tyler shrieks with delight, and Frank's face transforms with pure grandpaternal joy.

"All checked in?" I ask as Sawyer settles beside me, his presence immediately calming.

"Flight boards in ten minutes," he confirms, slipping his arm around my shoulders.

"Tyler's going to miss them more this time. He's old enough now to really understand when people leave."

Sawyer pulls me closer, unconcerned about public displays of affection. It's been over a year since the custody hearing, since he learned the truth about Drew's violence and nearly lost himself to guilt and self-recrimination. But it's also been a year of learning to trust each other completely, of falling deeper in love each day while building something real and lasting.

It hasn't been easy. Some days the guilt still hits hard—Drew's birthday, the anniversary of his death, unexpected moments when Tyler does something that looks exactly like his father. But Sawyer and I don't run from those emotions anymore. We face them together, honoring Drew's memory while refusing to let the past poison our future. Drew's compass still lives in Sawyer's pocket, a reminder to stay true to what matters most.

When the gate agent announces boarding for the Los Angeles flight, Doreen wraps me in a fierce hug.

"Thank you for having us, Alma. Frank and I had such a wonderful time," she says, and I can hear the genuine warmth in her voice. "We appreciate you and your friends making us feel so welcome."

"We love having you. Tyler most of all." I turn to Frank, who gives me a quick embrace before shaking Sawyer's hand with the respect that's grown between them over these months. I mean every word. Despite our rocky beginning—their initial disapproval of me, the custody battle that nearly tore us apart—what matters most is Tyler's happiness. But beyond that, we've found genuine moments of connection. Sawyer and Frank discovered a shared love of fishing when Dax and Daniel took them to Arroyo Seco for wild trout. Frank may prefer deep-sea fishing, but as he said, "Saltwater or fresh, a fish is still a fish, and it tastes great grilled with good company and cold beer."

"Three months, little prince," Frank says, pressing a kiss to Tyler's forehead. "We'll be back to see you again, okay?"

"Okay, Grampa."

As Frank sets Tyler down, he runs straight to Sawyer, who beams with pride as he kneels to meet him at eye level. Together, they watch Frank and Doreen head toward the gate, the grandparents pausing to wave one final goodbye before disappearing through the jetway doors.

We wait until the plane pushes back from the gate before Sawyer straightens up. I reach for Tyler's hand to guide him toward his stroller, but he stretches both arms up to Sawyer instead.

"Da-da, carry!"

As Sawyer lifts him effortlessly, I give him a look of mock disapproval. "You're completely spoiling him."

Sawyer pulls me against his side as Tyler settles contentedly on his shoulder. "Of course I am. Just like I'll spoil his little sister when she arrives in three months."

I laugh, my free hand instinctively moving to my rounded belly where our daughter grows strong and healthy. There's no doubt Sawyer will spoil both children outrageously, but I'm not complaining. Half the nursery is already decorated in soft pink while Tyler's half remains his favorite blue—all courtesy of Sawyer, who can barely contain his excitement about becoming a father to a daughter.

We've already chosen her name after many long conversations: Andrea, or Drea for short. It feels right somehow, a name that's entirely ours while still honoring the journey that brought us here.

Soon we'll need more space, which means Sawyer and Todd's next project is expanding the Willow to add two more bedrooms. Construction won't start until after Drea's birth—for now, our earthen home with its hand-painted wooden sign above the door is perfect exactly as it is.

Like our growing family, like the community that's embraced us, like the love we've built from the ashes of grief and guilt.

As we walk toward the parking lot, Tyler drowsy against Sawyer's shoulder and our daughter moving gently beneath my heart, I think about how far we've come. From that terrible day in the courthouse to this moment of quiet contentment, surrounded by the vast New Mexican sky and the promise of tomorrow.

Drew will always be part of our story—Tyler's father, Sawyer's brother-in-arms, the man whose death taught us both how precious and fragile love can be. But he's no longer the ending of our tale. He's become the beginning, the reason we learned to choose hope over fear, healing over hiding, love over the safety of staying alone.

Together with Sawyer, our children, and the chosen family who've woven themselves into the fabric of our lives, I know we'll be more than fine. We'll be happy, messy, complicated, and real.

And it's exactly what we're meant to be.

*Thank you so much for reading **Breaking the Rules**.*

Loved your time in New Mexico?
Stay here for Gabe's story, a friends to lovers romance in
Where She Belongs

*and Dax and Harlow's rocky beginnings in **Everything She Ever Wanted***

*Go back to where it began with Sarah and Benny in **Other Side of Love**.*

*Curious about Heath Kheiron, the billionaire? Read his story in **A Collateral Attraction**.*

Stay informed of what I'm working on next and their release dates by visiting my website at lizdurano.com or you can find me on Facebook at @lizduranobooks

ACKNOWLEDGMENTS

During my two decades as a massage therapist, I was honored to work with many veterans seeking relief from trauma stored in their bodies. Their willingness to try alternative healing approaches—often encouraged by spouses, partners, and family members who recognized their pain—opened my eyes to the hidden battles that continue long after military service ends. While no client's specific story appears in these pages, their collective journey toward healing deeply influenced my portrayal of characters struggling with invisible wounds. I am grateful for their trust and inspired by their resilience.

My eternal gratitude to Michelle Jo Quinn for being an extraordinary friend and for consistently challenging me to grow as both a writer and person. To Charity, for your relentless accountability that kept me focused on this story instead of chasing every shiny new idea that crossed my path.

Thank you to Carly Quinn for falling in love with Sawyer and Alma's journey and for gifting me the perfect phrase: "earthy and hard-won romance."

My deepest appreciation to Ellen Hawrylciw, Susan Hosek, Evelyn Martha, Cherry Shrestha, and Belinda Bauknecht for your invaluable support and guidance throughout this process.

OTHER BOOKS BY LIZ DURANO

DIFFERENT KIND OF LOVE: TAOS
Everything She Ever Wanted

Breaking the Rules

Where She Belongs

Other Side of Love (Prequel)

Every Breath (Sarah & Benny)

Nothing But Love (Valentine's)

Undaunted (Claudia)

DIFFERENT KIND OF LOVE: NEW YORK
Falling for Jordan

Friends with Benefits

Until We Fall (original title Lucky Charm)

LOVE BEACH EVER AFTER
Summer with a Navy SEAL

Merry with a Tycoon

Spring Break with a Bodyguard

WORTH IT ALL
Worth the Risk

Worth the Wait

Worth the Fight

ABOUT THE AUTHOR

Liz's start in storytelling got its rocky start in 8th grade when the "play" she was writing landed her in the principal's office for being a bit on the NSFW side. Since then, she's done penance by writing romance and chick lit–with a dose of naughty on the side if you look hard enough.

She lives in Southern California with her family, a Cocker Spaniel mix rescue named Annie, and way too many books and handspun yarn.

Let's Connect!
Lizduranobooks.com
lizduranobooks@gmail.com

facebook.com/LizDuranoBooks

instagram.com/lizdurano

bookbub.com/authors/liz-durano

amazon.com/stores/Liz-Durano/author/B013JB0L28